STORK

STORK

WENDY DELSOL

CANDLEWICK PRESS

Copyright © 2010 by Wendy Delsol

First paperback edition 2011

The Library of Congress has cataloged the hardcover edition as follows:

Delsol, Wendy.
Stork / Wendy Delsol. — 1st ed.
p.   cm.
Summary: After her parents' divorce, Katla and her mother move from Los Angeles to Norse Falls, Minnesota, where Kat immediately alienates two boys at her high school and, improbably, discovers a kinship with a mysterious group of elderly women — the Icelandic Stork Society — who "deliver souls."
ISBN 978-0-7636-4844-2 (hardcover)
[1. Supernatural — Fiction. 2. High schools — Fiction. 3. Schools — Fiction. 4. Minnesota — Fiction.]   I. Title.
PZ7.D3875St 2010
[Fic] — dc22   2009051357

ISBN 978-0-7636-5687-4 (paperback)

11 12 13 14 15 16 BVG 10 9 8 7 6 5 4 3 2 1

Printed in Berryville, VA, U.S.A.

This book was typeset in Granjon.

Candlewick Press
99 Dover Street
Somerville, Massachusetts 02144

visit us at www.candlewick.com

This book is dedicated to
my mother, Elaine Peck,
who gave me wings.

CHAPTER ONE

One moment I was fine, and the next it felt like an army of fire ants was marching across my head. Seriously. Fire ants wearing combat boots — heavy, cleated combat boots. I'd never experienced anything like it. I scratched at my scalp until my hand cramped. It didn't help. I turned, and the mirror behind the cash register confirmed my suspicions: along with the crazy rash creeping from under my hairline, I also had claw marks. Any other head of hair would conceal such blemishes. Not mine. My towheaded, sun-fearing ancestors had seen to that.

I opened the cupboard under the register. Where was that woolen beret I'd seen? Crimson red with a small loop on top. A bit of a fashion stretch, even for me. Oh, well. This town already thought I was odd, the suspicious package dropped at their door. I shrugged the hat over my head. It provided no relief, but at least it covered the damage.

Where the heck was that delivery? My *afi*—my grandfather—had told me I could close as soon as Snjosson Farms delivered the apples. I looked at the old clock above the candy counter. Nine o'clock. Afi had said the bushels would arrive at seven.

Hoping to see headlights barreling down Main, I looked outside. Across the street, a light in Hulda's Fabric and Notions caught my eye. No way. I'd been waiting for a sign of life in the place for weeks. The going-out-of-business sign and unclaimed bolts of fabric, glorious pristine fabric, had been taunting me as a bargain opportunity. I quickly scribbled *Back in five* on a piece of paper and taped it to the door. Snjosson Farms and their golden pippins could wait.

Clutching my Juicy Couture velour jacket to my throat, I hurried across the road. Dang, it was cold. Mid-September and already something the Minnesota yokels called an Alberta Clipper was bearing down from the north. In California I'd still be in shorts, spaghetti straps, and flip-flops.

A chime tinkled above my head as I stepped over the threshold.

Holy crap. It smelled worse than my grandfather's store, something I hadn't thought possible. Like something died. No. Worse. Like something got caught in the act of dying—some long, lingering, putrefying fade. I knew the feeling. For me it was junior year at Norse Falls High School. Exile High, as I liked to call it.

"Who's there?" The voice sounded cracked with age.

I looked up to see an old ball of a woman with skin more crushed and textured than the bolts of velvet she stood over. Tufts of charcoal gray hair escaped from under an orange hat with floral trim. She looked like a shriveled root dangling under a flowerpot.

"I saw the light," I said. "I've wanted to look at your shop for weeks now." I took a hesitant step farther into the store.

The old lady, dressed in a drab gray skirt and dull gray cardigan, checked the time. "No. Is too late. You come back again."

"But when?" The scalp condition grew worse. "I've been working at my grandfather's store for a couple of months now." I wanted so badly to scratch my head. "I've never seen you open before." What would the woman think if I dropped to the floor and started rolling like some flea-bitten mongrel? And no wonder they called them boils. My whole head felt like it was churning with hot foaming bubbles.

"Next time. You come next time." Once more, the old lady checked her watch.

I heard the creak of a rear door, a howl of wind, and then footsteps descending stairs, but I didn't see anyone. Kinda creepy. Then again, the old lady probably had more friends on the other side than on this one.

She pointed to the front door. "So sorry. You go now."

On a low shelf, I spied a tartan wool that would be perfect for the cape I was designing. I leaned down for a better look, and the red beret tumbled to the floor. I scooped it up and quickly replaced it on my head. I heard a gasp.

"You have the cap," the old lady said, wagging a trembling finger in my face. Her eyes bulged as she stared at my head.

I tugged the beret over my ears. "Not really mine. Just borrowed it." The itching got worse. It felt like fingers of angry red streaks were escaping down my forehead and across my neck. I fought the urge to reach under the hat and yank my hair out, handful by miserable handful.

The old lady looked at me as if I had jabbered in some long-lost Icelandic dialect. Of course, that was probably her native tongue. Half the town, my mom's family included, had descended from the same band of Vikings blown off their little iceberg of an island.

"Not borrowed. Cap is a sign. Follow me." The old lady started shuffling toward the back of the store.

Definitely creepy now.

"I really just wanted to look at the fabric. I sew, and I'm into design, but I could come back another time." My head was screaming with pain. I wondered if scalping was ever medically prescribed. I would do it in a heartbeat, just lop the whole thing off, no anesthesia necessary.

"Time is now. Follow me."

I obeyed like some sort of heeled dog, though how this little old lady could conjure such authority was beyond me. My mom couldn't even get me to pour milk into a glass. I just hoped there was Dupioni silk or pebbled crepe for which the "time is now" phrase was intended.

"Is there something back here you wanted to show me? Mrs. Hulda, is it?" Common sense told me to make like the yards of fabric and bolt — still, I followed.

"Is Huldabrun Vigarthursdottir. You call me Fru Hulda."

And I thought my name was bad. Plus Fru? I shook my head in wonder. *Fru,* I knew from my mother, was Icelandic for *Mrs.,* but seriously, who else would know that? In addition to the English word for *Mrs.,* maybe Fru Hulda should learn the word *assimilation.* Though I supposed the melting pot theory didn't apply when you came from one frozen climate to another. And as for the rest of the name, what a load to carry through life. No wonder the old betty was bent in two.

The back of the store was a maze of low shelves holding boxes of gleaming buttons, skeins of lace, and spools of ribbon. The quantity and quality of fringe, rickrack, sequins, and trims was unlike anything I'd ever seen — not even in the garment district of downtown LA. And such a riot of colors. My eyes glistened with delight. Then again, it might just have been smoke clouding my vision from the whole head-on-fire thing.

Hulda stopped at a battered old door. Faded letters spelled out OFFICE on a paint surface so crackled I could have scraped the whole thing away with one swipe of a spatula. She opened the door. A step or two of warped wooden stairs were visible, after which there was nothing but black. Hulda pulled on a simple metal chain, and a bare bulb illuminated the descent.

"Now we go down," she said.

CHAPTER TWO

Hulda looked at me expectantly.

No way was I going down there. Nothing good happened below the earth's crust. Just poll the local residents of any cemetery on that one. I raked my left hand deep into my scalp.

"Quick. Is time," she said, squinting at her watch.

Not only was I expected to head into the heart of darkness — I was urged to go first. She nudged me with a sharp knuckle to the small of my back. Though my head said "Don't," my legs said "No," and my stomach said "Up, if anything," I descended.

The staircase was narrow and turned three times before opening into a dark corridor. Hulda stepped forward and beckoned me with a nod of her head, motioning to the only door off the wide hallway. Clutching at my arm with surprising force, she pushed the door open.

Some of the oldest women I had ever laid eyes on were seated at an oval table. And if not the oldest, then definitely the oddest. Hardly the horror pic that'd been looping through my head, although the room itself was dank: low ceiling, stone walls, and lit only by thick white candles of varying heights surrounded by what could only be described as straw and twigs in the center of a massive table. The women all turned as Hulda pulled me into the room. *It must be some sort of costume party,* I thought. One of those crazy red-hatter clubs like my grams in Santa Monica belonged to. And hats off to this bunch: the assortment of bonnets, and beanies, and pillboxes — and one which could only be described as a horned wimple — was impressive, though oddly enough not a one was red.

I suddenly remembered my own hat, probably the mistaken passkey that had gotten me into this Knights of the Round Table meets Golden Girls Reunion. I was about to excuse myself, politely, when one of the women stood, scraping a heavy chair across the flagged floor. She was tall and dour, with a mouth that gathered in angry folds. She looked at Hulda as she spoke. "What is the meaning of this?"

Hulda pointed to one of the chairs, which, I now noticed, faced backward and away from the table. "The second chair can be seated now."

A chorus of gasps rebounded off the damp walls, as every one of the old women reacted to this statement.

"I can't stay," I said.

They all stared at me with wide eyes and open mouths.

Tall-and-Dour was clearly not pleased by Hulda's announcement, or invitation, or whatever it was. She slapped her hand to the table, causing the candles to flicker and the room to fall silent. "Have you no respect, Fru Hulda? You know the statutes. Youth is strictly forbidden. You risk exposure. And certainly not the second chair."

Talk about reverse age discrimination.

"I really gotta go," I said. "I'm waiting for a delivery." I pointed in what I thought was the right direction, though all the crazy turns of the staircase had me disoriented. "Across the street at my *afi*'s store."

"She has the cap," Hulda said in a voice as flat as the prairie.

Again with the cap. Double the trouble at this point: its musty wool was probably teeming with vermin, and it seemed to somehow be my ticket into this masquerade. I yanked it off and balled it in my hand. Another round of gasps, pointing, and nervous twitters circled the room. These old women seriously needed to get out more. Sure the skin condition was a nasty, festering mess, but wasn't it rude to gawk?

Another woman stood. "It is the cap."

Tall-and-Dour shook her head. "Impossible. She's just a child."

I'd had enough. I gave Tall-and-Dour the most adult-like look I could muster. "I'm sixteen, hardly a child." I turned and held the hat out to Hulda. "But anyway, you guys can keep the cap. It belonged to my *amma,* but she's dead now. I'm sure my *afi* wouldn't mind." I shoved the hat into Hulda's hand. "Like I said, I gotta get going."

"Is not the hat," Hulda said. "Is the cap." With this she removed her own hat, and I was shocked to see the same raging red rash afflicting her scalp, visible under thin wisps of gray twisted hair. One by one, the others in the room, except Tall-and-Dour, removed their hats. They were all suffering from the same mottled skin condition.

"Is this thing contagious?" I asked, a hand flying to my hairline.

Hulda shook her head. "Is not contagious. Is a sign. As is your youth. As is your arrival this night, the final night, of a three-year deadline to appoint a second chair."

All of a sudden my whole head started aching. Not just the scalp. Pain radiated from the base of my neck to my eyebrows. I'd had headaches before, but nothing like this. The room spun like a carnival ride, and I needed to sit down or drop to the floor. Hulda must have sensed this, as she quickly put a hand below my elbow and inched me into the room. I sat with a thud and put my head to my knees. Many minutes passed before I recovered enough to sit up and take stock of the situation. I was in the empty chair, which had been turned to face the table. The women looked at me expectantly.

On top of everything else, I thought I might hurl. "I don't feel well." I clutched my stomach. "And I don't understand what's going on."

Hulda, who was seated to my right, stuck a white bowl of what looked like dried leaves under my nose. "Breathe deeply," she said.

It smelled sharp, and the tip of my nose went numb, but I felt better. Both the headache and nausea were instantly gone.

"Where am I?" I was disoriented and momentarily wondered if I was hugging another type of bowl.

Hulda's voice was solemn. "You are at a meeting of the Aslendigas Storkur Society."

"The what?" I asked, realizing I was addressing my new best friend—the bowl.

Tall-and-Dour interrupted. "No more. There has been some mistake. She should never have been seated. And certainly not in the second chair."

I crouched into a backbreaking pose, whereby I could keep both nostrils sucking in grass clippings while my eyes raked the surroundings.

A short, plump woman said, "But Fru Grimilla, she was sick. Nearly fell over."

Tall-and-Dour, I thought, *must have been born with that scowl; how else would her parents have known to name her Grimilla?*

Aha moment: I can lift the bowl, a clever maneuver that allowed me to stretch my neck and shoulders in relief.

"Enough," Grimilla said with a slash of her hand. "Too much has been said already."

Hulda stood. "Fru Grimilla!" she said with surprising ferocity. "Do I need to remind you that I occupy the first chair, the Owl's chair, the Ugla's chair?" On closer examination, Hulda's chair was larger than the others and raised on a small platform. It had a large ornate owl carving, which made the bird appear to be perched atop the chairback. "We have waited three years for a new member to find us. And for it to be one so young is a sign."

I attempted to lower the herbs from my numbed nasals, make my apologies, and scram, but a mere inch of separation between my nose hairs and the weeds caused a relapse. I looked down and noticed that the arm of my chair was carved with perched birds, all kinds of birds.

"Youth is forbidden," Grimilla repeated. I noticed that everything about her sagged: her shoulders, her bottom lip; even the peacock feather of her teal-blue cloche hat drooped to her brow. "And Fru Hulda, second chair? You pass over many worthy of such an honor."

"We live to see many changes." Hulda spoke with authority. "It is not for us to question. It is for us to accept."

I didn't feel well enough to respond in any way to the madness surrounding me. I was rooted to the mysterious bowl by pain and nausea. I thought of fleeing, stealing their dinnerware and its contents, but my jeans had turned Judas on me. They just sat there shaking uncontrollably. Traitors.

Hulda turned to face me. *"Velkominn, vinur.* Welcome, friend."

A chorus of *"Velkominn, vinur"* was repeated.

All eyes fell on me, and I felt cornered and scared. It was definitely time to go. I'd had enough of the secret society of yodel sisters, and Afi would kill me if I missed the apple guy. "Sorry, but I can't stay. I'll be late," I managed to say, thinking if I could make it to the back door, away from the stink of those candles, the stares of these strange women, the fresh air might revive me.

"No need to worry about time," Hulda said. "Check your watch."

Weird. It had stopped at 9:03, the time just before I entered the shop. All the more reason to scat. I tried to leave; it took a great deal of effort, but as soon as I stood, my symptoms returned: blazing hot scalp, pounding head, and nausea. I sat back down, plunging my nose to the bowl.

"What is wrong with me?"

"Nothing is wrong. When the cap appears, you must come at nine o'clock to council. As for the other discomforts, your gifts are settling in. And always worse with the cap." Hulda nodded to a woman across the table. "Fru Birta, our Lark, are you ready to record?"

Birta, of the chartreuse wimple, opened a very large, very tattered leather book. "What is your name?"

"Kat."

"Your full name?"

"Katla Gudrun Leblanc."

Birta looked up from the book. "Katla Leblanc? That can't be."

"Only my mother is Icelandic. My father's side is French." Again, the room echoed with murmurs. I looked at the woman to my left. The arms of her chair were carved with what looked like pelicans. Were they bird watchers? Mad-hatter bird watchers?

Fru Hulda nodded to the room. "Yes. This is the granddaughter of Fru Valdis. And yes, this is the girl of the lake."

Huh? OK. These crazy ladies were driving me nuts. First I thought it was my non-Icelandic last name they were questioning. Now it seemed to have something to do with my poor dead *amma*. And what lake? Unless you considered the Pacific Ocean a lake.

"Let us continue with the records," Hulda said. "What is your father's first name?"

"Greg."

"Enter her as Katla Gudrun Gregorsdottir," Hulda said.

I was at least familiar with this confusing Icelandic custom. A boy's last name was his father's first name followed by *son,* and a girl's last name was her father's first name followed by *dottir,* for daughter. My mother, for example, was Lilja Olafsdottir because her father, my *afi,* is Olaf Vilhalminsson. And a woman didn't take a husband's name in marriage. But just because I understood the tradition didn't mean I bought into it. Nor did my dad. He accepted the name Katla, which he morphed into Kitty Kat. He begrudgingly tolerated the middle name Gudrun, because, as my birth story goes, my mom stopped pushing and refused to continue unless she got to pick my first and middle names. My dad agreed — though claimed the nurses bullied him — but he drew the line at the surname. He was French, and his child was a Leblanc.

"I prefer Leblanc," I said.

Birta looked up momentarily and received a nod from Hulda. I stretched my neck to get a look at the faded yellow parchment, but the Lark scribbled quickly and turned the page. Roll was then called, and the book was shut with a heavy thud.

"Perhaps listening to the meeting will best explain our purpose," Hulda said. "Fru Dorit, our Puffer, do you have an essence to bestow?"

Huh?

Dorit, the short, plump woman who had interrupted Grimilla before, rose solemnly from her place. "May I first commend you on this momentous decision, Fru Hulda, our Owl, our Ugla." Dorit ducked her head coyly toward her right shoulder. "And I'm sure it is not lost on one so wise as you, Fru Hulda, that the Icelandic word for *little owl* is *kattugla*. Her very name, another sign. Yes? Fru Hulda?"

Boy. It was clear that the suck-up position in this group was already taken.

"This I noticed," Hulda said, granting no particular favor to Dorit's doughy face. "Let us continue with our duties. Do you have an essence to deliver?"

"As always, I am honored to serve my sister Storks. And I wish to thank you all, in advance, for your consideration of tonight's recommendation."

"Please, Fru Dorit," Hulda said. "What say you?"

"A boy. He'll be breech, and late," Dorit said.

I looked around the room. Were these women midwives?

"What else can you tell us?" Hulda asked. "And remember, be brief."

"He's impatient to settle. He'll be gifted in music, but someone to whom words will come slowly."

OK. Even a really good midwife, with the ultrasound equivalent of the Hubble Telescope, couldn't know that.

"What vessels are there?" Hulda asked.

Vessels? Like ships?

"A thirty-four-year-old mother of three girls. Her husband pines for a boy. A twenty-nine-year-old single woman, who has lost herself in her career. A thirty-eight-year-old who has, four times, endured artificial insemination. The husband has been incredibly patient."

"And have you a recommendation for us?" asked Hulda.

"The thirty-eight-year-old," replied Dorit. "She has waited so long."

All of a sudden, something Hulda had said pre-
viously clicked. "Did you say Storkur Society? As in
stork?" I asked. "As in big white bird? As in baby delivery service?"

Hulda nodded. "Yes. Aslendigas Storkur Society. Icelandic Stork Society, Local 414."

"You guys are joking, right?" I said. "This is some kind
of prank. Am I being punked by someone?" My friends in
California were capable, but no way they'd go to this kind
of trouble. And I didn't have friends here in Minnesota.

I tried to stand, but—again—ended up in the
weeds.

"If you are to join our society, you will learn protocol
and patience," old sour-faced Grimilla barked.

"Who said I was joining anything?" I said into the bowl
of grasses, my nose ice-cold and my scalp smoldering.

"Fru Grimilla, our Peacock, you judge too quickly."
Hulda turned to me. "Is never a choice," she said with
resignation. "Is a calling."

"Yeah, well, nobody called me," I said. "Trust me. I'd
remember."

A twitch of a smile flashed across Hulda's face, but
was gone in an instant. "You will come to understand. I
will help you."

"Fru Hulda," old Grimilla said, "I fear we digress."
She and her bobbing feather wouldn't allow me
another interruption. Peacock, eh? I'd heard of whole

neighborhoods in Palos Verdes whose common goal was to rid their streets of wild peacocks. Reportedly the birds were loud, aggressive, territorial, and full of crap—literally. Made a lot more sense to me now. I half listened as the women adopted some sort of agreement regarding the musical boy and the test-tube mom, though I was simply too overwhelmed to fully understand the significance of the moment. Next thing I knew, I was herded up the stairs with the group, my scalp blister-free, my head pain-free, and my stomach settled. The women turned left at the stairs and disappeared out the back door. I hesitated, standing with Hulda at the rear of the store.

"What just happened?" I asked.

"Katla, you are very special girl. I know never of one so young to be given these powers."

"Powers?"

"Yes."

I looked around the shop, filled with such beautiful materials. "I'm seriously hoping this is all a dream, but if it is, what a waste of fabric."

"Is no dream. You go home. Next time you see my store open, we talk again."

Before I knew it, I stood in front of Hulda's dark store with no one in sight, my scalp as cool as the night air, and my brain twisting like taffy.

CHAPTER THREE

I turned the key in the lock, pushed open the door, and looked at the large clock on the wall. Six minutes after nine. Only three minutes had passed since I'd walked over to Hulda's store. How was that possible? I put a hand to my muddled head; no angry red bumps, and the hat was gone. I glanced back across the street through the still-open door. The fabric shop was dark. I was either going crazy or had just had an up-close-and-personal with a coven of witches or a gaggle of Stork ladies. Given a choice, I'd take crazy.

An old junker of a truck came belching down the road and pulled into a parking spot in front of Afi's shop, the Norse Falls General Store. I noticed the apples in the back of the cab and watched as a guy, lean and lanky, unfolded his long legs from under the steering wheel. Though it was a bitterly cold evening, he wore only a T-shirt.

I stepped back outside and crossed my arms. "You're late."

"Sorry. Engine trouble." He closed the car door with a back kick of a crusty boot, walked the few steps to the back of the truck, and lifted out a bushel of green apples.

Nothing like bad service to jar you back to reality. "You could have called."

"No cell phone. Where you want 'em?"

"Afi wants them in the back storeroom."

It took the guy about fifteen minutes to unload, all the while leaving a trail of mud across the plank floorboards I'd already swept. I used the time to work on an English assignment. When finished, he approached with papers to be signed. As he smoothed the crumpled sheets onto the counter in front of me, I could feel his stare.

"Aren't you even going to say hi?" he finally asked, removing his cap and looking at me.

I clicked a ballpoint pen in and out. "Uh, sure. Hi." He continued to look at me so intently that I became nervous that the rash or claw marks had returned. I fluffed my bangs over my forehead.

"You know me, right?"

I didn't recognize him. Then again, the school was filled with flannel-clad, John-Deere-capped, boot-shod farm boys, one indistinguishable from the other. Though as he held his gaze, which was becoming pretty awkward, there was definitely something familiar about the guy. I'd always liked the unexpected combination of blue eyes and dark hair. Didn't he go to my high school in California? No, that couldn't be it. He looked like that guy from the TV show about the Valley. Or was it the one about that prep school? Jeez, did the guy never blink? Or was he the local kid who cut my mom's grass over the summer? By this point, the guy had me so flustered, he was starting to look like a cross between my *afi,* Jack Sparrow, and Bono. There really should be a law, or at least some sort of strict etiquette, regarding lingering stares.

"Should I? I'm the new kid," I said, knowing for certain that it was a singular distinction. "I barely know anyone."

"But you know me."

I was starting to pick up on his tone: a mixture of arrogance and entitlement. He was probably the prom king or quarterback. And I'd put money on him being one of Wade Ivarsson's buddies. "Sorry," I said, shrugging.

He didn't seem satisfied with this response. "Seriously? You don't know me?"

Man, this guy didn't give up. "Am I in one of your classes?" I was not going to give him the satisfaction of guessing him as class president, or captain of whatever sport was king around here—probably bear wrestling or log rolling.

He seemed let down. "From before?"

Before what? I'd only been here a couple of months. I was pretty sure he hadn't been in the store in that time. And I remembered that the kid who cut my mom's grass was freckled and younger. "I doubt it. I haven't been here since I was eleven."

He looked at me with what could only be described as disappointment, though what I could have possibly done to him I couldn't guess. "I must be confusing you with someone. And I'm sorry if I kept you waiting." He extended his hand. It looked dirty, but I didn't see any way around shaking it. "I'm Jack Snjosson."

At least they taught manners alongside tractoring. "Kat." I touched his warm fingers. "Ouch!" A surge of cold shot up my arm, leaving me with a sudden ache. He must have experienced a similar jolt because we both pulled our hands away quickly.

He looked up to the lines of exposed wiring stapled to the wall. "When's the last time you guys had an electrician out here?"

"I wouldn't know," I said, rubbing my arm and looking suspiciously at the jerry-rigged fixture dangling just a few inches above my head.

"Something you may want to mention to your grandfather."

"Yeah. I will," I said, though the shock didn't feel electric to me. I shivered. It got a little more awkward, because he was the one who should have offered an exit line. Yet he kept standing there, all rigid, like he expected something of me, like he was daring me to do it — whatever *it* was.

I sighed, trying to think of something to diffuse the tension. The guy was in such an internal headlock that it really did look like he might hurt himself. "Can I ask you something?" I pointed across the road with the pen. "Have you ever seen that fabric store open?"

He replaced his cap, tugged at its brim, and seemed to come out of his trance. "Kind of a sore subject around here."

"Really? Why?"

"Old Hulda's the only holdout among the merchants on Main. They all have an offer from some developer, but she won't sell. And hasn't been seen for months, so she's holding the whole thing up. The developer won't buy unless it's a complete parcel. Why do you ask?"

I didn't know how much to reveal. "I thought I saw a light on over there."

"I hope not. I hope she foils the deal."

I had heard my *afi* talking about "cashing out," but he'd never mentioned an obstacle. "Why? Isn't it what the shops want?"

"Not the rest of the town."

"Why not? What's the developer going to do with it?"

"They're talking about leveling the whole downtown and building some big-box shopping center."

"Sounds good to me." Visions of Starbucks and Jamba Juice flitted across my lashes.

"There're a lot of people who depend on selling to these businesses. My dad sells apples and cider to the store; my mom sells pies, and strudels, and jellies to the café. And it's not just our family." He lifted his none-too-clean hands in a sweeping motion. "Take a walk through the shops one day. Most everything is local. You won't see too many 'Made in China' labels." He was working himself into a lather, which I hoped he'd at least use to clean the grime from under his fingernails. "And besides, you wipe away a town, you wipe away a piece of history."

"But if the stores aren't making it, that's just the way it goes. Right?" I knew I was grinding his gears, but, seriously, strudels and jellies? And apples were computers, period. "People like to see the quaint downtowns, sure, as they drive by in their SUVs on the way to the mall. It's the natural selection of economics; if you can't adapt, you go extinct." I gestured toward the rear of the store. "Just take a look at the old abandoned railroad back there, if you need an example."

That did it. He snatched the paperwork from the glass countertop. "What the hell would you know about it, anyway? If people like you had their way, the whole world would look like Disneyland." He stomped more mud across the floor and slammed the front door on his way out.

I sat and replayed his remarks, chafing under his tone. *Testy, testy,* I thought. Someone needed a visit to the Happiest Place on Earth. I shook my head in bewilderment. What a night. First the Stork ladies, and then eye-locking, freezer-zapping, angry Apple Boy. I *so* had to get back to California.

CHAPTER FOUR

The next morning, Wednesday, I felt chilled, even though a southerly had arrived with bags of balmy air and warm breezes. I hoped I wasn't getting sick, though at least an illness would have explained the hallucinations from the previous night. Maybe something nasty and viral was a good thing—a symptom, not a psychosis. I dressed in jeans I'd slashed and then lined with polka-dot panels, a Michael Stars tank top layered over a thermal T, a silver Burberry quilted jacket, three black crosses, and a Cole Haan turquoise belt. I sat down at the kitchen island to a bowl of Kashi Nuggets and my mom's scrutiny.

"A little warm for all those layers, don't you think?"

"It's cold in here," I said. "Did you leave the fridge open all night?" For longer than I could remember, I'd had an almost pathological aversion to cold. Even in LA, I was known for my jackets and sweaters.

My mom wore a short-sleeved polo, cropped khaki pants, and Birkenstocks. My style gene definitely came from my dad's side, the French side. From my mom, besides the blond hair, I got my ability to recite pi to the twentieth place, not necessarily a skill I would have chosen. "No. And it's not cold." She put a hand to my forehead. "Are you feeling OK?"

A loaded question. Technically I was miserable. Hated Minnesota. Hated school. Hated Kashi Nuggets, for that matter. I dumped a heaping spoonful of sugar onto my cereal. "Yes. Fine."

I wasn't. There was more on my what–sucks list. My seriously stupid hot and heavy with Wade Ivarsson, for one. I thought, with dread, about that night two weeks ago—the night before school started—at the abandoned quarry. Also making the list was the way he and his stuck-up girlfriend, Monique Tomlin, had since shunned me. The capper, of course, was my parents' divorce. But why worry my mom, who had cried for three months after Dad moved out? Especially now that she was finally acting happy.

"You sure?" she asked.

"Of course."

My mom moved back to the kitchen counter. She sliced open a package of beef and plopped it into a Crockpot. She added a bag of baby carrots, diced onions, wine, beef broth, and a heaping spoonful of paprika. Pot roast meant only one thing: Stanley. I was grateful for the warning.

"You'll be home for dinner, honey, won't you?" She ground pepper into the pot.

"Can't. I'm helping Afi again tonight," I lied.

"You've been doing that a lot lately. It's not cutting into your studies, is it?"

"No." Not a lie. Norse Falls High was, if nothing else, academic pabulum.

"Too bad. Stanley was hoping you'd be here."

Then he was even more of a doofus than I thought he was, because I'd been giving him the stink eye ever since he burst into our lives like gum on the face. The whole thought of my mom having a boyfriend made me want to retch. For starters, it was way too soon after the divorce. Plus, Stanley was a bore and a nerd. But worst of all, he tethered her to Minnesota, which made a return to California unlikely. Stanley, therefore, was a sore subject.

As was the ink-still-drying-on-the-paper divorce. Ten days ago, my mom had to track my dad down at the San Francisco Airport to get him to sign the final papers. He had been on his way to Vancouver to meet with a project engineer for his newest venture. She had returned all flushed and in the mood to celebrate. My dad is an entrepreneur, and he can't help it if his job requires him to travel a lot. The affair he definitely could have helped, and it still pissed me off, but he had said he was sorry about a thousand times. And he really was a good guy and a good dad. If I could forgive him, so could she. She just needed more time and space, without complications like Stanley.

My mom checked the clock on the stove. "Yikes. Gotta go. Eight o'clock lecture." She kissed the top of my head and hurried out of the room with a jangle of keys and a rustling stack of graded papers. My mom is a mathematics professor who left a tenured position at UCLA to return to her hometown and the nearby podunk Walden College, in a post-divorce molting of everything she associated with southern California: crime, traffic, materialism, and my dad. And as much as I loved my mom — and knew she was heartbroken, and wanted her to be happy — I had never been, and was still not, on board with the move.

The back door slammed and I sighed, dreading another day of torture at school.

I dropped my satchel on the worktable and fell into a chair. English had been a joke. Social Science had been a snore. And the butchery Madame Klabber, the French teacher, committed to the French language was, as *ma grandmère* in Santa Monica would say, *un massacre*. At least fourth period was Design, the only class and teacher I found remotely interesting.

Ms. Bryant leaned against the front edge of her desk, crossing one booted calf over the other. Her look that day, a chunky brown belt over a rolled-at-the-sleeve tweed jacket, was one I'd be borrowing. I asked myself again how this smart, attractive native Chicagoan had settled in Norse Falls.

"Today I'll be assigning partners for the semester project." Everyone quieted down. You know a teacher's cool when she doesn't have to shout for attention. "We'll be helping with the drama department's spring production of *The Snow Queen* by assembling a portfolio of costume and set designs. Does everyone know the story by Hans Christian Andersen?"

I sat wondering how even a high-school play in this alpine village had to be Norse-themed and snowbound, when I heard my name called.

"Katla Leblanc and Penny Peturson will be our last team." Ms. Bryant closed the folder she had been reading from. "Why don't you take the rest of the hour to meet with your assigned partner?"

"I'm Penny," said a perky redhead who took a seat in the chair beside me. I recognized Penny but hadn't known her name. She had bushy, copper-colored hair that lifted from her head and was shaped into something topiary-like, and she owned, I now recalled, an unusually large number of woolen vests. Today's was green with a band of pumpkins encircling her waist. At least she was thin enough to wear a design of bulbous gourds around her midsection.

"I'm Kat."

"I know. Everyone knows you."

I groaned.

"We don't get many new kids. And everybody knows your grandpa. We all have to go into his store sometime or other. Plus, I remember the . . ." Penny paused, biting her bottom lip. "I knew your grandma, too. She was so sweet. She used to be good friends with my *amma,* until they had that dumb fight. We even live on their block."

I figured anybody who knew my *amma* and liked her got the benefit of the doubt, though I wondered what was up with the granny catfight story. It almost made me giggle, picturing some silly altercation: the clash of the church ladies, the famous tea-party tussle, the great baked-goods brawl.

Penny and I spent the rest of the hour recounting what details we could of *The Snow Queen:* the arrival of a mysterious woman, her abduction of the boy character in her beautiful sleigh, and the girl's journey to rescue him. The bulk of this came from Penny; I mostly remembered fur coats with matching muffs.

When the bell rang for lunch, Penny stood and gathered her things. "You wanna walk together? To the cafeteria?"

Lunch. I hated lunch. Two weeks into the school year, and lunch was the code I just couldn't crack. The first day of school — the very next day after playing backseat Twister with Wade — I'd approached his lunch table, certain I'd be welcome. He hadn't even looked up. As I stood there, like a dork, waiting for him to acknowledge me, I'd been summarily shooed away with a haughty "This table is reserved" from a strikingly beautiful girl, who I would later learn was his girlfriend, Monique. I got the impression it was the sort of reserved that would hold through a ten-, twenty-, and even thirty-year reunion.

I waited for Wade to correct the misunderstanding, but he just stared at his food. I walked away slowly, still thinking he'd call me back. That's when I heard him say to the table, "Who the hell was that girl?" I'd turned around, a natural reaction to something too awful to believe. Monique locked eyes with me and bug-swatted the air in front of her. I spent the rest of that lunch in the bathroom. Over the next few days, I plopped down with groups of kids who looked friendly enough, only to be ignored—or worse, the subject of whispers and curious looks. Eventually, I found it easiest to sit alone and bring a book.

Penny and I were still discussing the project as we entered the cafeteria. I followed her through the line and was surprised when she waited for me to swipe my lunch card.

"So, can you write?" Penny asked.

"I read, too," I said.

"Follow me," she said. I shuffled behind her. As we passed the lunch monitor, she motioned with a backward hook of her thumb and said, "She's with me."

"Where are we going?"

"To the journalism room."

"The huh?"

"You're our new fashion columnist for the school paper," Penny said. "Congratulations."

"Oh, no, Penny. I really don't think so."

"Just come and see what's up. I think you'd like it. It's a good group. Plus, Mr. Parks, our staff liaison, writes us a pass out of lunch for the whole year. We get to hang out in his room and skip the whole cafeteria scene." Penny took a right past the senior lockers. "All of the staff are twelfth-graders. We'll be the only two juniors. Cool, huh?"

As much as the Get-Out-of-Lunch-Free card sounded good, not to mention that my mom would puddle over an extracurricular to pad the college apps—a 4.0, according to my mom, wasn't enough anymore—it sounded like work. Penny looked at me hopefully.

"I'll eat lunch with you guys today, but let me think about it. There's a bunch of other stuff going on right now. I don't want to feel pressured."

I followed her into the room, thinking maybe it wasn't such a bad idea, maybe I needed a diversion, until I got a look at the occupants. Not only were they a collection of misfits, but chief among them sat Jack, the angry Apple Boy, still sporting a seed cap and flannel shirt. If I had felt slightly chilled all day, I was now downright iced. And blue lips look cadaverish on ultra-pale blondes.

"Guys, this is Kat. She's in my design class." Everyone said hello except Jack, who kept his eyes lowered to a sandwich. "She's considering taking on the fashion column." I glared at her as we sat down at side-by-side desks, part of a larger semicircular configuration. She was oblivious to my look, more intent on Jack, whom she must have thought hadn't heard her. "Jack, did you meet Kat?"

"We've met," he said, balling his crusts and wax paper into a brown bag. "I gotta go check the printer." He walked out of the room without another word.

Everyone got all spooky quiet, as if something eventful had happened. They looked at me like I'd done something wrong. I felt like I'd just dropkicked a puppy. And I hadn't even said anything. He was the one who stomped out of the room. I gnawed on the inside of my cheek instead of the rubbery chicken strips, and watched as grease marks soaked through the small paper plate. What was it with guys in this town? I'd had plenty of guy friends in LA, and Ethan Milken and I had managed to go out for six months without the least bit of drama. Even our breakup had been easy. So why was it that the only two guys I'd even said boo to here wouldn't acknowledge my existence?

Penny nudged me and put a stack of school newspapers at my elbow. "Jack's our editor."

Of course.

"And I'm assistant editor," she continued with the bluster of a second-in-command. "Why don't you have a look at some of our back issues? You can get an idea of what we're looking for."

I pretended to shuffle through the old papers, but all I could do was sulk. How could I have gotten off to such a bad start here? How was I already a persona non grata?

My mind drifted to Wade. I thought about how he had started frequenting the store the last few weeks of August, buying sodas, magazines, and packs of gum. He seemed to have a knack for showing up just after Afi shuffled home. It had been a lonely summer; my mom and I had moved in late July, so I hadn't yet had school as a way to meet people. The first thing he ever said to me was, "Cool boots." Sure, I had been wearing leopard-patterned UGGs with jean cutoffs, but "cool boots" was a phrase my friends and I in LA used for everything, and "CB" was text for a range of affirmations, anything from "OK" to "I'm there" to "got it"—so he got my attention. For a hick, he wasn't bad-looking, a tall, barrel-necked linebacker type, who filled a room with both his stature and self-confidence. At first his size made me nervous, but when he'd leaned on the counter with his thick forearms resting casually, I'd relaxed. And he did have a certain charisma or charm that I found compelling. He wanted to know about California, beach life, and surfing. And he said he had a thing for blondes, real blondes.

I knew that a player's a player, no matter the geography. The only difference was the ones in LA had better tans—and better cars. But Wade offered me the one thing I wanted more than anything: introductions to his friends. I could tell that he was full of himself, and not really my type, but I was in no position to be choosy. School was starting, and I didn't know a soul. I never should have gotten in his car, and not just because it was a Camaro. And I never should have had that first beer. Bad enough it was a school night, but I barely knew the guy, and I have like zero tolerance for alcohol. I wasn't a complete innocent, but for whatever reason, drunk and stupid just didn't gel with my personality. Plus, the cheap stuff tastes like crap. I learned that much from my dad.

The second beer with Wade was plain old dumb—and the third, insane. He drove me out to an abandoned quarry. We made out. I also remember drinking something out of a flask, but after that, my memory gets a little blurry. Clarity returned the moment my knee made contact with Wade's groin and he rolled off me, calling me the kind of names that could shut down a TV station. But at least he'd stopped. Something in my resolve and awareness had thwarted him. I was sorry about the ball bruising, and said as much. I'd been told, on more than one occasion, that I was stronger than I looked. When he had recovered the use of his voice and limbs, and I had tucked in my blouse, he drove me home. The next day, I had a killer headache, my stomach was rolling, and my mouth tasted like mothballs. Seriously, my spit could have lined a linen drawer. And instead of apologizing, or at least blaming it on the beers, the lunch shunning took place. Later, I watched him strut through the halls with his arm slung around Monique.

The bell rang and Penny popped up, startling me out of my daymare. "So?"

"I'll think about it." We walked out of the classroom.

As if somehow summoned by my recent brood-fest, Wade passed us in the hallway. He looked left and then right, as if scouting. He then broke into a horsey grin, brought his hand to his lips, and blew a kiss in our direction.

Penny looked at me like she'd just seen me walk on water. "Do you know him?"

"No." If he didn't have to own up to the stupid hookup, neither did I.

"Then why would he blow you a kiss?"

"I thought that was for you."

Now she looked at me like I'd parted water. "For me? Hardly. We don't exactly hang out with the same people. Not to mention that Monique would make life miserable for any girl who messed with Wade."

"Good thing I don't know him, then."

Penny lowered her voice. "If you're smart, you'll stay away from him. I do. I have ever since kindergarten. He was mean even back then."

I could actually picture a younger pug-faced, yappy-voiced version of him.

"They have an on-again, off-again relationship, but they always get back together. And nothing good comes of anyone who comes between them. Wade and Monique may be king and queen around here, but they're not exactly benevolent."

"Probably best then to set out for the brave new world." Ironic that I could even use the word *brave*. The whole thing with Wade had left me shaken. Why had I been charmed by him? How could I put myself in such a dangerous position? What kind of guy would try to take advantage and then deny even an acquaintance? "Maybe I'll find some followers and we'll give that democracy thing a go."

Penny laughed, and I had to admit it had a contagious quality to it. We started walking again.

Penny hitched her backpack up over her shoulder. "I couldn't help but notice a little tension between you and Jack."

"Oh. That."

"Well?"

"He delivered some apples to my *afi*'s store last night. We shared opinions on topics ranging from evolution to economics to progress in the form of bulldozing Main Street. Needless to say, we didn't agree. I was for and he was against. I guess I rubbed him the wrong way."

That summed it up nicely: I'd managed to alienate both the monarchy and the peasantry. We stopped at the intersection of the school's north and south wings. Penny waved and headed in the opposite direction. I watched her walk away, wondering what she thought of me. Acquaintances for only two hours, and the only concrete things she knew about me were that the school king was blowing me random kisses and that I was in favor of leveling their town. I just hoped I hadn't scared her off; I really needed a friend, and should topiary hair and woolly vests be part of the package, so be it.

I leaned against my locker, hugging my arms to my body — being the new kid was stressful. No wonder I was imagining Stork ladies.

CHAPTER FIVE

I headed to Afi's store straight from school. As soon as I got there, he went to the back to take inventory, which I knew was code for nap. He'd been running the store alone since my *amma* died three years ago, so had earned himself a power nap or two. It wasn't like the place got the foot traffic of the Whole Foods in Westwood, but still, he worked hard for an old guy.

I sat on a stool behind the front counter with my Rocket Dog clogs propped up. I pulled a Mary Jane out of one of the glass canisters lined up along the antique mirror and thought I saw the reflection of movement across the street. Relief flooded my system when I realized it was just a car pulling out of the alley next to Hulda's store. I was really starting to lose it. I snuck another peek. Nothing. Activity would mean Hulda was around, and that my memories—which I'd fairly successfully convinced myself to be nothing more than an anxiety-induced delirium—were real. I busied myself with a chemistry worksheet and then turned my attention to Design. I was certain that everyone would submit something traditional: period Scandinavian costumes and quaint village settings for the term project. I was hoping to talk Penny into something hip and futuristic and edgy. *The Snow Queen* meets *Blade Runner*. I sketched a few quick commando-chic costumes.

Afi woke up from his nap and was hungry for dinner. "Wednesday's beef stew at the restaurant," he said. "You fly. I buy."

Walking down Main Street, I passed the used bookstore. A woman waved to me from where she was setting gourds and pumpkins among the stacks of paperbacks in the front window display. I knew she'd introduced herself in the summer and asked about my mom, but I couldn't remember her name. A few doors down, a man wished me a pleasant evening as he swept the sidewalk in front of the hardware store. I had no clue what is name was either.

Two doors past the antique store was the Kountry Kettle, my favorite hangout, mostly because Jaelle waitressed there. Jaelle was from Minneapolis and had more sass and presence than the whole town huddled on the green. I hip-checked the door open and stopped to savor something pumpkin. Idabelle, the café's owner, had no eye for interiors—as evidenced by the ruffled curtains and milk-can decor—but the woman sure could pipe out some delicious aromas. Jaelle looked up from the counter and instantly her mouth stretched into a wide grin. She had a great smile, but one she didn't spread thin the way so many of the adults around here did. Minnesota-nice, or whatever you want to call it, was like Michael Kors at Macy's: the more you offer it to just anybody, the more it loses its appeal.

"Hey, Ice." The first day we met, back in the summer, Jaelle had taken one look at my blond hair and proclaimed it ice-white. And as far as I could tell, Jaelle didn't give out nicknames easily. Kind of ironic that she called me Ice, given my dislike of the cold. Jaelle leaned against the counter. Idabelle made the waitresses wear yellow button-front dresses, but Jaelle had a way of making it her own. A black lace-trimmed undershirt pushed through the V created by unfastened buttons, and black bicycle shorts and long brown legs pedaled under the shortened skirt.

"So what's Mr. Vilhalminsson in the mood for tonight?" Jaelle asked. I always thought it interesting that someone as jive as Jaelle was so formal with elders.

"I'll take two stew specials to go." I sat at the lunch counter and spun the vinyl-topped seat a full three-sixty, something I could never resist.

Jaelle wrote the ticket and clipped it to the order wheel.

"Where is everybody?" I asked.

"Russ and the crew left on Saturday for a job up near Baudette. Don't know about anybody else." Russ was Jaelle's husband and the big hunk of a lumberjack for whom she had uprooted her life and moved north of civilization. It was a sore point with Jaelle that Russ's work often took him away for weeks at a time. They'd only been married a year, and Jaelle was an outsider here, too. No wonder she was bored and restless and spent her tips at Tinker's Tap, the local bar out on Highway 53. Rumor had it Jaelle liked tequila. And Norah Jones. And six-ball pool. Just give these townies something to yammer about and it spreads like mustard on a foot-long.

The door opened, and a waft of cool air blew in. I looked up to see Wade holding the door for middle-aged male and female versions of himself, complete with cropped hair and pig cheeks—even the mother. He continued to play doorman, and I was surprised when none other than Fru Dorit, Hulda's suck-up, walked in. Wade ushered her in with a well-mannered, after-you gesture. Huh? A submissive Wade?

The parents passed solemnly, nodding terse good evenings to Jaelle. Dorit graced me with a lopsided grin, wacky enough to pass for old-lady eccentric but lingering enough to make me think we shared a secret. My stomach did a small flip. *Uh-oh. Did we really share a secret? Like membership to a clandestine organization?* Wade managed a suggestive smirk, quick and smug. *Jerk.* They settled into a booth in the far corner of the restaurant.

"Do you know the Ivarssons?" Jaelle asked. "Wade must go to your school."

"I've seen him around."

"They're an odd bunch," Jaelle said in a low voice. She stacked the two containers of stew in a paper bag, wrapped two corn muffins in bakery sleeves, and then added napkins and plastic soup-spoons. "I guess it's understandable, given the tragedy."

I snuck a peek at their table, catching the father reaching across the booth to give Wade an upside-the-head smack. Some words were exchanged, but we were too far away to hear. I turned back quickly, not wanting to be caught staring—and wondering if "odd" was a comprehensive enough adjective.

"What tragedy?"

"The death of the little girl, Wade's sister, years ago."

"Really? How?"

"On a camping trip. She fell down a hillside and hit her head on some rocks. She was only nine."

"That is sad."

"Wade was with her. Can you imagine anything so awful?"

"No." I couldn't.

"The grandmother, Dorit, is a hoot. When she's on her own, she dishes on everyone and everything. That woman can yak, and that woman can obsess. She really loved that little granddaughter of hers, Hanna. I guess because she never had a daughter of her own. Wade's dad was her only child, so she dwells on the loss sometimes. She was in here this June and just beside herself about it being the first day of summer and the anniversary of Hanna's death. She really couldn't have been any sadder. But most times she's got a lot of spunk, and there's no mistaking who rules the roost in that family."

I took another quick look at their table, where Dorit was talking with a pointed index finger. Even Wade's father had his head lowered. *All righty, then. Order up. Scoop du jour. One big steaming bowl of dysfunction.*

Jaelle folded the to-go bag neatly and handed it across the counter, sighing and rubbing her temples.

"Are you feeling OK?" I pushed Afi's twenty across the counter and waited for change.

"I guess so," Jaelle said. "Had a little headache since I woke up, but have only myself to blame."

So maybe there was a little truth to the tequila rumors. I gave Jaelle a sympathetic look and noticed something above her head. Was it a bug? Did a throbbing headache actually bend air? I must have stared at the spot hard, because Jaelle started patting down her thick black curls. "What are you staring at?" she asked. "Is my hair that bad today?"

"No. Sorry. It's me. I'm tired. My eyes can't focus right."

45

"You stressed out at school again?"

"Again? That would imply the stress had stopped and restarted."

"OK, Miss Semantics. Are you *still* stressed out at school?"

"Yes."

"Remember. It's a pit stop."

I shoved a wad of bills and coins into my back pocket and made toward the door. "You mean it's the pits."

Jaelle pushed her hands into the pocket of her lace-trimmed apron. "Just don't let 'em get to you."

"I'll try." I tucked the paper sack under my left arm. "See ya, Jaelle."

Afi waited at one of the checkers tables, technically a row of barrels flanked by rickety wooden chairs, set up for a crew of old-timers who liked to come in and push reds and blacks across a board. The tables had been out on the covered porch all summer, but had recently been moved close to the cast-iron box stove in the center of the store. Afi rubbed his hands in anticipation as I pulled his stew from the bag.

"Atta girl."

I looked around the empty store. "Not too busy, huh, Afi?"

"Had a couple sales while you were gone."

We ate in silence, which was normal. My grandpa

was a quiet guy. Amma had been the chatty one. Talked enough for two or three, truth be told. In her presence, Afi's silent nature hadn't been noticeable. I wondered what he'd been like with her. Had he always been the ear to her voice, or had she been able to oil his jaw hinge on occasion? He had to have made conversation once upon a time, right? You couldn't go out with someone—what would have been called courting back then—and then marry them, I supposed, without some chitchat. Then again, I didn't remember much talk between me and Wade. Ugh. Thinking about that stupid mistake rolled my stomach end-over-end. Afi dipped his corn muffin into the bowl, sponging up the last dribble of gravy. Maybe he just needed a little prompt, and I was curious about what Jack had said last night.

I leaned back and picked an apple out of the bin. "These any good?"

"Best in the county."

"Jack Snjosson delivered them last night." I rubbed the apple up and down my pant leg, polishing it to a nice shine. "So what's the story with him? He seemed all cranked up about that development deal."

Afi lifted the paper napkin from his lap and dropped it over the empty Styrofoam bowl. "The Snjosson kid?"

"Yeah. Jack."

"Lars was supposed to deliver them."

"Well, he sent his grandson."

"Son," Afi corrected.

47

"Whatever. What difference does it make?"

Afi took a long time, even for him, to answer. "It doesn't really, but do me a favor. Don't mention the Snjosson kid to your mom."

"Why not?"

"Just an old bit of family business. No big deal, but your mom's got enough on her plate these days."

Wow. That was more than I may have ever heard my *afi* speak on any topic. And of course it got me thinking that the "old business" was why Jack expected me to know him already. "What old business?"

I could see the topic close in Afi's squinty eyes. "Never mind about that."

I knew better than to press. But maybe if I came at it from a different angle . . . "Jack is definitely against that development deal."

"He's entitled to his opinion."

"What's yours?"

"Gonna sell if I can."

I cracked a bite out of the apple. Tart, just how I liked them. "Then what would you do?"

"Rest. Find me a view over some water."

Afi started to gather the trash. Either Amma had been way better at crowbarring information out of the old guy or that was as much as you got. Period.

"Would they really level all of Main Street?"

"Oh, that's just one of about twenty different plans floating around. I've been to enough of the city council meetings now to understand that the whole thing is a mess. All I know is that this old building and little scrap of land is mine, and I can sell it to whomever I darn well please."

Another long oration from Afi. Quite the occasion. He yawned and stretched his legs. I knew I wasn't going to get anything else out of him for the night. "You want me to close up again for you, Afi?"

He looked up at me with milky blue eyes. "You wouldn't mind?"

"No."

"You OK driving in the dark?"

So far the only good thing about Minnesota was that I got a car. A little used VW Bug, but I wasn't complaining. Now that I had my license, the real thing, not some bozo learner's permit, I had a newfound sense of freedom. "I'm a good driver. Besides, it's not far."

My mom had rented a house from a colleague who was on sabbatical. It was about a mile out of town and close to the highway my mom took to work. The house was nice enough. I could still hear my mom trying to sell it to me: two floors, three bedrooms, kitchen with granite countertops, formal dining room, hardwood floors, and a yard that backed onto a city park. And trees. She'd been over the moon about bushy, leaf-dropping, color-changing trees. I was just glad it wasn't old and smelly. The agreement was that we'd give Minnesota a year, see how we liked it. And then talk about where I'd do my senior year. I wished I'd gotten that one in writing. Two weeks in a row I'd caught my mom with a highlighter and the Sunday real-estate section of the paper.

"Why don't you go ahead and walk home, Afi?"

He yanked on his thick lopi sweater with the patterned circular yoke. With his tufts of white hair, ruddy cheeks, and wiry build, he looked like an old fisherman. All he needed was a net thrown over his shoulder. Afi came from a long line of seafarers — mariners, as he liked to call them. Fishermen, whalers, boatbuilders, merchant traders, and explorers with a lineage going back to the Vikings.

He left, and I took my usual spot up at the front register. I pulled out my sketchbook, envisioning a costume for Kay, the boy character in *The Snow Queen*. At Hulda's, I'd seen a bolt of russet brown suede which would be perfect for a field jacket. I instinctively looked across the street to where the material was shelved, and a flicker of light caught my eye. It wasn't the overhead lights, the way it had been yesterday. It was more like a lantern or flashlight moving through the store.

I froze, a confusion of emotions. My logical side had told me to ignore the store entirely and had talked myself, deeper and deeper, into an illness theory, possibly stress-induced and with very strange symptoms. This logical side, I discovered, to a combination of dismay and thrill, had a counterpart that was highly curious about all things mystical. What if I hadn't been dreaming? What did "Icelandic Stork Society" mean, exactly? How had I been chosen?

How on earth could they possibly influence who a baby was placed with—and not *with* really, more like *in*!

There it was again, a flash of light moving slowly. I sat paralyzed with fear. I finally wrenched my eyes away, covering my face with my forearm and taking big gulping breaths of air. After a few minutes, I lowered my arm by a mere fraction of an inch. I'd take one last look and then close early, exiting through the rear. Afi wouldn't want me to go crazy all for the sale of a dozen eggs and a gallon of milk.

Holy cow! Hulda was pressed against the front window staring right at me and waving a lantern back and forth.

I tried to swallow, but my mouth was dry as chalk, and tasted like it, too. At least in LA you knew the basic shape of your worst fears: a drive-by, a carjacking, home invasion, or Zoey Simmons showing up to Mark Hall's party in the same alice + olivia batik print blouse as yours. This, however, had a whole new eerie supernatural side to it, and made riots and earthquakes and wardrobe malfunctions seem mundane. With an upright bolt, I steeled my shoulders. The woman was old, BC old. And small—heck, there wasn't enough of her to stuff a pillow. Just spooky with all her "The cap is a sign" ramblings, but not dangerous. It was time to get to the bottom of this. I grabbed the key out of the drawer, locked up the store, and marched across the street.

Hulda opened the front door and looked furtively up

and down the street. She pulled me inside with a finger pressed to her lips. "Follow quickly" were her only words.

I trailed the swinging lantern to the back of the store. Hulda shuffled quietly between the rows of fabric. I let a finger brush over their surfaces: nubby wools, cool silks, plush velvets. Once again, Hulda led me through the door marked OFFICE, down the rickety stairs, and into the chamber with the oval table. She motioned for me to sit. I went for the closest seat, but Hulda flapped and clucked and puffed until I scooted over to the second chair. And I had thought my ninth-grade biology teacher was uptight about assigned seats.

Hulda sat in the high-back she'd occupied the night before, the Owl's chair. Everything about this room gave me the willies. The carved back of my chair was jagged and uncomfortable, the lit candles cloyed the air with the smell of smoke and burning wax, and I had always disliked windowless spaces, basements in particular. I shifted in my seat, glancing down at the wooden arm, which was now carved with only robins, judging by their painted red breasts.

"Uh, Fru Hulda, is it me, or is this a different chair than I had last time?"

Hulda looked at the figures of robins perched among branches in the bloom of springtime. "Ah, so you will be our Robin. How appropriate."

"I thought I was *kattugla,* little owl."

"The chair picks the bird for each member of our

society. Though there is symbolism to be heeded from the little-owl reference, you are, from now on, our Robin."

Sounded better than puffer or peacock, anyway.

Hulda straightened her skirt. "It is highly unusual for us to meet outside of the council." She looked around like we were being watched, which did not help my overall feeling of unease. "There are those who would disapprove. We never like to arouse suspicion. But I could think of nothing else all day, and I knew we were destined to connect. When the bones ache, there's a friend to make."

Afi's bones hurt, too; he called it arthritis. But whatever, at least she used the word *friend*. I relaxed enough to breathe, though only one quick ragged intake.

"Tell me. Have you noticed anything unusual?" Hulda clamped bony fingers under my elbow.

Yeah, I thought—*you, for starters.* "Uh. Not really."

"You will. Your powers will grow. You will be contacted."

"By?"

"By the essence awaiting birth."

"Could you be a little more specific? Contacted how? Phone? Text? FedEx?"

"The child always comes as a dream."

I rubbed my cheeks. "I've pretty much convinced myself that you are a sickness-induced dream. So that would be a dream within a dream."

Hulda finally released the hold she had on my arm with a soft tap. "I know this must be very difficult for you.

Especially in these modern times, so many have forgotten the ancient ways." She looked at me with such furrowed intensity that her long gray spiky eyebrows rose like antennae. "Tell me, do you believe you have a soul?"

Nobody had ever asked me about my soul before. I'd had conversations about God, angels, ghosts, UFOs, and even the Loch Ness Monster and Bigfoot—but not my soul. It felt somewhat personal, but I didn't hesitate to reply. "Yes."

"And do you believe in fate?"

A little trickier. A master plan for this spinning ball of billions? "Just for the big stuff, I guess."

"And would one's birth be included in your list of big stuff?"

"Sure."

"Finally, then, would you allow that there are those among us with special powers?"

Crossing Over with John Edward was one of my favorite shows. "Yes. I suppose. But not me!"

"Why not you?"

"It's just, I'm not . . ."

"Not what?"

I wanted to say *special*. I wasn't special. At least not in that way. Maybe in other ways. Right? Everyone thought they were. Or was made to believe so, anyway, by those who loved them. My *amma*, my personal cheerleader, had always made me feel exceptional about anything and everything—ironically, even my childhood fascination with birds. From a very young age, I'd sketched them, pulled books about them from the library shelf, and made up stories about their winged adventures. That much I remembered. My *amma* liked to tell stories about my childish claims to understand them, translate their chirps to language. That part I didn't remember, but knew she had been quite amused by—even boastful of—this purported bird-whispering skill. Though I wondered what she ever made of my professed love for and intentions to marry Big Bird, the hottie of Sesame Street. Regardless, I'd outgrown such flights of fancy and delusions of grandeur a long time ago. "Not interested," I said.

Hulda sat back in her chair with crossed arms. "Not interested, you say. Your pupils are large, your breathing is rough, your cheeks are flushed, and your ears are ringing."

"How do you know my ears are ringing?"

"Same way I know you don't like clowns."

That helps. I exhaled loudly. My ears were ringing, and it was very annoying. Plus nobody really liked clowns, right? "Fru Hulda, do I have a choice?"

"No." Hulda's answer was kind, but definitive.

I lowered my head to the table and tapped my forehead lightly against its rough hewn surface. So many questions. So confused. So totally bummed it wasn't a serious illness. I sat up.

"So let's say I have a dream about some soul, or essence, or baby, what then?"

"Then, if they haven't already through the dream

cycles, the vessels who are candidates will be made known to you."

"Made known how?"

"Is different for everyone. For me, is always smell. When a woman is a prospect, she smells like crushed arnica root."

Right, that's a big help, I thought, *because when you crush the arnica root, that makes all the difference.*

"Fru Grimilla feels vibrations," Hulda continued. "Fru Birta sees candidates in colors, red too hot, blue too cold. She looks for something in a very specific shade of yellow-green."

Which at least explained Birta's chartreuse wimple — the color, anyway.

I was still unsure of the timing of the whole process, though it seemed a fairly delicate question. "So, the essence gets assigned, for lack of a better word, when exactly?"

"Two weeks after."

"After?" I asked.

Hulda looked at me impatiently. "Coupling during ovulation."

"So assignment comes right about the same time as . . . ?" I thought I knew the answer, but it wasn't like I had committed the whole reproductive cycle to memory.

"A woman's menses. No essence, she menstruates. An essence, the pregnancy continues."

"Does every soul require a meeting and vote? I'm not sure I have the time. I've got homework, a social life." Technically I did not have a social life, but what did she know?

"No. Only those in need of guidance."

"And what is the significance of second chair? Fru Grimilla made it sound important."

"Second chair is second-in-command and makes decisions when the first chair is not present."

Forget baby on board, more like baby at the wheel. "Fru Hulda, I'm not ready to be second chair."

"You will learn quickly. This I know. And what's done is done. Besides, I haven't missed a Stork meeting in twenty years. You will have plenty of time to observe."

I'm sure my mathematician mother had a formula to calculate the likelihood of an event after a prolonged — say twenty-year — period of inactivity. Kind of like ninety-nine years without a hundred-year flood. At least Hulda looked healthy, for her age, anyway. "What if I have more questions? Can I get ahold of you?"

Hulda took a deep breath. "For one so young, I must make an exception." She reached a leathery hand into the pocket of her long gray skirt, producing a large old-fashioned key, which she handed me. "This will open the back door. Wait for me inside, but do not open the door to the office. I will come along soon." Hulda, again, looked side to side as if under surveillance. "Something else. It's important."

"What?"

"You must tell no one. Not your family. Not the vessel, not the vessels who still wait. And certainly not the child, ever."

"Uh. OK." I couldn't imagine getting that conversation going, anyway. Uh, excuse me ma'am, but you smell like dried unicorn dung, so I'm going to beam a hovering soul into you. It's a girl, by the way. She's going to like butterflies and be lactose-intolerant. Congratulations!

"Your thoughts are swirling."

Jeez. It was bad enough when she knew my ears were ringing and that clowns had Charles Manson eyes. "So when I figure all this out—if I figure all this out, what then?"

"You call a meeting of the council."

"How do I do that?"

"You start scratching."

"Scratching what?"

"Your scalp."

"What will that do?"

"Once you start scratching, we will all get the cap, and we meet at nine p.m. And it is very important that you waste no time. It must be as soon as you have sufficient information. You must not hesitate. Do you understand?"

"Yeah. But I don't get it. By clawing at my own head, I'm gonna give you all a rash?" It seemed too stupid to believe.

"Yes."

There had to be a better way to communicate. Hadn't these old gals heard of e-mail? "Will I still get it?"

"Yes."

I rolled my eyes. "That thing hurt like nobody's business."

"The first time is always the worst."

"And the second time?"

"A little better."

"Only a little?"

Hulda shrugged in reply.

"Do I get to have a normal life in the meantime?" I asked.

"Of course."

"Then can I look at some of your fabrics?"

Hulda nodded. "For you, twenty percent off."

CHAPTER SIX

At breakfast the next morning, my mom wanted to talk about Stanley. Why did I avoid him?

She had made it clear to me, months ago, that the divorce was inevitable, that she could never forgive my dad for being unfaithful, and that the return to Minnesota symbolized her new start. Still, I couldn't help but think that my dad was a big drink of life, whereas Stanley was a sip, as in insipid. Anyway, it was just the wrong time for a heart-to-heart. I hadn't slept well. Hulda had me so paranoid about the essence coming to me in a dream that I couldn't relax. Branches had tapped at my window, and a nightjar may have been going for Guinness Book bragging rights on number of calls by a single bird. All night it sang its name: *Whip-poor-will, whip-poor-will, whip-poor-will.* No wonder it was of the species *vociferus.* If it were going for the record, it would have to best 1,088, one of the stranger facts I knew. Another thing I knew about the whippoorwill, that I had lain awake thinking about, was that its song was considered a death omen.

In this sleep-deprived state, I was no match for my crafty mom, who extracted a promise from me to have dinner with her and Stanley that night. He had offered to cook. What a sucker.

School that day was a grease fire. Wade, it appeared, was not content with Monique as the only chew toy dangling from his muzzle. He cornered me at the drinking fountain between second and third periods. I hadn't heard anyone behind me, so I had lifted my head and turned quickly after my drink. He was too close, uncomfortably close, forcing our chests to bump. The bastard stepped back, dropped his eyes to the point of contact, and had the audacity to lick his lips. Nasty, little thin lips that they were.

"The new girl," he said as if nothing had happened between the hours he spent lingering at Afi's counter and that moment. "We finally meet, but you really didn't have to throw yourself at me." He looked down at me. Dang, he was tall. "I would have found you."

"Wade!" a voice that could chip marble called from our left. I turned to find Monique with her hands on her hips. "What are you doing?"

"Keep your panties on," he said gruffly. "Just introducing myself to the new girl."

"They're staying on," Monique said. "I can promise you that."

"Relax," Wade said, stepping around me and coiling his arm around her waist. "You got nothing to worry about."

Monique looked over her shoulder, her brows lifting in scrutiny. "Nice outfit," she said in a phony voice.

I looked down at my Anthropologie floral shirtdress, striped tights, and Pucci flats. What would she know? She wore Old Navy. I took a big bracing breath of air and looked around. We had attracted onlookers, one of whom, naturally, was Jack.

In Design, nervous lines crimped Penny's forehead when I mentioned my idea of a *Blade Runner* look for our project. Not even the flash of tawny faux fur or russet suede from my book bag had piqued her interest. And I told Penny I'd write the dumb column. At least it was better than sitting by myself at lunch, though I still thought appointing a Norse Falls High fashion columnist made about as much sense as funding a Hawaiian interstate.

I followed Penny through the lunch line and to Mr. Parks's room. We were the last ones in. The desks were arranged in a circle again, and I had no choice but to take the one next to Jack. At least today he was without the cap. I noticed that his espresso-brown hair had a cowlick, which sprayed above his left brow in a fountainlike arc. He ignored me by shoveling his food, hand to mouth, with the rote mechanics of an oil derrick. He appeared to be eating some sort of brown-rice casserole with lumps of indistinguishable meat and a few branchy clumps of green, presumably broccoli stalks, but quite possibly pine boughs. It did not escape my notice that, unlike the rest of the room, Jack's meal was a sack lunch, definitely home-made. No flash of cellophane wrapping, nor scrap of card-board packaging to be seen. He drank from a thermos. Even the sack itself was of sturdy cotton cloth. When finished, he dropped the Tupperware container and bent silver fork back into it and extracted two green apples.

If I was going to continue eating lunch with this crew, I figured I'd better make an effort. I turned to Jack. "I had one of your apples yesterday. It was pretty good."

Jack stopped chewing for about a half second and then took another huge bite without responding. Nothing. He let my compliment just hang there like an open fly.

"Eat up, people," he said aloud to the group. "We start working in five."

"I read your editorial, chief," Penny said.

Did she really just call him chief?

Penny pulled out a copy of the paper, *The Norse Falls Herald,* from her folder. "The changes you made from the version you submitted prepress are great, and really pulled it all together."

Jack mumbled, "Thanks" between bites. Penny, at least, merited a reply.

"I wonder if anyone at Pinewood has heard about it yet," Pedro, a small guy with thick dark hair and large brown eyes, said. "You quoted two members of their school board, so it's bound to get back to them."

Tina, a tall girl with bangs curling-ironed into an unmoving barrel of molded hair, said, "Better watch your back at the homecoming game, Jack."

I had no idea what they were talking about. Pinewood was another small town about ten miles west, but they appeared to be discussing more than just a sports rivalry. "Is there a problem between the two schools?" I asked.

Penny passed the paper to me. "You should read Jack's article. It's really well researched. The bottom line is that both communities have declining enrollments. The two school districts are negotiating a merge. The sticky point is which high school to use. Both towns want their building to be spared."

"Which one's better?" I asked.

Jack made no attempt to hide a complete three-sixty of his eyeballs. "You wouldn't understand."

"Try me."

"Our school is bigger, but theirs is newer," Penny said.

Given the proximity of the high school to the downtown business district, I thought I already knew the answer, but asked anyway. "If the other were chosen, what would happen to this building?"

"It would be sold as part of the development deal," Penny said.

"And?" I asked.

"And flattened. What do you think?" Jack finished with an exasperated toss of his head.

I thought I might like to literally toss his head, out the window. "Sounds like one has the updated facilities, while the other has the space." I shrugged. "I guess that makes it a fifty-fifty."

Jack froze, his mouth wide open, an apple just inches from his teeth, which were, I noticed, very straight and very white. "A fifty-fifty?"

I didn't like the way he was looking at me. Jeez, he was smug. "Then again, if they've got computer labs, science labs, a gymnasium with level floors, tennis courts, and a cafeteria that can crank out more than pizza and chicken nuggets, then I don't know why we're even discussing it." I dropped a napkin over my half-eaten lunch.

Jack stood and threw his apple cores, one after the other, in perfect lobbing tosses into the nearest trash can. "Except ours is a hundred-year-old structure with architectural integrity and historic significance. Shiny and new isn't always better." He opened the folder on his desk. "Deadline is a week from Monday. Why don't we all get to work?"

It was more of an edict than a question. And what was the word for he who issues decrees? Edictor? Edictor in chief. Hmmm. I, challenger of authority, doodled clothing designs until the bell rang.

"Wait up," Penny called from behind me in the hallway.

I slowed for her to catch up.

"What is up with you and Jack? Can't you cut him some slack?"

"*Me* cut *him* slack?" Was she kidding?

We walked together toward our lockers.

"It's just that there's . . ." Penny bit her bottom lip and attempted to start again. "I've never seen a girl get under his skin the way you do."

"So?"

"So, he's usually the easygoing type."

I laughed. "I'd hate to see what you consider uptight."

"Seriously, he's not normally like that. He's a really good guy."

I found that hard to believe. Yeah, sure, he was kind of good-looking, if bullheaded plow-hands were your thing. "*Good* is a relative term," I said after a long pause.

"I don't know; he's good at everything he tries. Did you know that besides editor of the school paper, he's quarterback of the football team?"

Logrolling must be a spring sport. "So, why doesn't he hang out with the royalty?" I asked. "With Wade and Monique and their court?"

"Actually, Jack and Wade used to be friends."

Oh? "What happened?"

"Last year it was total drama around Valentine's Day. Wade and Monique broke up the week before, because he got caught with Lindy Vanmeer. And then Monique was all over Jack, playing the victim, tricking him into comforting her." Penny swung her backpack from one shoulder to the other. "On Valentine's Day, the student council sells Cupid's arrows. Most of the kids wear them over their heart, but it becomes this whole funny scene with kids wearing them sticking out of their legs and arms and butts."

I gave Penny a get-on-with-the-story look. She tucked a big clump of hair behind her ear and continued. "The arrows have a little dangling heart on the end for the sender to write their name, so it's the one day all year when everyone knows who's with who. Last year, Lindy was walking around with Wade's arrow sticking out of her chest. Monique took one look and went running to Jack. I saw the whole thing. It was one bad acting job, but Jack was just too nice to call her on it. And then after third period, Monique was walking around with about twenty arrows sticking out of her. Honestly, she looked like target practice gone bad." Penny giggled. I did too. The image was simply too wonderful.

"The little dangling hearts were left blank," Penny continued, "but she told everyone who asked that they were from Jack. Later on, Wade had this big confrontation with Jack. Wade accused Jack of planning to move in on Monique all along. I heard they actually came to blows. And then, boom, Jack and Wade aren't speaking and Monique and Wade are back to normal. Well, normal for them, anyway."

"What happened to Lindy Vanmeer?"

"Her family moved away. Kind of abruptly."

This town was like a little bubbled snow globe that had to shake itself up every now and then just to feel alive. "Seems pretty clear-cut to me. Jack, the really good guy," I said, charading quotation marks around those last two words, "got himself a whole bunch of arrows, but didn't get the girl."

Penny looked offended. "I don't believe that version of events. I think Monique sent herself those arrows. Plus, Lindy made some accusations against Wade." She crossed her arms. "And anyway, Jack isn't the type to get ... I mean, he's never really acted like any girl ... it's more like he's either oblivious or above all the immaturity of high school."

I wanted to ask more about Lindy's accusations, whether there was a flask involved. How could I, though, given my claim that Wade and I were virtual strangers?

We had reached my locker. Penny waved and kept on walking. I spun the combination thinking about her description of Jack — oblivious, a technique I resolved to master.

Instead of heading straight to Afi's store after school, I stopped first at the café. Jaelle was marrying ketchup bottles by stacking one upside down atop another.

"Coffee, Ice?" Jaelle asked me before I could even sit at the counter. I couldn't help thinking that it would really confuse things if the café served iced coffee, which it didn't because the menu was probably penned before freezers were invented.

"Sure." My mom didn't like me drinking coffee. She thought there'd be plenty of time for that later. She also claimed that caffeine was a growth-stunter. At five-three, I figured I'd squeezed all I could out of the height chart, and a cup or two of coffee wouldn't make a difference. Back home, I was practically addicted to Starbucks. Just like my dad, who was a card-carrying regular. His usual was a double-shot soy latte. Grande nonfat caramel macchiato was my Fourbucks of choice. If there were one single thing I could transplant to Norse Falls, besides my dad, it would be Starbucks.

"How're you doing, Jaelle?" I asked after completing my customary full spin of the stool.

"Just OK. Not feeling so great." Jaelle placed a thick white mug of coffee in front of me, along with a small silver jug of cream.

"Out again last night?"

Jaelle blew a big puff of wind out her cheeks. "Yeah, but didn't get crazy. Takes more than two drinks to fry me like this."

"Flu's going around. There were five kids out sick today in English."

"That's probably it." Jaelle wiped a dribble of red from the side of a bottle and replaced the cap. "Though I'm hoping for something else."

"Like what?"

"Like a visit from the stork."

I nearly spit my coffee all over the clean counter. Jaelle had not just said *stork,* because that would be graveyard spooky.

Jaelle laughed. "I forget sometimes how young you are. It's probably not appropriate for me to discuss with you."

"I just took too big a sip." My eyes grew to the size of beach balls. I could feel them inflating. "That's great news, right?"

"Could be."

"But that's what you want. You said so."

"I just don't want to get burned again."

"Have you tested yet?" I asked.

"No. Too chicken. Last three times were false alarms and I got my hopes up so high, I kinda crashed with the news. And I think I took Russ down with me. This time I'm not peeing on the stick until I'm all but certain."

I drank my coffee, ordered Afi a chicken potpie to go, and sat tapping my toes while Jaelle bagged up his dinner. As Jaelle bent down to the stash of napkins under the counter, I noticed something above her head again. Like last time, I thought it was a bug, but when I looked closer I saw squiggly little pulsations, like the air was corking. Holy cow. It hit me like a dropped piano. For real. I heard the splinter of wood and the jangle of scattering keys. This was a sign. *Jaelle was a potential vessel.* I sat back in shock, wondering if she smelled like shaved willow bark or mulled mugwort, or how she'd look in chartreuse. She'd look great, of course. The girl had perfect skin and mad style.

Jaelle must have noticed me staring. "Is something wrong with my hair again?" She patted down her bangs.

"Actually, Jaelle, I was just thinking how nice you look today."

"Aren't you the sweetest thing," Jaelle said with a smile.

CHAPTER SEVEN

I pulled into the driveway. Darn it. Stanley's car was there. I'd hoped he'd been called away at the last minute to some emergency Star Trek convention or abducted for a Geek Squad intervention.

They were in the kitchen. My mom was arranging cheese slices on a tray, while an aproned — good God, the guy had no dignity — Stanley stirred something on the stove. He was a redhead, flaming at that, with bits of gray fuzz coiling his sideburns. My dad's hair was nut brown and sleek. And Stanley was slim and on the short side, five-ten tops. My dad was six-two and toned. What did she see in him?

"Oh, good. You're home," my mom said.

I sat down at the kitchen island and watched her flit about like a hummingbird — slicing bread to go with the cheese, pouring wine for her and Stanley, tossing a salad, and brushing up close to him every chance she got. She was dressed up, too. Dressed up for her, anyway. She wore a wrap-front blue sweater and pleated print skirt, which suited her curvy figure. Her giddiness was irritating. As was her flirtatiousness. I could tell she was trying to bring it down a notch, for my sake, but she couldn't. She honestly couldn't. And Stanley was no better. At one point in this little pre-dinner show, he squeezed her butt as she pushed past him. They didn't think I saw, but I did. Yuck. Appetite gone.

Though we sat in the formal dining room with the good china and cloth napkins, it felt more like a torture chamber. The stroganoff Stanley had made was like wood chips covered with gull guano. The only way to get out of eating it was to feign interest, meal-diverting rapture, in his conversation. It wasn't easy. Stanley taught environmental studies. Hardly titillating stuff. His area of interest was climate change and greenhouse gases. *Woohoo.* I pushed what may have been a mushroom, though it looked suspiciously like the ear of some small varmint, across my plate.

"Tell Kat about the ice packs," my mom said.

"Did you know," Stanley said, waving his fork like a pointer, "that billions of tons of methane gas lie trapped below the permafrost, the byproduct of decaying ancient Arctic plant life?"

"Trapped gas?" I asked. "Like flatulence?"

He laughed, a deep throaty haw-haw for a not-so-big guy. "Good one. Do you mind if I borrow it?"

"All yours," I said.

"Tell her the rest," my mom said, sipping her wine. I could tell she was enjoying the conversation.

"I'm working on a model that predicts the release rate of methane as the polar ice packs melt, and the acceleration it will have on global warming."

"Sounds pretty important," I said. Although it was a side of doomsday to go with my meal and I still didn't want the guy at my kitchen table, I guessed it was good that there were smart people looking out for the earth.

"Speaking of important," my mom said, "how's school?"

"Good. I kind of made a friend. She asked me to write a fashion column for the school paper."

My mom perked up. "That's great news."

"I'm not so sure."

"Why not? It's perfect for you. And the writing portion of it will be good experience."

My mom was not a huge fan of my interest in fashion. Not as a future career, anyway. She claimed my aptitude tests predestined me for something more challenging. Our compromise was that I'd get a bachelor's degree before becoming the next Stella McCartney. She was certain it would be from UCLA, both my parents' alma mater, but my dad and I were cooking up a college choice that was a lot more interesting or, rather, *beaucoup plus intéressant.*

"I'm just not sure they're the kind of kids I want to hang with."

My mom gave me a look. Before moving, she'd given me the have-an-open-mind lecture.

"Plus, it'd be a tall order," I said. "Writing about fashion up here. I saw a guy today in overalls. Honestly. And a girl with white shoes and dark panty hose. Panty hose!"

"Kat," my mom said. My rant had embarrassed her. I could tell.

"Family budgets around here can't afford too many trips to the mall these days," Stanley said. "Maybe that's your angle. A way to make a difference. Fashion for the budget-conscious."

The guy looked at me like he wanted to be congratulated. Like he'd had some sort of epiphany or mentoring moment. I stared at him for a long time. It became awkward. I continued to stare. "Great idea, Stanley," I said finally. "And maybe I could do a nutrition column and call it Donuts for the Diet-Conscious." I'd gone too far. I knew it immediately. My mom looked at me like she didn't know me, or want to, anyway. She was either too mad to discuss it right then or didn't want to make Stanley feel any more awkward. I'd knew I'd pay later, plus interest.

With her face pulled tight, my mom stood and cleared plates. Stanley stood and proclaimed the scouring of pots and pans his specialty, holding up two big hands like ruddy mitts. I sat at the table listening to my mom rattle dishes and slam cupboards. I overheard Stanley say, "I don't take it personally. Divorce is tough on kids."

I got up and logged on to the computer in the family room, leaving them to their domesticities. Normally, I considered Twitter the greatest invention since slingbacks—there was something about that little blue bird I couldn't resist—but that night I just couldn't focus.

My mom came into the room, mentioning dessert and a movie on the Lifetime Channel. The Lifetime Channel! She had an avowed weakness for love stories, extra cheese, tissues on the side. My dad used to run from the room with his hands covering his ears. The good news—my mom couldn't be too angry if she was talking to me; the bad news was plated and carried in by Stanley. Any log-shaped chocolate concoction is gross. A couple of PhDs should have been able to figure that much out. I excused myself and went to my room.

CHAPTER EIGHT

Crying. Incessant crying. A newborn in distress. But where is it coming from? To my left? To my right? No, behind me, definitely behind me. The baby needs help. Now.

The wails lengthen, an unbearable crest of despair. I need to find the baby, but something is wrong with my legs. They swell to twice their size, until I have to muscle one around the other by lifting with my arms. Hair, ropy strands of matted hair, grows over my forearms and hands; it tangles in my fingers as I struggle to wrangle my elephantine legs. The baby is gasping for air between heartrending sobs. Then the baby is just gasping. And then silence, momentary silence, is followed by rushing air. This is no ordinary wind; something ancient and angry is rustling through a grassland, which rises under my feet as I still struggle to maneuver my lifeless limbs. Seedlings sprout at my feet, then grow to my knees, burgeoning and expanding until broad flat fronds slap at my face and block my progress.

Darkness gathers as leaves the size of patio umbrellas unfold above me. And all the while the wind increases in intensity, a roaring tunnel of air, lifting me off my feet, my grotesquely swollen toes floating like red balloons, and then slamming me to the ground with a menacing peal of laughter. I land hard on packed dirt frozen solid. The chill instantly sends sharp coils of pain drilling deep into my bones. "Please, not cold," I shout out loud. The gale whips above my head, a swirling mass of blowing leaves and twigs, until it becomes a determined mistral river flowing in a single direction. I have no choice now but to crawl, snakelike, using the currents of air to propel me forward. I grasp, with Neanderthal arms, at stalks of plants the breadth and width of barrels, until my chest and legs are scraped raw on the icy ground.

Again, a child's cry; it's muffled by the wind but pulsing, tauntingly, before me. How could an infant survive, even a moment, in this harsh and foreign jungle? It needs protection; it needs shelter; it needs warmth. I drive forward. Along the darkest of forest floors, I make one final advance, my legs dragging behind me like the tattered train of a moth-eaten gown. Again, the sharp mew of a newborn, and I, finding a last bastion of strength, claw myself forward another ten feet. Suddenly, the wind subsides and then there is light, glorious light. Newly energized, I manage two more pulls and then feel something warm ladle over me until my legs grow lithe and slim, and my arms smooth and sleek.

I am at the edge of a clearing; enormous stalks encircle a ring of soft grass. In the center lies a tiny babe, naked atop a bed of soft leaves and petals. Tufts of dandelion fluff float in the air, which is perfumed with flowers. The child's arms flail and her legs kick. A girl, I realize with a glance at the crease between her legs. She holds in each hand, and even with her fisted toes, a curled vine laden with purple flowers, which close as they draw my attention and ribbon slowly over the child's body.

I am so entranced by the scene before me, I fail to notice the perimeter of the clearing. As the baby settles into a contented coo, my gaze falls on four large stump-carved seats surrounding the grassy ring. The rough chairs are spaced evenly apart, seemingly at the four points of the compass, with the child equidistantly centered to each. Then there is a rustle in the trees, and I watch as Jaelle, wearing a long flowing white gown, walks quietly into the clearing.

"Jaelle," I call. She can't hear me. "Jaelle, it's me, Kat." No reply. "Jaelle!" My voice increases in volume and intensity, yet Jaelle still does not respond. She takes a few steps farther into the ring. She approaches one of the stumps, runs her hands along its rough-hewn surface, and lowers herself into the chiseled seat. She then reaches behind this

79

forest bench and pulls what appears to be an orange cape over her shoulders. She settles it comfortably about her shoulders, so that I am at first fooled into thinking it's a cloak of sorts. As I watch, though, flames lick up the back and onto Jaelle's neck. She doesn't seem to notice. Terrified for her safety, I call to her: "Jaelle, be careful!" She still doesn't hear me, nor does she appear burned or even aware of the heat. She adjusts the fire cape, seemingly luxuriating in its warmth. She sits back, crosses her legs languidly, settles her gaze upon the newborn, and falls into a pleasant, sleeplike sentry of the beautiful child.

CHAPTER NINE

I woke disoriented, but filled with a sense of wonder. There were so many confusing elements to the dream, if that's what it really was. It seemed so much like a vision, or alternate world. Even I had been somehow different there—primal and instinctive. The clarity of the images and the degree to which I could remember details were unlike anything I'd ever experienced. It had been so tantalizingly real: the baby's cries, the howling wind, giant plants, and the child—a girl, surrounded by four stump-carved chairs. The essence had contacted me. As I sat puzzling out the clues, realization spilled over me like a bucket of cold water. Not only had my vision introduced me to the child, but it had confirmed a vessel as well: Jaelle.

I collapsed back onto my bed in both relief and bone-rubberizing shock. So it was true. I was a Stork. I, Kat, was special. I, Katla, was the youngest to have such powers. I, Katla Gudrun Leblanc, had influence on the placing of souls. It was like when my sixth-grade teacher selected me to welcome the visiting congressman in front of the entire school assembly — times a thousand, then squared, then cubed. Then and now, I was both honored and scared out of my mind. I took a deep breath and focused on something small, and manageable, and positive: Jaelle. She wanted a baby and was my friend. This was a no-brainer. Part of me wanted to start scratching then and there. Gather up, girls, we have a winner, but then old Tall-and-Dour, Grimilla, came to mind. She had already warned me that I must learn "protocol and patience." The wrath of Grim would rain down on me were I to call a meeting before I'd seen the occupants of the remaining chairs.

And besides, I didn't fully understand what had been revealed to me about the baby. A girl was all I could announce for certain. I didn't think reporting "she clutched vines" much of a description. And what was up with Jaelle and that cloak of fire? I trusted that Hulda would help make sense of the dream.

For now, I'd just have to follow Grim's advice and be patient. First chance I got, though, I planned on scratching my darn head until blood and pus trickled down my neck. And this, I thought with a groan, was what I had to look forward to.

Nonetheless, I bounded up the concrete steps to Norse Falls High that day, another unseasonably chilly one, with a kick in my step — not easy in Doc Martens that probably each weighed more than some of the smaller freshmen I passed. Big buckled boots contrasted with a woolen kilt and my black leather motorcycle jacket was a combination I loved. A few kids did double takes, something I was getting used to and nothing that could spoil my mood. I, girl with gifts, simply needed to have another dream, jam three more women into the log-chairs, send a bouncing baby girl Jaelle's way, and then the whole ordeal would be behind me, special me.

A glint of hope charged through my system. Or were those my powers surging? Talk about a head trip.

A big group of kids gathered around the school's front bulletin board. A large sign reminded students that voting for Homecoming King and Queen was just a few days away. I overheard one girl say to another, "Monique will be such a pretty queen." I coughed, a big rheumy hack. The two girls moved away quickly. I noticed a folding table set up to the side. Penny was one of two students staffing it; a spool of tickets and a metal cashbox sat in front of her.

"What's up?" I asked.

"The Homecoming Dance is one week away. The committee just announced this year's theme, and I'm selling tickets for Saturday's bonfire."

I craned my neck to get a look at the large silver lettering at the top of the corkboard. *"Enchantment Under the Sea?"*

"Isn't it great?" Penny sat high in her chair.

"Sure." I was pretty certain that was the theme, the exact theme, in *Back to the Future.* And if I remembered correctly, it tampered with the whole space-time continuum, but who was I to split atoms?

"I'm on the committee."

Of course she was. She was probably on every committee and in every club, from the Back-to-School Cleanup Crew to Teacher Appreciation Week Cupcake Captain to Spirit Squad Battalion Chief. Penny was a genuine go-getter, the sign-me-up type. "That's nice."

"We probably do things a little differently from your school in California."

"How so?"

Penny scooted forward in her seat. "The theme is always a big secret until the Friday before."

Ground-breaking.

"And then Saturday night is the big Asking Fire," she said with bright eyes.

"The what?"

"See," Penny said. "I knew I'd get you. It's a tradition. The Saturday before the dance, the school throws a big bonfire event. Girls write the name of their chosen guy on a piece of paper and throw it into the fire. Then the boys have until the bonfire burns down to ask someone. The fire is supposed to have magical properties. If a girl has true feelings for a boy, the fire will grant her wish." Penny looked at me with a sort of rapture. She was, obviously, a believer.

Goody, goody, I couldn't help thinking. And when we're done with that, we can ask the Sorting Hat to divide us into houses. "Wouldn't it be easier to just take the initiative and ask the guy yourself? It'd save on paper."

I couldn't read the look on Penny's face. She was either offended or concerned. "I've heard of it happening before, but not very often. Anyway, there's a Sadie Hawkins dance later in the year. Why? Is there someone you want to ask?"

I took a step back. "No."

"It'll be a fun night," Penny said. "There's a really popular local band scheduled to play."

A kid with a five-dollar bill in his hand stepped in front of me. "I'll take one."

Penny ripped off a ticket, placed his five in the cashbox, and handed him two singles. He walked away.

Penny drummed her fingers on the tin box. "So you wanna go?"

"Where?"

"The Asking Fire."

"Oh." It wasn't like I had anything else to do, but then again, it would take more than a magic fire to get me excited about Homecoming. For one thing, I wasn't home — far from it. For another, the whole thing was a prelude to a dance I had no chance, or desire, of attending. Though the bonfire thing did sound like the sort of oddity you couldn't help but rubberneck, like Mormon prairie hair or extreme lowrider pants. "I don't know."

"Come on. Tina and I are going. You can come with us."

I recalled tall Tina, master of the curling iron. Who could pass up an invitation to hang with two such hair specimens? Penny and her hedge head and Tina and her barrel bangs. I was about to say no when I thought of my mom's have-an-open-mind lecture. Maybe I needed to give the place a chance. So what if it was a little hokey? So what if I had no intention of going to the dance? It was nice of Penny to include me. "I guess."

"How about we meet at your grandpa's store at seven? We can walk from there." Penny held out her hand. "That'll be three dollars."

I unbuckled a side pocket of my satchel. "You're a smooth salesman."

"You *are* smooth," a cloyingly sweet voice interrupted. I turned to find Monique and one of her friends behind me. "And have you done something different with your hair today? It looks . . . I don't know, fluffier." Monique smiled as if her perfect white teeth could conceal the sarcasm. "I'll take two." Monique dropped a five and a single on the table.

Penny made an effort to flatten her hair.

The pair sauntered off, but not before I overheard Monique say, "Chia Pet Penny smooth? Now, that's a joke."

I turned back to Penny. She pulled her mouth into a fish-kiss, tucked a big section of frizz behind her right ear, and looked down at her hands. I felt terrible for even thinking like Monique.

"Remember what I said about getting rid of the monarchy around here and giving that democracy thing a go?"

Penny lifted her shoulder with a small shrug.

"That one is evil and wicked and deserving of an overthrow," I said.

"Not likely," Penny said.

"I'll take one." I recognized Jack's voice and turned to see him holding three crumpled bills. He looked at me curiously and, as usual, for longer than is acceptable in polite society. Were we gunslingers in the Wild West, we'd both have had fingers on the trigger. Something dark passed over his impossibly blue eyes.

"I thought you couldn't go." Penny's voice was strained.

"Change of plans," Jack said, finally wresting his gaze away from me. He swallowed hard, and his neck muscles tightened. Gads, the guy really couldn't stand me.

"We're all going." A wash of pink crept up Penny's neck and over her cheeks. "Tina, Kat, and I." So she had a thing for Jack. How did I not pick up on this before? But good for her, though she seriously needed to play it a little cooler. "Who are you going with?"

"Pedro."

"We'll see you there," Penny said.

Jack walked away, but not before throwing a glance in my direction. A chill ran through me. I handed three dollars to Penny and sat on the edge of the table. "So how long have you liked Jack?"

The red in Penny's coloring moved into even deeper territory, something in the purple family, violet or possibly plum. "What? Why do you ask?" She handed me a ticket.

"I have pretty good radar about these things."

Penny opened her mouth as if to contradict me, but then snapped it shut and folded it into a look of defeat. "It's hopeless. We've been friends too long. He doesn't see me that way. He doesn't see anybody that way."

"Maybe he needs to see you in a new light." And maybe I could atone for being so judgmental.

"What?"

"I'll come to your house at six tomorrow. Have your hair wet and your closet open. We're gonna change things up a bit."

"We're what?"

"And tell Tina to be there, too. We'll make it a two-fer."

"I don't know. What's the point?"

"The point is you have pretty hair — people pay their stylists big bucks to get that color — and you have a cute figure, but if you want him to see you differently, if you want everyone to see you differently, then you have to give them something new to look at."

"I'm not so sure."

I crossed my arms. "You didn't answer my question. How long have you liked him?"

"Forever."

"And how's that working out for you?"

She blew a big puff out of her cheeks. "Not so good."

"Hair wet. Closet open." I walked away before she could argue any further.

CHAPTER TEN

The rest of that school day was blissfully incident-free. Penny was warming to my *Snow Queen* costume ideas and looking forward to our appointment the next day — what she was calling Extreme Makeover: Minnesota Edition. Gotta love a girl with the sense of humor. And Jack completely ignored me at lunch, which was fine by me.

After school, I walked to Afi's fighting a head wind. The tails of my scarf whipped about my head, and leaves skidded across the downtown sidewalk. Some squawker of a Canada goose was blaring at me from across the street. If I didn't know better, I'd think it was trying to tell me something. Like, we're all heading south — wanna catch a ride?

I had the creepy sensation that someone was watching me when an old woman swept past on a bike, her sharp profile making my breath catch. Grim. She did not smile or wave or acknowledge me in any way. The Wicked Witch of the East's theme song from *The Wizard of Oz* played as she pedaled away. It did. I heard it. It made me giggle. My cell phone rang.

"Hey, Dad."

"How's my Kitty Kat?"

"OK, I guess."

"It's Friday. Got any big plans?"

I didn't know if hiding out in my bedroom from my mom and her okely-dokely boyfriend was big, but it sure was my plan. "Nah. Tomorrow, though, there's some sort of bonfire going on, a school tradition. Some band's gonna play."

My dad chuckled. "Pagan sacrifices? Viking reenactments? The Icelandic Sagas: The Rock Opera?"

I went all rubbery. I had to stop for fear of bouncing off the sidewalk. If only he knew the half of it. "Something like that." Had we been speaking in person, I might have told him more about the Asking Fire. He would have scoffed loud and long. I missed him. "Where are you?"

"Still in Tokyo."

"How's it going?"

There was a long pause on the other end. "Not so good."

"What happened?"

"The contract with the factory, it fell through, so looks like our financial backers are pulling out."

"Oh, no. After all your hard work." For months my dad had been working on a start-up deal for a factory that would manufacture a newly patented design for small- and medium-size wind turbines. Last I had heard, they had a rental agreement to take over an abandoned plant in Long Beach.

"This whole trip's a waste," he said. "Without a contract to prove we have a facility, the deal will fall through."

"It might still work out." The goose had now crossed over to my side of the street. It was big and waddled toward me with authority, still squawking.

"It would take a miracle at this point, honey."

"What are you going to do?" I worried about his funding falling through. It was a really big deal to him. Another goose circled above and then dropped in next to its buddy. The two of them walked behind me, jabbering away.

"Try to buy us some more time. We've got one more meeting. Then we fly home." I could hear the strain in my dad's voice. "And start all over again."

"Will there be time to come see me?"

The triangle formed by me and my parents was rubbed raw on all three sides. My dad hadn't wanted my mom to move from California, though there was no way he could have fought for custody. Even without the affair as a blemish, he traveled too much and worked too many hours. My mom didn't want to take on our home's mortgage alone. But more than that, she wanted to go home, as in Minnesota. Wanted to spend more time with her widowed father. Wanted a fresh start.

Dad was the quintessential Californian. He surfed, played beach volleyball, drove a convertible, and wore shorts and flip-flops year-round. My mom used to describe him as fun-loving, but that was before she knew the full extent of his fun. The rip in my gut flapped every time I dwelled on the whole thing. Still, I wanted desperately for the two of them to just find a way to deal. And I wanted my dad to visit. And I wanted my mom to be OK with that.

"I'll try."

"When?" I turned a corner; so did the birds, still tail-feathering me. *What the hell?* "And don't say Thanksgiving, because that's too long from now." Plans were in place for me to visit him in November, but that was over two months away.

"Soon as I can."

Which was post-divorce-speak for "no promises." A truck rushed past me. It was the old faded green junker with SNJOSSON FARMS painted on the side of the cab. I couldn't tell if it was Jack in the driver's seat, though. A cap obscured the identity of the driver, as did the speed of the vehicle. Suddenly, a rush of wind came out of nowhere. It blew my hair into my eyes and mouth. I had to stop and turn my back to the squall. My dad must have heard the howl through the phone.

"Was that what I think it was?"

"Yes. Humans have no business living in this climate."

I could hear my dad laugh all the way across the ocean. He had a great laugh, the kind you hope for, and work for. All the more special, given the setback in his business deal. "Heck. Sounds like we should set up shop right there. Who needs a ridgeline when you've got Canada blowing down your neck?"

"That's a great i—" There was a bunch of static, and then the line went dead. I looked up to see Wade and Monique coming my way. They were ticker-tape parading their conjoined status. Honestly, a start-of-game Jenga tower didn't touch at that many points. It was too late to cross the street. I pocketed the phone and wrapped my scarf around my face. As if it wasn't bad enough with the two carping geese still following me and winds battering me from above, I had bad news headed straight for me.

As they approached, forcing me off the sidewalk and onto a grassy strip, I found myself growing wary. Wade, I could see, had a vile twist to his mouth. They passed, and I momentarily locked eyes with Monique until something drew my attention upward. Around the crown of her head bounced little corking spools of air. I stopped suddenly, startling the geese. They honked angrily and flew off with great flaps of wings just a few feet above my head. I saw Wade duck his big head at the thunder of their takeoff.

After they turned the corner, I stood in the same spot for many minutes, shivering. Monique — could it be? She had the same vibrating spirals as Jaelle. Monique — could it *really* be? Or was I going crazy?

CHAPTER ELEVEN

The wind howls as if wounded. I can't see; leaves the size of beach towels encircle me, flapping in the gale and blocking my view. I look down. My feet are bare and cold. I inch forward, first on tiptoe and then the balls of my feet, anything to avoid full contact with the frozen ground. My dress, a long flowing gown of a gauzy red linen, is tattered and frayed and bunches at my ankles, twisting and wrapping itself until my gait becomes geisha-like. All the while the maelstrom of cold air continues, lifting my hair and holding it aloft as if it were flotsam in a raging river.

Obligation nags at me. Am I late? Am I lost? A test at school? Curfew broken? My mom worried? Something compels me. Someone compels me. Someone needs me. The child. Dear God, where is she? Still alone?

Still unattended? The clearing. I must find the clearing. The insistent bleat of a newborn rises above the noise of the storm.

Something taps my shoulder. The tendril of an intrepid vine snakes over my shoulder, and as I turn away from its creeping fingers, I lose my balance. Tumbling to the ground, I tear the bottom of my dress on a thorn the size of a rhinoceros horn. Still, the vine continues its crawl across my shoulder and over my stomach, pinning me to the cold, hard ground. I kick one leg free of my shroud, then the other, and claw desperately at the encroaching vine. Struggling to my knees, I pull myself upright by grasping a clump of berries, frozen hard and hoary. The berries then lift. Airborne, I cling to them, kicking my legs as I adjust to this woodland zipline, crashing through leaves and thick stalks. Needly pines tear gashes across my forearms. Pinecones rain down on me as if launched with slings. I am losing my hold on the swinging clump of berries; my hands are raw against their frozen surface, and my arms sore from the effort to remain aloft. I worry I'll be thrown to the forest floor, when with a final crash through a wall of leaves I find my toes touching grass. Soft, warm grass. I let go and pull my aching arms to my sides. A delightful sound, cheerful and melodic, tickles my ear. The coo of a contented baby. I turn to see the infant once again on her perch of pillowy leaves and velvety petals. As before, she bats her fisted hands and kicks her feet at dandelion fluff as it floats above her. And as I stare at the cottony seeds, they transform before my eyes to snow, thick crystalline flakes that dust my shoulders and cling to my eyelashes.

I spin in wonder at the sudden powdery shower and in doing so, scan the entire clearing. Again, the four stump-carved chairs are present. Jaelle, with her crackling fire-cape over her shoulders, still sits in a trancelike state. Within a moment or two, Monique walks into the clearing.

"Monique," I call. "Monique, can you hear me?" No reply.

Monique walks to one of the seats, circles it contemplatively, and settles herself onto its coarse bench. She reaches behind the stump, lifts up a cottony substance, and pulls it over her shoulders. I think it's gauze or wool of a dove-gray tint, but as I watch closely the cape shifts and moves. It's a curl of smoky mist, a fog bank, a puff of cloud. Monique adjusts her airy cloak, folds her hands primly across her lap, turns her gaze to the newborn, and settles into a pleasant, sleeplike sentry of the beautiful child.

CHAPTER TWELVE

I woke with a start, vivid images still playing on the backs of my eyelids like some old-fashioned movie reel. I bolted upright, swiveled to find a notebook, and began writing down every strange detail of the dream. Monique. It was too good to be true. I held the match that could light the fuse to the rocket that would send Monique's perfect little world into orbit. To maternity and beyond. What a choice: one vessel who wanted it, another who deserved the complications. Though I couldn't call a meeting until the other two chairs had been filled, in the meantime I had questions.

I grabbed a granola bar, scribbled my mom a note, and headed into town. It was one of those mornings when a cup of Starbucks seemed as vital as oxygen, and possibly more so than my spare kidney. I parked in the alley behind

Hulda's store, careful to keep my car off Main Street. Afi would be opening up soon, and I didn't want to provoke his curiosity. Approaching Hulda's back door like a rookie thief, I looked left and then right, until I chided myself for such shifty behavior. Heck, I might as well shrug a ski mask over my face and carry a tire iron. On second thought, the large brass key Hulda had provided me was big enough and heavy enough to forgo any tool or weapon. I stopped, took a deep breath — muttering, "Hulda, here I come" — and slowly turned the key in the lock. The door opened with a long groaning creak, and I stepped a few feet into the dark back hallway. Hulda had instructed me to wait inside, but not to open the door to the office, which wasn't an office anyway, though its faded lettering said so. I shuddered with cold. A weak morning light filtered through the transom above the back door, and I could see a very large brown spider busy at his loom. I heard something and took a few tentative steps toward the door just as Hulda poked her head out. She motioned for me to follow her back down the stairs.

"You have need of me?" Hulda asked, gesturing for me to take my spot, none other than the robin-carved second chair.

First of all, I was curious how she even knew I'd arrived. If Hulda had been in the basement, how could she possibly have heard me from that thick-walled and windowless room? Furthermore, it seemed an odd coincidence that she was even on the property, never mind down in the dungeon at the very moment I came calling. I hadn't phoned ahead; we had no set appointment. What could she have been doing down there? It sure wasn't my idea of a cozy nook.

I settled into my chair. Was it my imagination, or had the robin carved into the wood of my backrest opened its wings?

"Speak, child," Hulda said with authority.

"I've had two dreams."

"Tell me."

"I'm always lost, and it's always windy, like a category-four hurricane, and I'm in some crazy overgrown arctic jungle. And when I say overgrown, I don't just mean thick. I mean Jack-and-the-Beanstalk-size plants. It's cold and there's always something tripping me up: legs ballooned to twice their size or a dress that knots itself around my ankles. And then I hear the baby crying, and I find her in a clearing. Around this grassy circle are four chairs—sort of rough and unmade. My friend Jaelle sits in one chair with what looks like a cloak of fire over her shoulders. And this girl I know from school, Monique, sits on another wearing one of mist. And they're in some sort of hypnotic state staring at the baby."

Hulda watched me with eyes that flitted back and forth, darting from my own eyes to my hands, to my lap, and once, crazily enough, to my wedged loafers. I couldn't help but be creeped out by the scrutiny. What was Hulda looking at? Or for?

"The baby is a girl?" Hulda asked.

"Yes. Definitely a girl."

"And the vessels, they are known to you?" Hulda stroked her chin.

"Yes. Is that normal?"

"Can happen. Yes. Tell me more about the baby."

"She's crying, but then settles down once I get there. She's on a bed of leaves and flower petals. And like I said, there're huge plants growing all around. Oh, and she has a curled vine twisting around her with purple flowers that close when I approach. And she's batting at dandelion fluff, which turns to snow."

Hulda supported her right arm with her left and tapped her forehead in concentration. "The child will be shy. The purple flowers are violets, shrinking violets."

"Oh."

"She will love nature and outdoors. That is why the plants are so large."

"I guess that makes sense."

"The snow signifies that she will live in a cold climate."

What I wanted to say was "poor kid"; instead I said, "I think I'm starting to get how this works."

"And the square of chairs is the four earthly elements, two of which — fire and air — have arrived. It would seem that earth and water are expected."

"Wow," I said. "You're good."

"But there are aspects of this dream, Katla, that are *unusual*." She dragged out the word *unusual,* as if the word itself weren't freaky enough. "Is *unusual* to journey to the child, but to struggle or toil even more so."

Perfect. Because I wasn't weirded out enough.

"And is normally three vessels, not four," Hulda continued. "Also troubling is location itself. Very strange, no?"

She was asking me?

"But the wind." Hulda pulled her folded arms into her body. "This is a new symbol." She rocked back and forth. "I must think on this wind. I must have forgotten something from many years prior."

The room went eerily silent. Hulda was pensive, still bobbing back and forth as she moved her lips up and down, though emitting no sound. Two minutes passed, then three; I grew uncomfortable.

"Is Saturday. You come back in two days," Hulda said. "This thinking will take long time. You come back on Monday. Seven p.m. I'll be waiting."

Hulda hurried me out as if there were a line of novice Storks all waiting their turn, or customers with purchases in hand and toes tapping impatiently. I looked confusedly around the empty fabric store and left with more questions than answers.

CHAPTER THIRTEEN

I checked the address Penny had given me. It was on the same block as Afi, but the houses on this end were smaller; even the trees seemed less stately.

Penny's house was squat and pale yellow with gray shutters. A brightly colored bird-feeder was perched in a low tree, and a pot of orange mums sat next to a welcome mat. I rang the doorbell. Heavy steps approached, and the wooden door creaked open.

"Fru Grimilla?" My mouth opened wide with wonder.

"You know my *amma*?" Penny stood beside her grandmother.

"What a good memory you have," Fru Grimilla said. "It has been many years since your own *amma* hosted our ladies' group."

Good save.

"I remember," I lied.

"Was that before the two of you had your fight, Amma?" Penny asked.

"It wasn't so much a fight as a personality clash," Grim replied sternly, without answering the question. Man, she was a black hole. Just being in her proximity made my shins splint. Kudos to my *amma* for avoiding the abyss.

"I'm ready for you," Penny said.

Indeed, her hair was wet, as instructed, and I was glad for the diversion. "Let's get started." I turned to Grim. "Nice to see you again, Fru Grimilla." I followed Penny out of the small entryway and past the living room and kitchen. The house was boxy by modern standards and the furniture was circa *Leave It to Beaver,* but everything was neat and the place smelled of cinnamon.

"Fru?" Penny said once we were out of earshot. "I didn't know you were into the old ways." Penny opened the door to her bedroom, revealing Tina sitting on her bed, also with wet hair.

"I'm not," I said. "I'm into what's new and hip and can blend on Rodeo Drive or Montana Avenue." I paused and took a quick look around the room. It wasn't bad, certainly nothing like the rest of the frumpy old house. Grim had about as much design sense as she had sense of humor. But Penny's room showed promise. The comforter was zebra-print. There were black-and-white photos of winter scenes matted in white and framed in black. A desk fashioned out of an old door occupied an entire wall and had an assortment of clear glass vases and apothecary jars containing pencils, scissors, rubber bands, and other various supplies. And the room was painted eggplant, a bold statement, and just as difficult to decorate with as it was to make palatable. I was impressed.

"Great room."

"Thanks." Penny tucked a strand of wet hair behind an ear. "My *amma* doesn't like it. She thinks it's too forward. She thinks out of respect for my mom, I should leave it the way it was. Except that I was two when my mom painted my room pink. I'm really not into pink anymore. And besides, a coat of paint is not disrespectful."

"Do you mind my asking where your parents are?" I asked. "You never mention them."

Penny's mouth twitched. "They died in a car accident."

"I'm sorry. I didn't know."

"It's OK. My *amma* takes good care of me. She's a little old-fashioned, but her heart's in the right place."

Maybe, but I'd like to see the X-ray. I wasn't as convinced as Penny. Anyway, it helped to understand the household dynamics. "Does your *amma* make your sweater-vests?"

"Yes."

"And who cuts your hair?"

"My *amma*."

This was good news as far as I was concerned. It wasn't necessarily that Penny had no flair, more that she had a roadblock. And how hard could it be to get around something so tall and so thin? My spirits did a little heel-kick at the opportunity to encourage Penny in her teenage right to freedom of expression. Defying Grim was just sprinkles on top. I pulled a pair of scissors, a hair dryer, and a hair relaxer, compliments of Jaelle, from my satchel. "Does she know why I'm here?"

"Yes."

"Did she disapprove?"

Both Penny and Tina giggled. "Big time," Penny said.

"And you're still willing to go through with it?"

"Hell, yes."

"Excellent." I had way underestimated Penny. Here was a girl with potential on several fronts. Number one: she could decorate. I have always appreciated an eye for design. Number two: she was willing to take a fashion risk, even at the peril of being grounded or shrugged into ill-fitting, handcrafted crochet wear. And three: we shared a basic philosophy. Democracy: enlightened, fair-minded, and stylishly New World. Monarchy: repressive, cliquish, and very Dark Ages. This had all the makings of a lasting friendship.

I dumped the rest of the contents of my bag onto Penny's bed. Blouses, belts, scarves, bangly bracelets, and thick necklaces scattered into a tumble of color and texture. Penny fingered a white blouse embellished with floral patches and mismatched buttons.

"Did you make this?" Penny asked.

"Yes."

"Where did you get all these crazy buttons?"

I hesitated, but then figured there was no reason to be secretive. "The store across from my *afi*'s, Hulda's Fabric and Notions."

"Recently?" Penny looked up with eyes the size and shine of spotlights.

"Yes."

"Hulda's in town?"

"She was briefly."

Penny bit her thumbnail. "I wonder if my *amma* knows. They're friends, but Hulda's kind of eccentric. She never married. No kids. Comes and goes as it suits her. Nobody knows where she disappears to. Just vanishes for weeks at a time. Then one day she'll just be there at church, or in her store. If she weren't so rich, she'd probably be called crazy."

"She's rich?"

Penny laughed. "Are you kidding? She owns half the town."

"Half the town?"

"That may be an exaggeration. Besides the store, she owns a big home, the abandoned paper factory, and all the land surrounding it."

Why didn't I know this? "What happened to the paper factory?"

Penny opened her arms in a gesture of futility. "That closed a long time ago. Cheaper to import, is what everyone says. Plus, it had been her father's business, and it wasn't like she needed the income."

"Hulda's rich?" I knew I was acting thick, but my brain was having a tough time processing the information. For starters, she dressed in rags. And the three times I'd been face-to-face with her, they'd been the same rags at that. And those heavy brown lace-up man shoes were vintage Dust Bowl, with the layer of dirt to prove it. I shook myself back to the job at hand, stating, "OK, girls, let's stay on task. We've got some hair issues to tackle."

Within an hour, and with enough hair spray to glue a cat to the wall and an arsenal of my own accessories, I had transformed my two subjects. Penny's hair was tugged into a single flip and had a sheen that even I hadn't thought possible. She wore jeans, heeled boots, a crisp white blouse, belted linen jacket, and a smile that could light Disney's Electrical Parade. Tina had promised—and had even written it out ten times on a tablet of paper—never again to lift a curling iron to her poor bangs. I couldn't help but wonder how such a simple tool could get the better of someone so smart and with such excellent penmanship. And it turned out that Tina had pretty hair, auburn with honey streaks that I scrunched into an attractive tumble of natural curls. She wore a long denim skirt, shirttails poking out from a corduroy coat, and a silky scarf wrapped stylishly at her neck. I'd been worried about finding the right look for Tina. Not only was she tall, five-eleven slouched, but she was a serious athlete: cross country, basketball, and track. For the school paper, she covered girls' sports and crusaded for equal time and equal coverage. I wanted to find a style that respected her sporty side, while adding a touch of femininity.

I stepped back and looked her over, rubbing my chin. "Hmmm. Something's missing."

Penny held up a thick silver bracelet. I shook my head no. The two of us stood scrutinizing Tina. "I know just the thing," Penny said with a clap of her hands. "I'll be right back." She returned carrying a cloth shopping bag full of hats. She rummaged through it, extracting the teal blue cloche with peacock feather that I'd have recognized anywhere. "It's my *amma*'s. Isn't it crazy?" She dropped it onto Tina's head. It looked ridiculous. We got the giggles.

"It's a showstopper, all right," I said. "Just not sure what kind of show." We got the guffaws. Penny snorted like a circus elephant. We laughed louder.

There was a knock at the door. "Is everything OK in there?"

Penny snatched the hat from Tina's head and kicked it and the cloth shopping bag under her bed. Grim opened the door and poked her horsey nose into the room. She took a long look at Penny, and then Tina.

"What on earth?" Grim said.

"What do you think?" Penny asked.

"I think you girls should get going." Grim closed the door with a thud.

We got the giggles again. I doubled over with spasms of laughter rolling through me. I couldn't have told you the last time I'd had anything to laugh about. I righted myself and looked at my two new friends. "You guys look great."

"Nobody's going to recognize us," Tina said, fingering her bangs. I promptly swatted her hand away.

"You could get community service hours for this," Penny said, checking herself out in a full-length mirror. "Or at least extra credit with Ms. Bryant."

I gathered my things and shoved them into my bag. "It was fun. And if you guys like the results, then that's all I need." I really did get a kick out of seeing them preen in the mirror. "Should we get going?" I asked, bundling myself into a thick cream-colored fisherman's sweater, knee-length down vest, nubby wool scarf, and fur-lined trapper hat with ear flaps.

Penny looked at me and giggled. "It's supposed to be pretty mild tonight."

I shrugged. "I take no chances with the cold."

CHAPTER FOURTEEN

It actually was a beautiful fall evening, and I probably was too warmly dressed. Still, it wasn't completely nightfall yet. And the weather here was more fickle than the Hollywood press.

The Asking Fire took place on a remote acreage. We walked along an old trail lit by hanging lanterns, skirting thick woods until we came to a wide-open field. The bonfire, a towering inferno of at least ten feet, was already burning brightly. It emitted a heat that gave the crowd golden complexions and rosy cheeks. There were benches and picnic tables set around the area, and a stage off to one side of the fire. Some kids had brought their own blankets, and these were laid out in front of the stage. Cups of punch and boxes of sugary donuts lined a refreshments table. At another table were boxes of pencils and colored squares of paper.

"So how does this thing work?" I asked.

Penny and Tina looked at each other with giddy expressions. "You write down the name of the boy you hope will ask you," Penny said. "Then you offer the paper to the fire. If your heart is true, then he'll ask you."

"You seriously believe that?"

Penny shrugged. "It doesn't hurt to try, even if it is a long shot." She picked up a pencil and a small square of light blue paper. She scribbled something quickly.

Tina also jotted something down and then folded the pink paper over twice. "Aren't you going to write down a name?" she asked.

"No way," I said quickly. "I'm just here for the show."

"What happened to you two?" I recognized Jack's voice and turned to find him standing behind me. He was staring at Penny and Tina, as was his friend Pedro.

"Don't they look great?" I said.

Pedro was the first to answer. "You both look very pretty." Though he used the word *both*, I noticed that his eyes were focused on Penny.

"Sure. I guess," Jack said. The guy obviously had zero appreciation for clothing or style. He wore a purple-and-gold Vikings T-shirt, under which the collar of an orange-and-blue plaid short-sleeved shirt was visible. I hadn't seen colors so misused since kindergarten. And short sleeves? It had to be in the forties. The work boots were OK, I supposed. And the jeans fit well, anyway. At least he wasn't wearing a cap and I could actually see his blue eyes, which I noticed, in the firelight, had flecks of green. Luckily, his lack of enthusiasm hadn't dampened Penny's mood. She was still smiling winningly. So much, in fact, that I worried the volume of aerosol hair spray had frozen more than her flip.

"So are you girls feeding the fire tonight?" Pedro asked.

Penny quickly stuffed the scrap of blue paper into her jean pocket. "We'll never tell."

"I'm not," I said, realizing immediately that I'd not only cut Penny off but had contradicted her as well. "Just watching." Jack gave me a long, hard look. You'd think I'd have been used to it by then, but somehow the guy still unnerved me. "I don't believe in magic anyway," I found myself saying. This from, of all people, a girl who had recently discovered she was a human Stork and had input on the placement of infant souls. Something about the guy caused my neurons to backfire, and made me say things and do things just to be contrary.

Monique and two of her orbiting moonies walked by. She glanced at our group dismissively and then did a head snap, taking in Penny and Tina's makeovers.

"Don't you two look nice tonight." She flashed one of her campaign smiles.

Of course, it was too good to be true. As they walked away, I distinctly heard Monique say, "Talk about lipstick on a pig." She and her friends then dissolved into a fit of giggles.

My concerns about Penny's exposure to harmful chemicals evaporated with Penny's smile. Even her hair seemed to droop a little.

"Don't listen to her." I dropped an arm across Penny's shoulders. "Evil. And wicked. And deserving of an overthrow. Remember?"

Penny managed the slightest of shrugs. "I know." I didn't detect much confidence in her tone.

"You're twice the person she is," Jack said, looking fondly at Penny. For the first time since I met the big doodah, he'd finished a sentence without me wanting to stuff his tongue down his throat. I nodded at him. In fact, I couldn't have agreed more. "Prettier, too," he continued. Had I a pardon to bestow, I'd have granted him one. Heck, if I had a sword, I might have knighted him.

It seemed a perfect opportunity to give them a few moments alone. "Tina, do you want to get some punch?" I took Tina by the elbow. "You want us to bring you some, Penny?"

Penny looked at us like we'd just dropped her onto a deserted island with only a nail file and a birthday candle. Now if only I had a way of hog-tying Pedro, the bothersome third wheel. I steered Tina toward the refreshments, noticing that groups of kids were starting to gather around the stage.

"Now what?" I asked.

"The class president will give a speech," Tina said. "And then the band will start."

"Speech? From the president?" Who I knew to be Wade. I wasn't sure I could stomach him pontificating. What I wouldn't give for a magic carpet ride to the Century City Mall or the Third Street Promenade in Santa Monica right now. And what would the Asking Fire think of that request? Tina was called over by a small group of girls. I watched as she fluffed her hair for them, obviously a reaction to their compliments. I felt like a proud mother hen, happy and peace-filled, until I noticed Wade hovering around the table. He nodded to me, reached for two cups of punch, and walked my way.

"Beverage?" he asked, holding out a cup for me.

"No, thanks."

"Suit yourself." He pounded down one, crushed the cup with his fist, and then gulped the other, finishing with a loud "Aaah." He looked around and then dipped his head forward. "I've been thinking about you lately. And I like a girl with a little fire in her. Maybe we should try again."

"Over my dead body."

He laughed menacingly. "You really are a little hell cat, aren't you?" He dipped his head closer. "Thing is, I don't mind a challenge. Routine gets boring, if you know what I mean."

I took two steps back; he took three forward.

I then heard a loud, shrill call from behind me. "Wade!"

I turned, though it wasn't necessary. Monique's voice was as distinctive as a sonic boom, and just as subtle.

"You're being paged," I said.

"Duty calls." He lifted his eyes toward the towering flames. "Don't forget to feed the fire."

I watched as he sauntered off and grabbed Monique by the waist with a playful growl. She squealed and wriggled to get free. It was very loud and very dramatic — so was childbirth, according to most accounts.

After they left, I took a cup of punch if for nothing else than to cleanse my palate of the aftertaste of arrogance. It didn't help much, but at least it filled my mouth with more than just unused stinging barbs. I took another sip and turned to find Jack at my elbow.

"Was he bothering you?"

"No," I said quickly. "Not at all. I don't even know the guy."

"Really? 'Cause it looked like . . ."

"Just seen him around is all," I said. "Barely know his name."

Jack stared in the direction Wade had walked off. I couldn't decide if the emotion twitching across his brow was anger or relief. "What you did for Penny was nice," he said finally, turning his piercingly blue eyes back to me.

I looked to where I had left Penny, who remained with Pedro — darn him.

"I didn't do much. A little hair product, a big round brush . . ."

"I was talking about the pep talk after Monique was so mean."

"Oh. That. No biggie. Monique will get what she deserves."

"You mean Wade?" Something dark inked across his irises.

A wind howled through the trees behind us. I gathered my vest to my throat. "That and more." *As in morning sickness, swollen ankles, and a squirming belly.*

Feedback from the PA system screeched through the air. I looked up to see Wade with a microphone in his hand.

Jack looked left and right. "I don't see Chris. I'd better make sure he's getting photos for the paper." He glanced up at the stage with a scowl and then hurried off.

Whatever had happened between them last year, it wasn't forgiven.

"Welcome, everyone," Wade said. "Just a few words about this year's Homecoming." He stood with a confidence beyond his years, his thick legs set apart in a boxer's stance. "Ballots for this year's king and queen will be available first thing Monday morning. Stop by the front table before or after school to vote." I noticed there was barely an *umm* or hesitation to his words. The gift of gab. A born salesman. "Tickets to the dance also go on sale Monday morning. Remember, they're only sold in twos, so make the right request of the Asking Fire."

What a crock. Only sold in twos? What, do they have a bouncer at the door checking? Couples' police? Ark patrol?

This was a boat that definitely needed rocking. Which at least went with the dance's under-the-sea theme.

Wade then slid from class president duties to those of football captain. He praised the team and its coaches, cheered their unbeaten record for the year, and announced that he and his defensive line were going to make Pinewood pay for last year's game. I noticed he spoke only of the defense, with brutish words like *crush, pound, wreck,* and *ruin*. It was clear that Wade took his tackles seriously. He didn't acknowledge Jack, the quarterback, or the rest of the offense. Whatever was between them was mutual. "And finally," he said, "Let me declare the Asking Fire open for bids." He lifted his arms in a wide gesture and affected a poet's cadence.

"Should your mind be open
And your heart be true,
Then let the fire's magic
Make a match for you."

I stood with my mouth open, unable to believe that even someone as oily as Wade could stand there and recite anything so corny. But nobody else seemed to think twice about the lame little poem, which must, I surmised, be tradition. I decided to find Penny and walked in the direction I'd last seen her. I skirted around the fire, watching bands of girls clutching pieces of colored paper in their hands and then releasing them to the fire with rapt looks in their eyes. It couldn't possibly work for everyone. The Asking Fire had to disappoint as much as it pleased. I stopped in my tracks, chiding myself for personifying the fire. I found Penny and Tina clutching their papers and whispering to each other.

"Haven't fed the fire yet?" I asked.

"We were waiting for you," Penny said. "I thought you might change your mind."

"No way."

"Can't think of anyone?" Penny asked.

"Not to save my life," I replied.

"Should we go ahead, then?" Tina asked Penny.

They approached the fire. I could see them elbowing each other and could hear their giggles from where I stood behind them. They both lifted their arms high and let go of the small chits of paper. I watched as Penny's light blue and Tina's pink rode the currents of air into the dancing flames. Then a strange thing happened. Penny's blue scrap blew out of the fire and landed in the dirt not far from where I stood. I bent to retrieve it. It was slightly singed, but intact. I called to Penny, but she had joined a gaggle of girls, talking and laughing and hoping for magic. As much as I didn't believe it myself, I didn't want Penny's evening ruined. I walked quickly to the edge of the fire and returned the pastel blue paper to the flames, ensuring this time that the fire consumed it.

"So you changed your mind?" Jack said. I turned to find him grinning at me.

"It probably looks that way, but . . ."

"So will you go with me?" He spoke quickly, as if the best approach was to get it over with fast, like a flu shot, or snapping a bone back into its socket.

"What?"

"Will you go to the dance with me?" Jack repeated.

"I think there's some misunderstanding. What about Penny?"

Jack looked confused, but pointed to where Penny was involved in a one-on-one with Pedro. "I think she's spoken for."

"What?"

"Pedro has wanted to ask her all night, all week for that matter."

I looked over again at Penny, who nodded her head affirmatively at Pedro, after which he broke into a big smile.

"So?" Jack was looking at me expectantly. Many things flashed through my mind in that instant. Why would he ask me? We'd been crash-and-burn since the moment we met. And what would Penny think? It looked like she had a date, but still, what would her reaction be? She'd liked Jack since forever, so this could really crush her. Plus, it was the sort of thing I would avoid on principle. Couples only. Guys have to ask. How Stepford!

"I guess," I heard myself say. Unbelievable, but true; my voice came from somewhere else. A ventriloquist's trick.

"Good." The wind picked up and was gusty enough to blow the long tendrils of my hair across my face and into my eyes. I felt Jack's warm hand brush a lock off my cheek, then a stab of cold pierced through me. I gasped as if plunged into an icy river. Something flashed across Jack's face. He looked hurt. Or in pain. And something went hollow in his eyes. Quickly, he turned and walked away.

What was going on? Who asks a girl out, zaps her with a cold charge, and then disappears like some caped crusader? I felt chilled to my core. Why did I say yes, when my internal dialogue had been all cons — and no pros? And what on earth was I going to say to Penny? Who was, for the record, heading my way. I think I stole your crush, but I'm not entirely sure. I think I'm going to the dance with him, but I could be wrong. There's a fifty-fifty he played me like a trump, but I guess I need a dress, just in case. Holy cow. What would I even wear?

"I got asked to the dance," Penny said.

"That's good. Right? I mean, Pedro seems like a nice guy."

Penny kicked at a clump of grass with the toe of her boot. "I guess it's OK. He is a nice guy, but I don't understand what happened."

"I . . ." I was interrupted by the arrival of Tina.

"Guess what?" Tina said. "It worked! The Asking Fire worked. Matthew asked me."

The Asking Fire, I remembered with a jolt. "There's something I need to tell you, Penny. Two things, actually. Your paper, it flew out of the fire. You had already walked away, so I picked it up and put it back in for you."

"What?" Penny looked startled.

"There's more," I said. "Jack asked me to the dance, and I kind of said yes. I don't know what I was thinking."

"You fed my paper to the fire?" Penny asked.

"Well, yeah, but . . ."

"So then the fire thought you asked for him."

"It was your writing."

"How would the fire know that?" Penny asked.

I couldn't believe I was having this conversation. "How would it know me from you or anyone else for that matter? Come on, let's get real."

"We told you. It's magic."

I exhaled loudly. Had rational thought, like In-N-Out Burger, not yet made it this side of the Rockies? "It was just some sort of weird, awkward moment. I'm not sure he even wanted to ask me. He barely said two words to me and then took off."

"He probably doesn't understand it any more than you do."

That was the first thing in this conversation that made any sense. "Good. Then he'll probably take it back."

"You really don't know him, do you?" Penny said. "If he's anything, he's true to his word."

It got very quiet between us. The band was starting up. My head was already on overload without the jarring drumbeat or screeching vocals. Out of the corner of my eye, I saw Wade leaning against the edge of a picnic table. He was all alone and watching me.

"I'm heading home," I said. "I have a headache."

Penny and Tina offered to walk with me, which I knew was just their proper upbringing speaking. They didn't really want my company at that moment. I was a boyfriend-stealing fire hog. Heck, I didn't want my company. I declined and started making my way toward the dirt path. I noticed Monique at the center of a group of girls. I assumed they were celebrating, or spreading rumors, or perfecting their nastiness, but as I grew closer, I noticed Monique was wiping away tears. One of her friends patted her on the back, and I overheard her say, "You're better off without him."

I kept my head down and trudged onward. The drum of a woodpecker tapped steadily nearby. Its sudden catlike call startled me. Not a woodpecker, after all. A sapsucker. My *amma* had once taught me the difference.

Not a moment later, I passed a clump of trees. The low-lying brush shook, I heard a scuffling of feet, and Wade stepped into my path.

"There you are," he said. "I've been watching you."

I looked around nervously. "What do you want?"

"For us to start over."

"Not going to happen. Just leave me alone."

He cracked his neck from side to side with big thrusts of his Neanderthal jaw. "Aw, come on. Let's be friends. Tell you what — I'll even take you to the dance."

"Too late," I said. "For being friends or the dance."

"What?" Something snapped closed in his eyes.

"I've got a date. And honestly, you'd be my last choice at this point."

"What date?" he asked, his voice low and gruff.

"Jack."

"Snjosson. That punk." He spat it out like a bloody tooth.

"Yes."

"That's not a date," he said. "That's a curse." With that, he brushed past me back toward the crowd. Something shrank in my gut. It did. My navel retracted. It probably wasn't a good idea to piss Wade off. Some dogs you just don't mess with. I shook my head as I scurried along the dark path. I heard the bird again and remembered another thing my *amma* had taught me—all sapsuckers in this region were yellow-bellied.

I had just made it back to where the long gravel path met up with the parking lot when I heard Jack's voice from behind.

"Kat, wait up."

I had been so absorbed in thought that I'd been blind and deaf to my surroundings. Truth was, I'd been thinking about him. Why was everything between us so charged? Enough that it seemed to even produce a physical manifestation. I was alarmed and confused. I turned toward him, not knowing whether he was the last person I wanted to see at that moment, or the only.

"Did you feel it back there?" he asked.

"Feel what?" I didn't know why I was playing stupid. He had clearly heard me gasp.

"When I touched you back there, something happened."

I swallowed hard. "Like the first time." I could barely look at him and had my eyes to the ground.

"What did you feel?"

I lifted my eyes to his. "Cold."

"Cold," he repeated, as if it wasn't the answer he was looking for.

"I'm sorry." I knew nobody would want their touch described as cold, even Jack. It wasn't exactly a compliment. "I know it doesn't sound nice, but your hands — they're warm enough to the touch, but they send icy shivers through my system."

"I want to talk to you about something," he said. There was an urgency to his tone. The tautness in his voice, the rapidity of his blinks, the rigidity of his every muscle heightened the moment. I knew, by some primitive internal alarm, that what he was about to say was important. Just as I braced myself for impact, voices reached us from the path. They were approaching quickly. Jack scowled, shoved his fists into his jean pockets, and turned to see who was coming.

Penny and Pedro were the first upon us. Followed quickly by Tina and Matthew. I was crushed to have our moment intruded upon. I also felt guilty. Not only had I misappropriated Penny's offering to the Asking Fire and

126

stolen her date, but there I was seemingly flaunting the betrayal.

"There you guys are," Pedro said. "We're pulling together some plans for tomorrow. Wanted to see if you were interested."

"What plans?" Jack asked.

"We're thinking of hiking out to Fletcher Lake."

"Where's that?" I asked.

"It's a hiking trail about an hour north of here," Pedro answered. "It's a little punishing, but worth the climb."

Punishing meant painful, and *climb* meant up, neither of which sounded good to me.

"You guys should come." Penny looked straight at me. "It's going to be fun. We're going to pack a lunch. And it's a really pretty view." I looked at her shyly, and she just kind of smiled at me. I was taken aback at just how sweet she was, and how much the clothes and hair-style suited her.

"We'll make a full loop of the lake," Pedro said. "About halfway, there's an observation tower. Bring your camera."

"And it's not too late in the season for a dip," Matthew said. "Or should we call it a plunge. Bathing suits optional, cojones mandatory."

Jack emitted a small growl of displeasure in response to what Matthew had said. I didn't know what to think about the invitation, especially given the way Jack was scowling.

Penny sidled up next to me. "I'm sorry if I wasn't excited for you back there," she said in a whisper. "It wasn't very nice. And Jack has always made it very clear with me, and plenty others, that we were just friends. And of course it makes perfect sense that you and Jack should end up together." Penny must have realized, by the look on my face, just how little sense that made to me. After all, she, more than anyone, knew about the tension between us.

"Perfect sense?" I said, almost under my breath.

"You just haven't figured it out yet," she whispered back. "But you'll see."

The only thing I could see was Jack looking at us like he wondered what all the secrecy was about. Before I could respond, Penny said to the group, "I just talked Kat into it. She says she'll go. How about it, Jack?"

Whatever his reservations had been before, he took a deep breath and replied, "Sounds like a plan," though I could still sense some hesitancy on his part.

After that we stood around for a few minutes finalizing arrangements. We'd all meet in the school parking lot at nine in the morning. From there, we'd pile into Pedro's mom's Suburban. I was assigned breakfast: coffee and muffins.

I was also reminded to dress warmly and wear comfortable shoes.

CHAPTER FIFTEEN

The pink sweater with the curled ribbon collar had seemed too girly, and the black zip-front one with leather piping — too formal. I yanked it off and dropped it onto the growing pile at the bottom of my closet. Sure, clothes were my thing, but even I knew I was overthinking something that would probably spend most of the day under my heavy parka. I settled on a simple hunter-green V-neck, hoping at least someone would notice it matched the paisley scarf I looped around my neck.

"You're up early," my mom said, laying down her newspaper. She looked at my outfit. "What are you dressed for?"

"A hike."

"A hike? Where? With who?"

"A few kids from the bonfire last night. The girl Penny I told you about, the guy who delivered apples to the store, and a few others."

"The Snjosson kid?"

"Yeah."

"I didn't know you knew him." She pulled at her bottom lip.

"Not well."

She took a quick sip of her coffee. "Then are you sure this outing is a good idea?"

Good thing I didn't mention the dance. "Afi said something about bad blood between our families. Are we the Hatfields or the McCoys?"

"We're neither." She picked the paper up and snapped it open. "And I, for one, don't listen to gossip."

We had a quiet breakfast together after that. I only had a banana, knowing I was stopping for muffins and coffee. My mom ate her usual bowl of high-fiber, certified organic bark. Honestly, you could landscape with the stuff. I swear I'd seen it used. It made a decent mulch. She and Stanley had plans to look at open houses. She added quickly that *he* was in the market, but still, I didn't like the idea.

The chime above the door to the Kountry Kettle alerted Jaelle to my presence, but she didn't flash me with one of her usual smiles. I approached the counter hesitantly. The place was busy, so I figured that was the reason for her less-than-enthusiastic greeting. I took a seat at the counter, forgoing my usual spin.

"Good morning, Jaelle."

"Hey, Ice."

"How are you?" I asked, because her eyes looked kind of bleary, like she'd been crying.

"Been better."

"Did something happen?"

"Just a stupid fight between me and Russ. We'll get over it." Jaelle asked why I was dressed like I was about to scale Everest. She had heard of the lake before, but hadn't hiked it. She was, admittedly, not the out-doorsy type.

One of the customers signaled that he needed more coffee. Jaelle picked the pot up from behind her. I took that moment to pull my mom's thermos out of my back-pack. When Jaelle returned, I ordered a dozen muffins and asked her to fill the thermos to go. She emptied the contents of the coffeepot into the stainless steel carafe and then took a long swig from her own mug, though it appeared to be filled with tomato juice and not coffee. She started bagging the muffins, and I could tell by the way she was pitching them into the bag that she was upset and, moreover, would have made a darn good softball player.

"What did you guys fight about?"

"Same old stuff. About his being gone too much. And me stuck in this dead-end job. I have a business degree, you know."

"I know."

"What am I going to do with it here?" She handed me the bag.

I shrugged.

"He left this morning without saying good-bye."

"But you guys always work it out."

"Except this time he thinks maybe we should postpone starting a family until we figure out a few things."

"I thought . . ."

"Joke's on him, huh?"

"Did you take the test?"

"No. Still too chicken."

"Wouldn't it be better to know?"

Jaelle looked into the contents of her mug and then lifted it in a sort of toast. "Here's to the great unknown."

"Jaelle," I said with alarm, "what's in that cup?"

"Just tomato juice. Let me tell you, though, if I knew I wasn't pregnant . . . oh, don't listen to me. I'm a mess this morning." She leaned against the counter on her outstretched arms. "Don't you have somewhere to be?"

"Yeah."

"Then bounce your butt outta here. You got friends, girl, and they're waiting on baked goods."

"Yeah, but . . ."

"Get going."

I left the restaurant with serious concerns about Jaelle—as well as the condition of the muffins tucked under my arm.

CHAPTER SIXTEEN

I met everyone in the parking lot right on time. Everyone except Jack, who was late. I poured cups of coffee and handed out lopsided muffins as we stood waiting. I was surprised at the effect his tardiness had on me: a crush of nerves had my tummy twitching. I was definitely interested in the guy, but interested how?

Pedro griped that Jack was the last person in the developed world not to have a cell phone. At a quarter after, the group came to a consensus that if he wasn't there by nine twenty, we'd go without him. I had to admit, I was bummed. And not just because I felt like it was a reflection of his interest in me. His absence took all the excitement out of the day.

Nine nineteen. I wondered if I'd sound desperate suggesting we give him a few more minutes. Or would I appear all the more pathetic when he still didn't show? I was shocked at how much I wanted his old truck to pull up. Now that he'd asked me to the dance, and there was something he wanted to tell me, I was—despite everything else going on in my life right now—thinking way more about Jack than I should. Especially as it was nine twenty.

Pedro sighed. "Looks like he's a no-show. Let's get going." As we were only five, I sat in the backseat with Tina and Matthew, while Penny sat up front with Pedro. It was awkward. It had become a sort of double date and I felt about as wanted as a big fat jellyfish between the swimming cones. We were just pulling out of the parking lot when I caught sight of Jack's old junker barreling at us from the opposite direction.

"I think that's him coming," I said, trying, and failing, to keep an even keel to my voice. If I'd sounded any more gleeful, I'd have needed choral robes.

Pedro made a U-turn, and Jack parked his car alongside ours. He climbed out from under the steering wheel, walked to the back of the Suburban, and stowed his gear. He then vaulted himself, quite effortlessly, into the third row of seats. Pedro pushed some sort of button that closed the hatch automatically. I was frozen in my seat. Would it look funny if I, too, scrambled into the back?

"So Kat, you gonna make me sit back here all by myself?"

My stomach did a jackknife. Just the sound of his voice, kind of breathy from rushing, but also playful, had every inch of my body trilling.

"Are you going to ask nicely?" I had to at least try to act cool.

"Will you *please* sit back here with me?"

Now I had to crawl into the back and not look like a complete spaz, in stiff boots that had about as much give as granite. I managed to land on my butt, hard, but at least I ended up on the seat and not the floor.

"Dude, you seriously need to get a cell phone," Pedro said.

"I'm sorry," Jack replied.

He looked straight at me, and I could tell that this was intended for my benefit more than anyone else's. His right hand stretched out and then balled into a fist, like he wanted to touch me as he said it. Of course, he didn't dare. Given the bizarre and chilly outcome the last two times we'd made contact, who knew what could happen? I was pretty sure Pedro's mom didn't have insurance for a freak pelting of hail and ice.

"My dad wouldn't let me leave until I'd finished my chores for the day. I've been up since four."

No one dared get on his case after that. I hadn't even made my bed before rushing out the door, never mind the pile of clothes I'd left on the floor of my closet.

In the front of the car, they began a conversation about the band that played at the Asking Fire. Jack and

I were quiet, though there was an intensity between us that screamed volumes. It was driving me flippin' crazy. I was on fire. Every neuron in my body was crackling. I wondered how no one else could hear it.

"Have you been up here before?" I asked finally.

"Once. A long time ago."

"Is it a long hike?"

He looked down at my boots. "Are those as new as they look?"

"Yes."

He shook his head.

"They're Timberlands," I said defensively. My grams in Santa Monica had bought them for me when she'd heard we were moving to what she called "north of nowhere." Nobody shopped like my grams. Born and raised in Paris, she claimed couture was in her blood. Her favorite thing, besides shopping for herself, was shopping for me.

"But have you worn them before?"

"No."

Again the head shake. I looked down at his boots, the leather of which had probably been tanned about the same time as Moses's sandals. I couldn't tell if he was teasing me or if he was genuinely concerned, nor which I'd have preferred. I decided to change the subject.

"What's the weather forecast for today?" I asked.

Something passed over his brow, like the start of a joke or remark, but then he just kind of shrugged.

Tina overheard my question. "I think it's supposed to stay fairly mild. Of course, we are hiking up to a higher elevation. I hope everyone brought layers."

Jack was in a T-shirt, as usual. "Is that all you're wearing?" I asked.

He looked straight ahead, but, again, I sensed some internal struggle on his part. "I don't feel the cold," he said matter-of-factly.

For the last portion of the drive, I stared out the window. I'd never seen so many trees. They bordered the highway, some encroaching within feet of the blacktop. Their leafy heights swayed in the wind, and birds — so many I grew dizzy watching — soared in and out of this lush canopy. We even passed a small herd of deer, ten or twelve together; they loped gazelle-like between a thicket of tree trunks. Finally, Pedro pulled into the parking lot of the state park. There were only a few cars. It was seemingly more of a summer destination. We piled out and grabbed our gear. The air was already cool, and I was glad to have heeded the advice about layers. I wore a long-sleeved Under Armour T-shirt, Eddie Bauer knit blouse and had the hunter-green sweater tied at my waist and a North Face parka balled into my backpack. Were the next ice age to suddenly hit the area, I'd probably survive.

Again, I looked at Jack's light apparel. "Is that seriously all you have to wear?" I asked. My paranoia of the cold, was, I discovered, transferable: frigiphobia by proxy.

"Don't worry about me," he said.

"It's the bears you should worry about," Pedro cut in. "I hope you brought your bear repellent."

"My bear repellent?" He had to be kidding.

"He's joking," Penny said.

"Are there really bears?" I asked.

"Black bears," Jack said. "Not grizzlies, and not the brown bear you have in California."

"Kinder, gentler bears," Pedro said with a laugh. "Even the wildlife around here is Minnesota-nice."

"You really don't need to worry," Matthew said. "We come up here hunting every year and never had a problem. They're more afraid of us than we are of them."

I did not like the idea of there being any bears in the vicinity, and I made no allowances between brown or black. I cast a wary eye all around me, and only settled when it seemed I was the only one with pre-hike jitters. I reminded myself, quite logically, that the Pacific Ocean — in which I willingly swam and surfed — was full of sharks, yet there I stood all limbs accounted for.

Several trails were marked on a large map, which was posted outside the small ranger station. It seemed we were taking the longest and most circuitous route; our trek would take us up the western side of Fletcher Lake, along a northern ridgeline separating it from Weaver Lake, and back down the east side, crossing a small river.

We started hiking, skirting meadowlands for the

first ten or fifteen minutes. The dirt path was wide and hard-packed, a good sign as far as I was concerned. Many had gone before us, and returned, presumably. We walked two by two, in the newly formed couples' groupings. Tina and Matthew took the lead, both long-limbed, though hers was the more athletic of the two builds, his teetering to a gangly or spindly classification. Penny and Pedro followed second. The four of them chatted easily. Jack and I, pulling up the rear, were quiet, which, at that moment, I preferred. I was drinking in the surroundings: air so crisp you could snap it with your fingers, and greens in every lush shade imaginable, offset by the autumnal flashes of red and yellow. I couldn't imagine a smell more invigorating than the wafts of earthy pine carried along the cool currents of air. OK, so Minnesota had its perks.

The trail then became rockier with trees, mostly evergreens, lining the path. And ever so gradually we started to ascend. If the air was this cool at nearly midday, I would certainly need my parka later.

Once again I looked at Jack. We were keeping up a fairly brisk pace, but still, I wondered about his lack of warm clothing. He was definitely in good shape, owing to football practices, I imagined. Though I supposed farm chores alone would be a workout. My thighs and butt were starting to sing a little. I regretted not having a fall sport and made a mental note to look into both volleyball and track for the winter and spring. At least my boots weren't giving me any problems.

The others were still talking in muted voices. An occasional giggle from Penny floated back, and it filled the air with so much light and joy, I couldn't help but think that she had no regrets about the pairings. It did make me wonder why Jack and I were so stubborn in our silence. I was normally a filler, someone who instinctually grouted the social cracks. A dozen little starts of conversation came to mind: books, music, travel, movies. Still I resisted, enjoying the tension heightened by our lack of communication. I wondered if he was always this way. Or was it something I brought out in him, as he did in me?

We were soon enveloped in thick trees and the path became narrow, forcing us to continue single file. Jack simply urged me into the second-to-last spot with a sweep of his arm, and then took the back of the line. I noticed that Pedro helped Penny over a few treacherous rocks that blocked the path. I could sense how close Jack got to me at these impasses, and I could hear his labored breathing, but he didn't offer me his hand. And then suddenly, around a bend in the path, we came to a small clearing and the lake. It was smoky gray, with a rocky shoreline and bordered by thick trees all around.

"Wow. Beautiful," Tina said.

We all agreed and paused to enjoy our first glimpse of Fletcher Lake. Penny reminded us to drink water. I perched on a large rock and pulled a bottle of Evian from my backpack. Jack looked long and hard at my choice of water, and I waited for him to make some comment. I was sure he'd have something to say about water coming all the way from Europe. Evian tasted better. That was fact. My friend Mindy did a science fair project in eighth grade. It won the taste test hands down. So what if tap tested the same for purity? Jack shrugged, pulled a large, refillable metal bottle from his backpack, and drank. It had been decided we'd eat lunch once we reached the observation tower, which, by Pedro's accounts, was only another twenty minutes up the path, but we'd all certainly made quick work of our breakfasts. Jack pulled a bag of apples from his pack and tossed each of us a shiny red ball. I wasn't sure if it was the apple or the source, but it was delicious, and a different variety from the pippins Afi stocked.

I looked over the lake. Something large and graceful soared into my field of vision. Even stories high above our heads, the size and power of the bird was impressive. As a newly discovered member of a Stork Society, a real bird society — not some binocular-sporting, Audubon-card-carrying bird watcher — I felt a connection to the majestic creature.

"That's a bald eagle," Pedro said.

It ducked and dodged above us in a show of speed and agility.

"Wow," I said. "It's so graceful."

We sat in silence for many minutes watching the

impromptu air show until the bird dipped his wings and soared, effortlessly, out of view.

Matthew looked out at the lake. "Who's up for that cold plunge?"

"Not me," Tina said.

"I dare you," Pedro said.

"I will if you will," Matthew replied. He looked at Jack. "How about it, Jack?"

"No." Jack's response was so abrupt, I was startled. Everything about him seemed suddenly tense and even angry, though at what I couldn't imagine.

Tina gave Matthew a nudge in the side, and he returned the prompt with a sheepish shrug. "I forgot," he whispered to Tina. I was seriously confused.

Just then a wind shear blasted us from above. It was cold and menacing, and I quickly untied the sweater from around my waist and pulled it over my head. The wind's timing couldn't have been any worse; an odd chill had already settled around our little group.

"Let's keep walking," Pedro said. I could tell he was trying to defuse the situation, but everybody got quiet and even the air seemed pressurized as we gathered our things and set back along the path. Even my boots stiffened to the mood. From behind, I watched Penny's white running shoes bend pliantly over rocks and roots and whatever else lay in our path. Sneakers, especially white sneakers, and jeans was a look I abhorred. Athletic footwear should pair with athletic apparel, period. But at this juncture, and as much as I hated to admit it, I envied Penny. My boots had about as much give as the Grinch, and I had definitely started to limp.

Much to my chafed ankles' relief, we finally made it to the observation tower. As the area was accessible only to hikers, not much had been done to develop the site. There were a few scattered picnic tables, a small wooden building housing rest rooms, a large outdoor map-board, and the wooden platform observational tower itself. It was a wonder that such a gem was so off the beaten track. In California, there'd be a restaurant, gift shop, and scenic tram up to the area, and, needless to say, an admission. I had to admit that the view was already worth the hike. And we hadn't even climbed the platform yet.

By unanimous vote, we decided to eat first. Penny and Tina unpacked a selection of sandwiches, Pedro threw out two large bags of chips, Matthew produced a container of homemade chocolate chip cookies, and Jack dumped another six apples onto the pile. We sat at one of the picnic tables, closest to the tower, chatting casually.

"What was your school in California like?" Tina asked.

"The biggest difference would probably be the campus," I said. "Year-round outdoor lunch seating, open-air corridors; even our lockers were outside."

"How far to the beach?" Matthew asked.

"Five minutes," I said.

"Nice," Pedro said.

I lifted my eyes up to our beautiful surroundings. "This is nice, too."

Here in the comfort of the group, I finally felt like I fit. We talked about the dance coming up next weekend. I debated internally whether Jack would confirm our date or break it, the latter seeming more likely at this point. He had hardly spoken during lunch, and I wondered what was going on. As I looked, again, to gauge his mood, I found him returning my stare with a funny expression on his face. Had I been ogling him that openly? And for how long? For some time was the unfortunate reply to my internal question. I hadn't a clue what anyone else had eaten, yet I could inventory — and probably calculate a fairly accurate calorie count — of Jack's lunch consumption: three sandwiches (two turkey, and one tuna), four handfuls of Fritos, three cookies, and one apple. How embarrassing. No wonder the guy had stopped talking to me. He was most likely thinking I'd go *Fatal Attraction* on him.

I looked away, probably guiltily, up toward the tower. A young couple had been on the platform when we arrived. Our decision to eat first probably had as much to do with giving them their privacy as with our own ravenous appetites. I watched as he pulled her into a hug from behind, protectively, and they took in the scenery from the same vantage point. Something caught in my throat as I spied on their intimacy. It seemed so natural, and painless.

"Did you guys hear about Wade and Monique?" Tina asked.

I went absolutely still.

"She turned him down for the dance," Tina continued. "He was flirting with someone else."

I bent down to retie my bootlaces.

"Give it till Monday," Pedro said. "They'll be back together."

"Except he called her some pretty nasty names," Penny said. "Said it loud enough for half the student body to hear."

"It's like the Lindy Vanmeer saga all over again," Tina said.

Again, out of nowhere, an arctic gust descended on our group, sending leaves scattering and blowing tendrils of hair into my eyes. Our trash went flying; Tina and Matthew jumped to collect our airborne empties. When the gale finally settled, I noticed that Jack had walked a few paces away.

"What is with this weather?" Penny shook a leaf from the hem of her pants. "Tina and I are going to check the maps. You wanna come?" She pointed to the large freestanding map-board posted in front of the rest rooms.

"No," I said. "I'm more interested in climbing the tower."

146

Tina and Penny set off. Pedro and Matthew were scouring the area for walking sticks, which they'd at first teasingly called "bear sticks," seemingly for my benefit. And Jack was still off on his own. Good. I was looking forward to a few moments alone with my thoughts and a bird's-eye view of such natural beauty.

CHAPTER SEVENTEEN

I ascended the stairs to the tower. It looked like an over-size and elevated lifeguard station. It was even painted the same familiar shade of light blue. Two stories, and two turns of rickety wooden stairs, led me up to a square open-air deck with a wooden half wall spanning its perimeter. The couple had departed, so I had the place to myself. Besides a vista onto the lapping waters of two steely-blue lakes, a dense forest of trees stretched endlessly in all directions. I marveled at the amount of open land. In LA every square inch of ground is developed into tidy, compact bundles. Even the open spaces are spare and trim. The neighborhood playground, where I'd spent hour after hour with my longtime nanny, Rosa, was called the Marine Parkette, *park* presumably too ambitious a term.

The call of a bird drew my attention to the west. The bald eagle had returned. I held my breath, amazed at the vantage point the observation tower provided. He circled two times, edging closer with each pass. His snowy white head was such a stunning contrast to the earthen brown of his body, and his wingspan was immense. The pull of his wings sounded like the wind-borne flap of a large flag. He settled onto the bough of a towering pine, not thirty feet from the railing of the platform where I stood.

"Friend of yours?" Jack asked.

I nearly jumped out of my boots, cursed things.

"We just met. And I'm not so sure *friend* would be the right word. I think he's eyeing me for lunch."

Jack laughed. "Nah. He wouldn't want to have to chew through all those layers of clothes, not to mention those boots."

I looked down at the damn things. As forgiving as concrete. My ankles were not looking forward to the balance of our hike.

"Take them off," Jack said.

"What?"

"Take them off."

"Why?"

"You'll see."

"I'm not taking them off. My feet will get cold."

He looked at me with exasperation. "You limped the last half hour and we're only halfway around the lake."

I grumbled, but bent to unlace the espresso-brown ankle-high hikers.

I handed them over to Jack, who proceeded to vandalize my property. He removed the laces in a series of efficient tugs and then twisted the leather backward in a flap, bending the high-top portion over the heel. He dropped them to the floor of the platform and continued to pummel them with his own heavy footgear. Kicking and stomping and grinding my two-hundred-dollar nubucks into a pulp. At one point he removed a large stone from his backpack and hammered on the ankles. Who carries a rock in their backpack? No one, of course, which was how I knew the assault was premeditated.

"Are you quite finished?" I asked.

"That should do it." He dropped the boots into my arms and playfully wrapped the loose laces around my neck as if to copy the scarf I had stylishly knotted at my throat. The leather was scraped, and cracked and creased where it had been bent backward. They looked awful and would never again complete the boot-cut Lucky jeans and brown leather bomber jacket ensemble.

I grumbled again and bent to relace and then refit my boots. I stood to find Jack planted above me with his arms crossed and a huge smile on his face. "Better?"

I took a tentative step. Damn him. They were better. Much better. Had some give to the ankle, finally. "A little."

The eagle remained at its nearby perch.

"My grandmother says it's a good omen to be eye-to-eye with a bird," Jack said.

As if it had been eavesdropping, the eagle flew away, its wings clapping like thunder. It distanced itself in a matter of moments, skirting the trees along the lake's edge. "I think it's mocking us." I looked down at my pathetic feet. "Pitying us our inferior means of travel. I'd take wings today."

"If you could stand the heights."

I looked to where the great bird had settled, a football field away and at the upper reaches of the towering pines. "No problem. The higher the better." It was true. I'd always scrambled to the top of the highest thing: slides, jungle gyms, high dives, and ladders. And I always took a window seat on a plane.

The others joined us on the platform. We spent a long time sharing Matthew's binoculars and snapping photos. They were sorry to hear they'd missed our up-close-and-personal with the eagle.

"We're atop an esker," Jack said.

"A what?" Pedro asked.

"An esker. It's an elevated ridge between two depressed surfaces formed by subglacial streams or tunnels."

Pedro laughed. "Dude, you sound like an encyclopedia."

Jack just shrugged. "Glaciers are interesting. They shaped so much of our landforms."

"Interesting to penguins and polar bears, maybe," Pedro said. "Me, I just think it's a nice view."

"We should get going," Matthew said. "It's still quite a hike back."

We kept with our plan to hike the full circular route around the lake. It definitely felt good to walk and generate a little body heat. The first few minutes back in the cool afternoon air had been a shock. I still couldn't believe Jack continued with no jacket. How could anyone be so impervious to the cold? I could actually see steam forming where my warm breath met the air's chill. My feet were still aching, though to be fair, the injuries were preexisting. I comforted myself with the thought that we were heading down.

We came upon a fork in the path, one side wider and obviously more traveled than the other.

"I saw this on the map back at the tower," Penny said. "We go this way." She pointed to the wider trail.

"The smaller one would run along the lake," Pedro said skeptically. "It seems more logical."

"Trust me," Penny said. "Tina and I checked the map."

We set off on the larger trail. Twenty minutes later, we came upon a good-size stream. We all stopped short, realizing that the means of traversing the running waters was a series of wet slippery rocks, each spaced about a foot from the other and spanning a distance of at least twenty feet. Our feet were definitely going to get wet.

Pedro went first, making quick work of the stepping stones. Penny followed him, and though she teetered at one point—balancing with one leg hanging precariously over the rushing waters—she also reached the other side with no more than a few splashes on the hem of her jeans. Matthew and Tina probably shouldn't have tried to hold hands as they crossed. Though deserving of points for chivalry, he probably did, in hindsight, drag her into the waters with him. They flailed about fairly comically and emerged on the other side with their pants drenched to their thighs.

I could see the muscles in Jack's shoulders tighten into a ripple under his T-shirt, and though I was impressed, I knew it wasn't a good sign.

"I'm going back to the fork," he called to the others. "There's probably a bridge on that trail."

Pedro was the first to react. "What? That's like a mile back, probably more. And who knows if that trail leads into this one?"

"Don't worry about me," Jack said. "I'll meet you at the car."

"Seriously, dude," Matthew said. "You saw us. It isn't that deep."

Something very dark flashed across Jack's face. The wind rifled through his hair. "I'll catch up," he said.

"I don't understand," I said to him in a quiet tone the others across the stream couldn't hear.

"I don't do water," he said.

"What does that mean, you don't do water?"

"I don't swim. I don't boat. I don't fish."

"Why not?"

He blew air through his lips in a half whistle. It seemed like a stalling tactic. "It's a long story," he said finally. "You go ahead with them. I'll catch up with you guys in a little bit."

I stood there frozen, not knowing what to do. My feet were aching, and all I wanted was the fastest way back to the upholstery of Pedro's mom's Suburban. I realized, with a start, that this was the first he'd spoken to me since we'd descended the tower. And a dismissal at that. A directive for me to leave him. A "go away" decree.

"I'll stay with Jack," I called across to the group.

Matthew made one last attempt at convincing Jack to cross, but it only seemed to anger and embarrass him. I reminded them I had my cell phone, and that we could call if we ran into any problems. With that, the four of them shrugged and continued down the trail, while Jack and I retraced the path back toward the fork.

I walked ahead of Jack, wanting to admonish him for being so quiet all day, but didn't dare darken his mood. I was also highly curious about his aversion to water, but knew it was neither the time nor place for that conversation. We reached the split and headed down the other trail. I hoped this path wouldn't take us too far out of our way. My feet were beyond pain now, and though I knew I walked with a decided hobble, I had no choice.

"You're limping," Jack finally said.

"I know," I said, none too pleasantly. "My feet are killing me."

"It's your boots."

"You don't say."

I could hear a muffled laugh behind me, and then he said, "Stop a minute."

I sighed good and loud, but came to a standstill under some low-hanging trees.

"You're in pain," he said. "Let's take a little break."

We came to rest under an overhang of pines. I sat on a fallen log and stretched my feet out in front of me.

"I feel responsible," he said after a minute or two of nothing but the forest crackling around us. "This detour is my fault."

"I wasn't forced into anything. Besides, even in the big city, they teach us about the buddy system."

"Buddies, huh?" he said with a grin. "Let me help you out there, buddy. Take your boots off again."

"What? No way. They'd end up in shreds."

He laughed. "I wasn't going to work on your boots. I was going to wrap your ankles."

"With what?"

"I could cut up that scarf of yours. I have a pocket-knife."

"Are you crazy?" My hand flew to my throat. "This was expensive."

"Suit yourself."

"Besides, aren't you forgetting something?"

"What?"

"The last two times we touched weren't so successful," I said.

He looked up at the sky. "I wanted to talk to you about that."

"Talk? Really? You talk? That would be something new."

"I'm sorry. I haven't been very good company today. It's just . . ." He paced back and forth. "You make me so . . ." He balled his hands into fists at his sides. "I have a theory about that thing between us."

"What kind of theory?"

"I think we just need to let it play itself out one time, and then we'll be over it." He took a step toward me. "How bad could it really get?" He wiped his palms, one across the other, in nervous pumps.

"Forget it," I said, rising to my feet. Damn. My ankles were rubbed raw. I slowly curled the scarf from around my neck and tossed it to him. "You cut. I'll wrap."

He did, indeed, have a knife with him and made quick work of my cashmere scarf. I unlaced my boots, took the two halves, and swaddled my bruised ankles. They felt immediately better. Cashmere has that effect. I stood and looked down at my altered footwear. It was a sorry sight. I just hoped the rest of my attire survived the day.

"We should press on," I said. "We don't want to keep them waiting."

The trail became narrow and densely forested. I wondered if we'd made a mistake. This was clearly a seldom-used route. We ducked under fallen branches, scrambled over large rocks, and, at times, bushwhacked our way through dense vegetation. Finally, the path skirted the lake's edge, where waves tumbled over a rocky shoreline.

"What's that?" I pointed to a round black dot in the water just fifty or so yards up the trail.

"Shit," Jack said.

"What is it?"

"Shit. Shit. Shit," Jack whispered. He stopped dead in his tracks.

I continued to stare at the object. It moved then, and splashed a little in the water. "Is that a bear?" I asked.

"Yes." Jack was looking about wildly, behind him, behind me, off into the trees.

I looked again at the furry mound. Even allowing for the distance, it didn't look very large. "Is it a baby?"

"Yes."

"That's OK, right?" I could hear a nervousness cording through my voice.

"No. That's bad. Very bad." Jack kept his voice low and continued to scan the area, looking for something.

"Why?" I whispered, following his cue.

"Black bears would prefer to leave us alone." He held his hand up as if gauging the wind. "They're not aggressive by nature, except . . ."

"Except?"

"When protecting their young. If we come between that cub and its mother, this could get ugly."

"Ugly?" Forget nervousness, there was now an open-throttled panic to my voice. I'd been promised Minnesota-nice bears.

"If only I knew where the mother was. What direction," Jack said, more to himself. Again he scanned left and right. "The right wind would help us. If we were upwind, she might not catch our scent. Never know we were here."

"Unless you brought a very large fan, I don't know what we could do about that right now. Don't you think we should just back away? Put distance between us and it." I pointed at "it" as "it" playfully splashed at something in the water. Hard to imagine that anything so childlike could be a threat, but I'd seen enough Discovery Channel and PBS to know better. I tried to remember something, anything, which would help in that moment. Making tea out of pine needles and lashing shelters out of palm fronds came, crazily, to mind.

"Make no sudden moves," Jack said, placing one foot slowly behind the other.

I did the same.

"Bears have a sense of smell a hundred times stronger than humans," he whispered, placing another foot warily behind him. "If we rush, we'll actually displace our scent."

I placed another foot, slowly, behind me. It was difficult to keep my balance at this awkwardly slow gait.

Our movements made *tai chi* look like the hundred-yard dash. We had both backed up about ten yards when the snapping of twigs and a low growl froze us in our tracks. Through the trees, between us and the cub, a big black mama bear emerged. *This can't be the end,* I thought. I'd never shopped for Chanel in Paris, or Prada in Milan — or fallen in love.

And then several things — bizarre, unexplainable things — happened simultaneously. A rush of wind so swift and sudden it produced a small boom came over the lake, ruffling the fur on the mama bear and causing the baby bear to lift its paws in a batting motion at this teasing funnel of air. The eagle, its wingspan stretching six feet at least, rode that same channel of wind and with an angry caw dove at the cub. And then a black bird, in some crazy kamikaze move, went after the eagle. Inside a single beat of my thumping heart, the mother bear lunged out of the woods and toward her unprotected babe and the bird of prey.

"Run," Jack urged, though still keeping his voice low. He waited until I was a few paces in front of him and then he followed. I could hear his labored breathing and the heavy thud of his boots behind me. We ran full out. My legs were seizing with cramps, and my lungs felt ready to pop. We came across a large tree fallen over the path. I stumbled, clumsily, my sweater catching on a spindly branch, and I fell, hard, backward. In the tiniest of moments, Jack was upon me. He ripped the bottom edge of my sweater from the tree's snatches and then bent to lift me from where I lay sprawled across the earthen floor. I felt his arms encircle me and it seemed like time itself was stalled, suspended in the space between us — and then a shocking burst of freezing pain. Scenes flashed in front of my eyes, obscured in a watery haze. Panic consumed me. I kicked, but my legs felt heavy and moved as if through something thick and cold. And I was sinking. Going down fast and hard. I struggled, yet it only seemed to hasten my fall. I tried to scream, but my voice was muffled, and my lungs filled with a horrible pain. And though there was light above, darkness grew as I descended. It was a cold like nothing I'd ever felt before, a chill that brittled my bones. I felt hopeless, utterly hopeless, and then resigned. Death. This could only be death.

"Let me go. Let me go." I was lying on my back on the gravel path, screaming.

Jack lay on the ground next to me. "Are you OK? Are you hurt?"

I tried to sit up, but the muscles in my stomach had turned to jelly. Still, we had to keep going, away from the bear. I took a deep breath, attempted to stand, and then everything started to spin. The last thing I remembered was a look on Jack's face that was pure agony. And then complete and total blackness.

CHAPTER EIGHTEEN

I came to feeling like I was on a horse. There was a constant jostling motion, which was making my head pound. I looked up to find myself in Jack's arms, and we were running.

"What happened?" I managed to say, though my voice was weak.

Jack stopped suddenly and dropped to his knees, still cradling me in his arms. "Oh, my God, I thought I killed you."

It took a few moments for it all to register. I remembered the bear, and the freezing jolt of pain.

"I must have fainted."

"You weren't breathing," he said.

I felt awkward in his arms, my face pressed against his still jacket-less chest, with his head bent to rest just inches from my own. But I was definitely weak, and somehow it felt warm and safe in this position.

"Can you give me a moment?" I asked in a faltering voice.

He continued to hold me. Many minutes passed. I couldn't believe how still he remained. And as I was suspended in this cocoon, I felt strength returning to my body. Finally, I wiggled to release myself, though it seemed he let go reluctantly.

I sat on the ground next to him, my arms around my knees. "I think I'm going to live." I tried to laugh, for his sake. I could see how pained he was. "What happened back there?"

"For starters, we had a bear encounter."

"I remember," I said, rubbing my head. "Are we safe here? Would she still come after us?"

"We're safe," Jack said. "She wouldn't abandon her cub to chase us, and those birds . . ."

"What was up with those birds?" I asked.

"I've never seen anything like it. They acted like . . ."

"Like what?"

"I don't know. It was just very strange."

"I'm not going to argue," I said. "It bought us time."

"Yes. It did," Jack said. "And then you fell. And I tried to lift you up, and you had a . . . reaction."

"If I remember correctly, you did, too."

"Not like you." He shook his head regretfully.

"But what did you feel?" I asked.

He seemed to fight some internal debate, but then began in a shallow voice. "I couldn't breathe. When I touched you, I couldn't breathe. It's as if a weight pressed down on my chest and I couldn't fill my lungs with air."

"That doesn't sound good."

"Your turn," Jack said. "What happened to you?"

"I froze, and then I sank, and then I died."

"Froze?"

"Yes. And I hate the cold. Have for as long as I can remember."

"You died?"

"That's what it felt like."

"Tell me," he said. "Did it seem like a dream, or a hallucination, or a vision, or . . ." He paused as if measuring his choice of words. "Or a memory?"

"Oh." This came out in a gasp. "How could it be a memory?"

He stood up and started pacing in front of me. It seemed he wasn't going to reply, or at least, not until he'd carefully planned the words. "Remember when I first saw you in your grandfather's store?" There was uncertainty in his eyes and voice. "Do you remember what I said?"

"You said, 'You know me, right?' You were pretty insistent." I realized then that I had replayed our first encounter over and over in my head. And I was pretty certain I had it verbatim.

"I'm not sure if I'm really the one who should be telling you this." He ran his fingers through his hair. "Maybe you should talk to your mom."

"About what?"

"I'm not sure I'm allowed."

"Allowed what?"

"To tell you."

"Tell me what? Seriously, Jack, you're freaking me out."

"Get up," he said, helping me to stand. "Just in case, let's put some more ground between us and that bear, and then let's talk."

We scrabbled over the path at a very brisk pace. I wasn't sure if it was distancing myself from the angry mama bear or propelling myself toward Jack's "talk" that fueled me. No longer did my boots hurt or my muscles cramp; I simply put one dogged foot in front of the other. Finally we returned to the section of the stream with the slippery rock crossing.

"We're back where we started," I said with surprise.

"Not much choice."

"But what about the water?"

"I'm not going to fall," he said. His fists were balled at his sides and his shoulders rod straight.

He insisted I cross first, and though I was exhausted and my legs were shaky, I made it across with only the slightest of balance checks. He started as soon as he saw me safely on the other side. I knew he would have no problem. We'd been through enough already. There was a determination that corded through the muscles of his thighs and the set of his jaw. I thought of what Penny had said, that he was good at everything he tried. There was, I had to admit, a confidence and capability about him that was reassuring. Once we were both high and dry on the other side of the stream, Jack pulled me to a fallen log and sat me before him, though he remained standing.

"I don't want to scare you," he began.

"Jack," I said, "I'm way past scared. Just tell me."

He kicked at a clump of grass, as if hesitant to begin.

"When you were eleven—the last time you were here—we were involved in an accident out on Elkhorn Lake." He spoke fast, as if afraid the words wouldn't come if he took the time to think them through. "It was right after Christmas. Your family had been visiting. A bunch of us kids were skating on the lake. You fell through the ice. I was the only one who saw you. I went to help, and I fell through, too. We were under for a long time. Too long. Some say as long as forty minutes; others say twenty. It doesn't matter though—either way, we should have died."

My heart was trying to escape my chest; it pounded to get out. This information was, somehow, more frightening than our bear encounter. "There's no way," I said. "I think I'd remember something like that."

"But that's the thing. You didn't. We were both in the hospital for a long time. You were in a coma. It was a huge story. Considered a miracle. Especially since we both survived not just the frigid temperatures but without breathing. When you woke up days later, you didn't know where you were and you remembered nothing. Your parents took you back to California as soon as you could travel. And you never came back. And all I ever heard was that you had some sort of trauma-induced amnesia."

"But my parents would have told me."

He shrugged. "I'm sure they did what they thought was best."

"How could I not know this?" It seemed like we were discussing a character from a book or a scene from a movie. All I could do was imagine. I kept trying to remember something, anything, but came up empty. "That's why you don't do water," I said slowly, glad to know I could process recent events. "And that's why Hulda called me the girl of the lake."

"You know Hulda?"

I realized I'd let that one slip. I never knew how much I was allowed to say. "We've met." Jack looked at me a little funny, but then again, he'd just told me we'd shared a near-death experience, essentially that he'd saved my life. I supposed the guy was entitled to look at me any way he pleased.

"I think you should hear the rest from your mom,"

Jack said. "I'm probably already in trouble for saying too much."

A storm of thoughts battered me. One was the realization that what I had felt when Jack held me — the fall, the darkness, the hopelessness — were memories, an unsettling reality. How had I survived? How had *we* survived?

"Are you OK? Do you think you can walk?" he asked. "The others will be getting worried."

"They don't know anything?"

"I couldn't find your cell phone, though I swear I heard it buzzing."

I patted the zippered inside pocket of my jacket. "It's in here."

"I gave up looking and just started running."

I stood and took a few steps and was surprised at how wobbly I was. Without the fuel of adrenaline, my limbs had turned slack. Jack cupped his hand under my elbow.

"Easy does it."

I leaned on his arm. "At least one good thing has come out of this whole we-touch-and-then-we-die experience."

"What's that?" he asked.

"Your theory — about getting it out of our system — it seems to be true. No more icy zaps." After the first few haltering steps, I got stronger.

He shook his head. "Talk about a silver lining."

We got a good rhythm going, if a bit slow. "What are we going to tell the others?"

"It's your call."

"I suppose the bear encounter is enough. I'll say I felt faint. I want to talk to my mom about the lake story."

"Bear story it is," he said.

I could see the shock on the others' faces as Jack and I came limping toward them. They had tumbled out of the car at the first sight of us coming along the path and were upon us in moments.

"What happened?" Pedro asked.

"Kat, are you hurt?" Penny's voice registered alarm.

"We had a little incident with a black bear and her cub." I was relieved that Jack took it upon himself to offer explanations. My mind was reeling in anticipation of the conversation with my mother. I didn't think I had it in me to placate this group in the meantime. "She probably suffered a mild case of shock. She just needs somewhere safe and somewhere warm." This from a guy who still was without a coat.

Jack helped me into the third row of Pedro's car, and it felt right when he pulled me close to him. I remember feeling very sleepy and my head starting to bob. Jack's hand firmly tilted my chin onto his shoulder, and his arm settled comfortably around my shoulders. I remembered nothing more of the car ride home, except that I did feel safe, and I did feel warm.

CHAPTER NINETEEN

"Oh, my God. What happened to her?" There was panic in my mom's voice.

"I'm OK, Mom. Just let me get to the couch."

Jack, my new guard dog, helped me over to the sofa, which Stanley had quickly vacated. I leaned back and sighed with exhaustion, not even bothering to unzip my parka. Jack sat gingerly beside me. Stanley pulled a fleece throw from off a chair and placed it on my lap. I hadn't even known I was shivering.

"Is someone going to explain?" My mom's voice was demanding.

I exhaled loudly. "I met a bear today. Two bears actually: one adult and one cub."

My mom gasped. "What happened?"

It took Jack and me twenty minutes, speaking in bursts and interrupting each other, to explain the bear encounter. A range of emotions played across my mom's face in reaction to the story: fear, shock, disbelief. It was like watching a silent movie. I was relieved and thankful that Jack had forgotten to mention the birds' role in the story, just as he had with the others. His recounting of the story had us backing away slowly and fortunate to have been upwind of the protective mother. It was just as well. I really didn't know, myself, what to make of the birds' involvement. And if the eagle had shown a kind of birds-of-a-feather solidarity, what was up with the black bird muscling in? But that was crazy thinking, right? Even if I was some kind of human Stork, it couldn't possibly mean that I had winged watchers, make that bird watchers—the real deal.

When my mom finally seemed convinced of our eventual survival, I said, "That wasn't the only adventure of the day."

"There's more?" she asked.

"I had a flashback. Of the skating incident." I leaned forward, unzipped my jacket, and pulled my arms slowly from the sleeves. I turned to look at my mom, who had settled herself into the chair opposite me. "How could you keep something like that from me?"

My mom went white. She pursed her lips and pushed up the sleeves of her cardigan. "What do you mean you had a flashback? Specifically?"

"I remember dying. Is that specific enough?"

My mom looked at Jack, but when she spoke, it was more to herself. "I knew it wasn't a good idea. You two spending time together."

"It's not his fault," I said. "And you didn't answer my question. How could you keep something like that from me?"

She shook her head defensively. "It was the therapist's idea. You'd been through such an ordeal. He was adamant that we let you work it out for yourself. Or let it stay buried if that was how your mind best protected itself."

"I have a shrink?" Ugh. How very LA of me.

"You haven't seen him in years. You've been doing so well. It really didn't seem necessary to continue."

I suddenly remembered a special doctor. "You mean Dr. Sherman?" I also recalled that I had always been confused about the visits; they had seemed so pointless. It had been explained to me that he dealt with "insides only." God, had I been gullible. "Correct me if I'm wrong, but this just seems like something I had a right to know."

"Honey, I'm sorry. Your father and I did what we thought was best for you." Stanley leaned down and rubbed her shoulders.

My mom then turned to Jack. "Thank you," she said, clearly trying to hold back tears, though not entirely succeeding. "Thank you again for taking care of her."

"You're welcome," Jack mumbled, embarrassed.

My mom must have seen us drive up in my car. "Do you need a ride somewhere?" she asked.

"Back to my truck, I guess," Jack said.

Stanley and his wiry red hair sprang to attention. "I'll take him. Let you two talk."

Jack seemed hesitant to leave. "See you at school," he said with a backward glance. I was surprised by how much it pained me to see him go; something fisted in my chest as I watched the door close behind him. I was, however, exhausted. And my bed seemed the perfect place to rest my spinning and aching head.

"Can I get you something, honey? I made a casserole."

"I'm not hungry. I think I'll lie down."

Though it was probably only about six p.m., I brushed my teeth, dressed in my warmest pajamas, and pulled the bed covers to my chin. My mom sat at my desk chair. At first she fiddled with the pens and pencils in the desktop mug, asking me if I wanted extra blankets or Tylenol. Then she started to explain the events of that fateful day.

"It was two days after Christmas. You were so thrilled to go skating outside. We usually visited in the summer, so the snow was very new and exciting to you. Amma gave you a pair of my old skates. You, of course, insisted on a proper skating outfit to go with them, so she dug up an old red woolen coat of mine from the attic. It came to your knees and had a matching fur-trimmed muff. She also found you a diamond-patterned knit hat that had pom-poms on strings, which I remember bobbed up and down as you spun around the ice."

My mom exhaled and crossed her legs. Her eyes were distant. It was as if she were transported to that moment and reporting back, a kind of play-by-play. I felt very small and far away listening to her.

"You'd had lessons at the rink in Culver City, so you could do a few spins and turns. It had been cold for weeks already. The first snows had come in mid-November and were still on the ground. All the local kids were skating. They assured us it was safe. Amma and I sat on a bench watching you. Afi was at the store that day. And then Amma's feet got cold, so we decided to wait in the Buick."

I felt fingers walk down my back. They needed filing. The image she was painting was so vivid. I remembered my mom calling out to me that they would be in the car. I pictured Amma in her short little black boots, dark nylons, and plaid coat trudging through the snow. It was all coming back to me:

"I remember now. I didn't know any of those kids. They weren't very friendly. One big kid almost knocked me over, so I moved to an area of the lake where I could be alone. It was just on the other side of some orange cones. I did a jump, and a girl in a blue hat called me a show-off, so I skated a little farther away. I remember falling through. And I remember the cold. More than anything, I remember the cold."

"Honey, if this is too much for you . . ." My mom must have heard the strain in my voice. She stood and came close to the bed, laying a hand on my forehead. "Don't struggle. Don't try to force it. If I remember anything from the therapist, it's that the mind needs to deal slowly with trauma."

I was suddenly very sleepy. "Mom," I managed to say. "Is the accident why we never came back here? Why you went alone to Amma's funeral?"

"Yes."

"Not because Dad hated it here."

"No. Certainly not. He didn't hate it here."

I rolled onto my side. My eyelids felt like they weighed a hundred pounds each. "I really, really miss Dad."

The last thing I remember is my mom looking down at me with a tenderness so keen it seemed to pulsate.

I run and soon realize I am barefoot. The path transitions from hard-packed dirt to jagged rocks. Each step is pure agony, but the wind is insistent. At times it carries me over the path, and for this I am grateful. At times it sets me down hard, and I wonder if it's laughter I hear echoing through the trees that tower on either side of me. Something wet now covers the surface of the piercing stones. I turn and discover red footprints behind me. I think crazily that I'm being followed, until I realize, with resignation, that I'm trailing myself.

The bleat of the child pierces the air. I am headed in the wrong direction. A trick of the wind! The cry came from my right. I must fight this storm. I know with certainty that I will do whatever it takes to find the child. Obligation fuels me. I will endure and defeat what comes between me and the baby. I release a sound so primal, so guttural, it could only be described as a growl. I glance into the thickest of forests. How could trees grow so densely? Can I even squeeze between them? I step from the path, shimmying between two thick trunks of coarsely textured bark. My coat, my lovely red coat, catches and rips. My hair, braided in two perfect plaits, pulls and tangles as twigs with spindly fingers crowd around my head. I push between tree after tree, as they seemingly tighten ranks.

The forest floor is strewn with sticks, and leaves, and acorns. I feel every jagged edge and pointy length radiating in pain up my ankles and calves. Soon the ground levels. It is ice, as smooth as glass, so slick I slide across its surface, and it is cold. Too cold. The pain travels up to my knees and thighs. Where are my boots? Where are my pretty white skates? My teeth chatter, and my shoulders rock with chills. To stop would be unthinkable; continuing, impossible.

Just then the terrain changes. I am on a decline. A solid frozen chute. I manage to stand for a minute, but then I fall hard on my backside. I fall and fall and fall.

With a crash, I am in the clearing. Jaelle and Monique sit atop their coarse chairs, unaware of my arrival, unaware of anything but the baby, who babbles contentedly in her earthen cradle. This time, the infant wears a wreath of bright-orange marigold blossoms.

I hear a rustle in the leaves to my right. I watch as my mother steps into the clearing. Her hair is a bird's nest, so snarled I almost don't recognize her. She fusses with the tangles, her fingers catching in the knots, clearly bothered by the disorder. And I realize that she, too, has fought the wind in her journey to this spot. She then approaches one of the chairs. I watch as she stares with curiosity, examining the interesting texture. She runs her fingers over the corrugated bark. She tests the seat, scooting to the left, then right, before leaning against the whittled backrest. She reaches an arm behind her, lifts a rug of sod from behind the trunk, and drapes this cloak of clover-green grass over her shoulders. She's in the same predicament as Jaelle and Monique, in some sort of meditative state. The baby continues to gurgle, happily, batting at dandelion fluff as it dances above her head and still gripping the curls of vine, even with her tiny toes. A bit of fluff floats in my direction and tickles my nose as it descends. I stretch to swat at the seeded parachute and find it wet and cold. Snow blankets me suddenly, and I discover, alarmingly, that my limbs are frozen. I attempt to yell across to my mother, but by then, I've also lost the use of my voice.

CHAPTER TWENTY-ONE

I woke with a start. OMG. My mother. How could that be? She was too old, wasn't she? Thirty-eight. She'd had me at twenty-two, senior year of college, six months after marrying. My birth was a feat my parents had never been able to duplicate, try as they might.

If the events of yesterday hadn't been trauma enough, this newest discovery plunged me into a deep funk. I lay in bed for a very long time. I was aware of the clock sounding out seconds, but I couldn't rouse myself—not for a shower, though my hair was matted to my head—not for food, though my stomach growled angrily. There was something else about the dream that was incredibly clear to me now. The maternal instincts I experienced were so brutish—I was the mama bear. Nothing and no one could have stood between me and the baby. I shuddered, realizing that Jack and I had been in mortal danger. Given only a split second to decide between lunging in our direction or toward her charge, the bear went the cub's way. What would have happened had we stood between them? How much could my guardian eagle have helped then?

It was all so much to deal with. I could barely keep the events of the last few days in chronological order, never mind make sense of them. And now the idea of my mother as a vessel was heaved to the pileup of brain junk, clogging neural pathways and blocking the flow of information. *No way,* I thought. *Not my mom!* And then it came to me. No way. Not my mom. I had some control here, didn't I? Not only was I on the steering committee of this decision, I was chairman, wasn't I? Just then, my mother knocked softly on my door and opened it slowly.

"How do you feel this morning?"

"Exhausted."

"What about school? Are you up to it?"

The thought of shuffling from class to class was unbearable. It felt trivial. And I had more important things to occupy my mind. Then I thought of Jack. No school meant no Jack. And though I felt my Stork duties were coming to some sort of thunderous head, I wanted to see him.

"I think I should go. That English paper is due."

My mom bit her lower lip. "If you think you're up to it."

"I'll be fine."

I walked across the wide expanse of lawn that fronted the school. The brick courtyard was teeming with kids, and I found myself anxiously looking from one group to another, seeking out Jack's profile. I realized, too, that I'd done this every morning since that first stupid argument at Afi's store. A subconscious memory? Realization of a connection? Something fluttered in my tummy. And then I spotted him, sitting on one of the low brick walls that edged the courtyard. All alone and obviously waiting for something, or someone. I advanced, unable to keep my smile in check. He got the full flash, gums and all. I was trying to think of something witty or clever to say. It seemed to be a pivotal moment. As I came close to him and opened my mouth—having decided to go with a simple "good morning," unable to come up with another coherent greeting—his long arms stretched out and pulled me into an embrace so crushing and intimate, I may have whimpered just a little. He then released me enough to look deeply into my eyes before he lifted my chin with his right index finger and kissed me quickly, but hungrily, on the mouth.

"Great morning," he said.

Dang, he even one-upped me there. "Best ever." I was instantly proud of my reply, which was, I thought, an artful mix of clever, encouraging, and game-on. Yay, me. Though the whimper was worth a demerit or two.

"I've been waiting for you," he said. "I was afraid you wouldn't show. Would be too . . . tired or something."

There were definitely a bunch of somethings going through me right then. My arms and legs had turned to quivering, utterly useless attachments. And my digestive system was going through some sort of emergency evacuation drill. "I wanted to be here today." I couldn't believe how breathy I sounded. Ugh. "Plus, I have an English paper due."

He laughed, a sound I could definitely get used to. The first warning bell rang. "Come on," he said, grabbing my hand. "You've got a paper due."

And I thought I'd been an object of curiosity on my own. That was nothing compared to the spectacle that Jack and I holding hands created. Jaw-dropping, traffic-stopping, bug-eyed stares. I was in a tug-of-war between pride and embarrassment. The only thing keeping me from splitting in two was that, judging by Jack's own glowing smile and viselike grip on my hand, he was enjoying himself.

He led me straight to the door of my first period class, English, and I wondered how he knew my schedule. And then I plumped upon realizing—*he knew my schedule.* Class was torture. Besides turning in my paper, I had no clue what transpired or what we discussed. I did or did not participate. I really couldn't say.

Jack appeared at my side, almost magically, after English. He hooked his arm around my waist and my right hipbone popped into place. I actually heard it. It'd been misaligned my entire life. It's a wonder I'd ever been able to walk.

He dropped me off at Social Studies, where we started a new unit. I only know this because we'd finished the old one the Friday before and had been tested. I vaguely remember turning pages in a book, my finger trailing over a picture of some place. Or was it a person?

My escort service continued, as did the stares, as did the whispers. Fourth period was Design. Penny settled into the seat next to me with an I-told-you-so grin.

"You guys are the talk of the school," she said.

"I noticed."

"Nobody's even talking about Wade and Monique's break-up."

Wade's name was still a sore subject, but today the burn lasted no more than a second. Not even he could spoil my mood.

"So what really happened between you two on the trail?" Penny asked.

We were sitting in two-by-two desk groupings according to our project partners, so although we had a measure of privacy, I still looked around to make sure no one was listening. "I had a recovered memory."

Penny gasped, and a couple of girls looked over. She covered fairly well, adding a dramatic, "That's brilliant" and pointing to the blank page in my notebook. "Sorry," she whispered. "Go on."

"After the bear encounter, I stumbled on the trail. He helped me up and, his touch, it triggered a flashback of the . . . incident."

Penny started to react, but the look I gave her could have muffled a jet engine.

"Anyway," I continued, "he told me the basics. And when I got home, my mom told me the rest."

"Wow."

"Tell me. Is this something everyone knows?"

Penny's eyes got wide, and she simply nodded her yes.

"I mean everyone: freshmen, teachers, the janitor?"

She nodded again.

"So when I was new here and it seemed like everyone was staring at me . . ."

"You were never new here," Penny said.

"So it was like some conspiracy that everyone was in on?"

Penny rolled her shoulders forward. "I wouldn't call it a conspiracy. It's just that there were a lot of newspaper articles. They all explained how you had a specific type of traumatic amnesia and that you had returned to California unaware of what had happened. And then the whole town shops at your *afi*'s store. Especially when your *amma* was alive, we'd get updates. It was common knowledge that you'd never recovered your memory, or been told."

I made a *hmmmph* sound. "Besides the aversion to water, how did Jack react?"

Penny breathed in deeply. "Jack is . . . resilient, tough. Not the type to talk about it."

That much I knew. "So he never discussed it, ever?"

"He gave a few interviews at first. He was considered a hero, you know. He went in after you."

"He told me." I thought of how quick a decision he must have made. And at what, age twelve? What kind of person plunges through a hole in the ice after a stranger? And there were adults around. I remember other parents skating with their little ones, or watching from the benches. "Did he have any sort of injuries or impairments?"

Penny shook her head. "No. That was part of the whole mystery. You both should have died."

I shuddered at her remark, and not just for myself.

Jack waited for me outside the doors to the cafeteria, and even though he had his usual sack lunch, he followed me and Penny through the line and then walked with us to Mr. Parks's room. At the meeting, Jack had everyone provide updates on their stories. They were all well researched, with interesting angles and relevant sources. When it was my turn, I merely reported that the column would have a Homecoming theme. Jack nodded and said, "Good work." It wasn't. He was playing favorites, which was fine by me.

The day continued in this way. Classes were unbearably long and bewildering, and then my heart would soar with each dismissal, as I knew he'd find me, and just those few minutes of hall time produced some sort of G-force emotional glee.

The only low point of the day was Wade. He'd cruised past us earlier, taking a long lingering look at Jack's hand intertwined with mine. Another time, immediately before fifth period, he'd brought an imaginary camera to his eye and clicked as I shuffled past him in the hall. I stopped, thinking I'd misunderstood, the gesture meant for someone else, when I could hear his laughter pealing from behind me.

After school, Jack and I had only a minute or two to say good-bye. Mr. Carter, the football coach, made anyone who was late to practice run the bleachers. We sat on the brick half-wall in the front schoolyard.

I pulled the John Deere cap off his head teasingly. "Why do you wear this thing all the time?"

He went to snatch it back, but I sat on it quickly. "Because I like it."

He tried to wrangle it from under my left thigh, but I swatted his hand away. Wade approached from behind Jack. The set of his jaw was ominous. My limbs locked. I heard the dead bolt.

"What do we have here?" Wade asked. "The talk of the school."

"Beat it," Jack said through clenched teeth.

"You want me to go, Kat?" Wade asked.

"Yes," I said quickly.

"What? We're not friends anymore?" he said.

"We were never friends."

"I don't know. We got pretty friendly that night out at the quarry."

Jack emitted a low growl.

Uh-oh.

"I even have a little keepsake of our time together." Wade reached into his pocket and pulled out a cell phone. "A photo for your album. You seem like the type to keep mementos like that."

"Go to hell," I said.

I looked at Jack. His mouth was clamped tight. His nostrils were flared, and he was taking deep, chest-expanding breaths.

Wade fiddled with his phone, smiling like a hyena. "This one's my favorite," he said, looking intently at the small screen. "You want to see?" To my horror, he held the phone up to Jack, but then pulled it back suddenly. Memories of that night pelted me. I drank too much, blacked out, and though I know I stopped things before they got really ugly, none of it was anyone's idea of a Kodak moment.

I lunged for a look, but Wade quickly pocketed the phone.

"Maybe that's not such a good idea," he said. "You girls can be so funny about photos."

The skies blackened. Thunder rumbled in the distance. A light rain started.

"What do you want, Wade?" Jack asked.

The rain fell harder.

"Just thought you might like to know that, once again, you get my leftovers."

Lightning surged overhead, emitting a flare that split the sky in two. I briefly saw every hollow in Jack's face glint like ice. Then a bolt touched down just across the parking lot from us, hitting a lamp pole and erupting in a fountain of hissing and bubbling sparks.

"Holy crap!" I said, lifting my feet as fiery tinsel danced over the brick courtyard.

Jack let out a sound so pained and raw I thought he'd been struck, though when I looked at him, he was still on his feet, clearly agitated, but physically able.

"The end of days," Wade said, laughing and holding his arms out to the elements. I wondered at his delight in this change in the weather. "But darn. An inside practice." He turned and jogged back toward the school.

I still sat like a stone on the brick ledge. Jack paced in front of me.

"Were you really with him?" he asked, his voice a snarl.

"Once. The night before school started." Mine was barely a whisper.

"At the Asking Fire you said you didn't know him."

The skies darkened, and the rain fell harder.

"I lied. I'm sorry. It's just . . . he was the first to act like it never happened. And after I figured out what kind of jerk he was, I was more than happy to play along."

I didn't like the look on Jack's face, mostly because I couldn't pinpoint the emotion.

"What happened?" he asked, his voice tense.

I looked at my shoes. "He took me out to the quarry. We drank beer." I paused, not wanting to own up to my behavior, not to Jack, anyway. "And some hard alcohol. There's a portion of the evening I don't remember."

Jack jumped up as if hit. For the tiniest moment, he frightened me. The rain was pelting us now. I could hear it drumming over the cars and rooftops. I saw every taut muscle in his jaw, neck, and shoulders ripple through his T-shirt, now drenched with rain. This had to be anger. What else would set him off like that?

"He's been accused by girls before. Why would you put yourself in such a dangerous position? You barely knew him."

"It was stupid. I know," I said. There really was no good way to defend my behavior. I'd gone willingly with a creep like Wade. And being duped by a bullish charm was no excuse for recklessness. I worried Jack would think I was that kind of girl. And if that wasn't enough to stress over, we'd also managed to unleash the wrath of Wade. "There's more. He asked me to the dance on Saturday. I turned him down, and wasn't too gracious about it. And I told him about us. I think it made him angrier. He called it a curse."

The rain started coming so hard, I felt like I was drowning: an ocean falling around us.

Jack started pacing back and forth in front of me; he seemed barely able to contain himself. His fists were closed tightly against his chest, and his shoulders balled into an angry forward knot. "Can't control," I heard him mutter. "Too close" was another fragment I picked up. The worst part of it was he couldn't look at me. His pacing continued, but at least he spared me any more comments. Jack then took a swipe at some invisible foe, like he was swinging at the cold rain that blasted us head-on. He turned to me, walking the few short feet that separated us with heavy steps.

Another clap of thunder, louder and closer this time, crashed against the gunmetal gray sky. Jack looked around wildly, as if searching for something in the roiling clouds.

"It's just that ..." he started. "Too much ... can't trust ... I can't ..." He went to touch my arm, but pulled away.

"Jack ..."

He started jogging toward the parking lot.

"Wait," I yelled.

He turned briefly. Lightning split the sky behind him, and then he was gone.

For many minutes I sat there in a fierce downpour, replaying it all. He was definitely mad—at me. He let himself get too close—to me. Chided himself for having trusted—me. Rain struck me like stones. I stood, and the John Deere cap tumbled to the ground. It was soaked through and now muddy. I lifted it, fingering its dirty band, and then tucked it under my arm.

I drove home in a fog. The storm got worse. The kind of maelstrom that pierced your soul. The skies grew darker still, the clouds themselves shading to an onyx black, as if pulling the sorrow right out of my chest. I went straight to my room. When things get bad, the bad go to bed. And I felt very bad.

CHAPTER TWENTY-TWO

I must have burrowed under my covers for only an hour, though it seemed a hundred years. Outside I heard the raging storm. Rain fell hard, a continuous wall of water. From time to time lightning flared and was followed by a jolting clap of thunder. I rolled onto my side. The clock on my nightstand read five p.m. I had two hours until my appointment with Hulda. Let's hope two days had been sufficient for her to do her "thinking." If so much about my dreams had already been unusual, what would Hulda say when I reported that my mom was now involved?

I sat up, but sadness tugged at my shoulders. How had Jack, in two days' time, become so important to me? Two days. It seemed hard to believe. He'd transitioned from an improbable request of the Asking Fire to hiking partner to fellow drowning survivor and twenty-four-hour boyfriend. And in that same compacted forty-eight hours, I'd survived a bear encounter, recovered buried memories, identified my mother as a vessel, and driven Jack away. Was this some sort of Stork sorority hazing? Cruel pecking order? All Hulda had to do was figure out what symbol the wind represented. Talk about executive privilege.

I was sliding my feet into a pair of Alegria clogs — backless the only option due to blisters from yesterday — and wondering why my feet hadn't bothered me at school, when I heard a familiar voice, deep and resonant, call my name.

Dad? At first it was a question to myself. "Dad?" This time called out loud.

I ran out of my room, down the stairs, and there he was, removing a black leather coat dripping with rain and dropping it on the sofa. I collapsed into his arms. He wasn't expecting it and had to take a bracing step to support me. I cried. It was pitiful, but I couldn't help it.

"Oh, Kitty Kat," he said. "What's the matter?"

"Everything."

He lifted me off the ground, just a little, and cradled me under his chin. It felt like I was five years old. I wished I was five years old. "Your mom called me last night. I got here as soon as I could."

The events of yesterday shuffled to the forefront of my to-deal-with list. I froze to death five years ago. He and my mom had lost me, found me, hid it from me, and finally lost each other. Ugh.

"I'm still processing it all." This was the truth.

He set me down. "We didn't know what to do. I always wanted to tell you, but the doctor thought . . ."

"I know. Mom told me." I took a step back. "But I'd have been able to handle it this year, or last year, even the year before that. How could you let me come back here without knowing?"

"I didn't want to, hon. And it was a hard secret to keep."

"That's the thing," I said, emotion building with every word. "It wasn't yours to keep. It was mine."

"I know that now. We didn't handle it right. We let a doctor make decisions for us as a family. I never liked that. I should have insisted." He pulled me close and rested the point of his chin on my head. It was heavier than I'd have thought it would be. "Can you forgive us?"

I liked that he said "us," even though I knew it was too late for the "us" to have any real meaning. "You did what you thought best, right?"

"Always, honey. Always."

"There's still a piece missing about that day. Where were you? Mom said she and Amma were at the lake, and Afi was at the store. But where were you?"

"Well, I was at home in LA. Working. I didn't make that trip with you two." He touched my cheek. "I flew out the moment I heard, and was at your bedside when you woke up, but I'm sure you don't remember any of that."

"I don't."

I knew there'd be future discussions of the events, detailed accounts of sleepless nights at the hospital and doctor's appointments. I wasn't going to let him, or my mom, off that easily. For now, it was nice to know that my dad would come when I needed him.

After a moment, he lifted his head, put his hands on his hips, and looked around the room. "So this is the place, huh?"

"Temporarily."

"Not too bad. At least it's not decorated like a back-woods cabin."

"It's OK, I guess."

"I called your mom when my plane landed. She told me where to find the extra key. She'll be home later. I'd have been here earlier, but we had to circle the airport twice due to this freak thunderstorm."

"Welcome to Minnesota," I said.

He pulled me over to the couch. We sat quietly for a few moments. I never felt awkward around my dad. He had this great charisma that just blended with anything: a raucous party or a prolonged silence.

"What happened with your business deal?"

"On hold. We have a lead on an empty factory out in Palmdale."

195

"And that's really all you need? The finances are squared away?"

"The rest will follow."

I traced my bottom lip with my finger. "Wind energy, huh?"

"Gonna be big, kiddo."

Hulda had spent the past two days thinking over the wind symbol in my dreams. It couldn't really be this, could it? That would be too easy, right? But why else would I be transported to this glacial outpost and drawn into the clutches of Hulda and her cronies? And Hulda owned an abandoned paper factory. Someone was spelling this out for me. Though just thinking about Jack made my heart heavy, it was also what he wanted for the town. Some way to preserve the place. New jobs would mean new families. The school district would see an increase in enrollment. It was at least worth mentioning.

"Hey, Dad. What if I told you there was a vacant factory here in this town?"

He gave me a look.

"I have a friend. She's old, like Afi's age, but we're sort of friends. She owns the fabric and notions shop in town, but she inherited the paper factory from her father. It's abandoned."

"Oh, Kat, we're not looking at Minnesota as a possible site."

"Why not?"

"This far north, there'd be additional trucking costs. We'd also have to factor in weather delays for most of the winter. We're concentrating our search out west. California, Nevada, or Arizona."

"But would you at least look at it?"

"Aw, hon, what would be the point?"

I sighed. Hulda had talked about my powers growing. She had asked about fate and destiny. Sure, it was a little outside of my Stork duties, but the signs seemed significant — to me, anyway. Maybe I just needed a different tactic. "The point is I'd get to see a lot more of you."

"You know I'd like that." He ruffled my hair. "But I don't think . . ."

"Would you just look at it, please?"

He exhaled a big puff of air. "Maybe. We'll see."

It was all I needed for now.

My dad and I had a quick dinner at the Kountry Kettle. Jaelle could only shake her head at him in wonder when he asked for a veggie burger with blue cheese crumbles, neither of which was on the menu. I could tell, though, that she thought he was cool — for a dad, anyway — and handsome. He wore Diesel jeans, a cashmere V-necked sweater, and Kenneth Cole shoes that had a slightly upturned toe. I wondered about the manicure. Not too many guys running around Norse Falls with buffed fingernails. Jaelle was very attentive to our booth. She was an excellent waitress, but still, it made me smile. More proof that my dad had mad charisma.

I made up a story about a study date at seven. I didn't dare break my appointment with Hulda. My dad had a twenty-minute drive to his hotel, anyway, and had some phone calls to make for business, so was fine with the early dinner. Jaelle returned hawking dessert. She recommended the apple crumble, which my dad took along with — although reluctantly — a cup of coffee.

"Who is this study date with?" he asked.

"A girl." Which technically would be the category Hulda fell into — sixty or seventy years ago.

He seemed kind of disappointed, or unconvinced. "Your mom said you were with the kid from the . . . incident. The Snjosson kid."

"He's a friend." My dad seemed to buy this line, though I squirmed and looked away. He had never been as skilled as my mom at factoring body language into a conversation.

Jaelle dropped off my dad's pie and my personal fave, the chocolate fudge cake, and two steaming mugs. After Jaelle was out of hearing range, my dad looked at the coffee suspiciously. "At least it's hot." He took a sip and scrunched his nose. "Blah." He then reached down into his leather briefcase and extracted two small cans of Starbucks espresso. He held them up for me to see and winked conspiratorially. "Emergency supplies for the morning."

He tapped the can affectionately. "My faithful Ariel"—his nickname for the mermaid on the Starbucks logo.

I looked at the familiar image. I'd never really studied it before. It was a mermaid, with a split tail and crown. Such a curious choice. Though I supposed it symbolized something.

I glanced down at my watch—just a few minutes to seven. "Yikes. Gotta go." I stood and kissed my dad on the cheek. "So you'll take a look at it? Yes?"

"At what?"

"The factory."

My dad sighed. "Listen, Kitty Kat, I'm not setting up shop anywhere I can't get a decent cup of coffee."

"But you said you'd look."

He sighed. "OK, but don't expect much."

CHAPTER TWENTY-THREE

I used my key at Hulda's back door. Again she emerged from the office-which-wasn't-an-office door. We nodded silently at each other and proceeded to the dungeon. I settled into the robin's chair, whose carvings had taken flight.

Hulda sat back in her seat, steepling her hands below her chin. "I have been thinking on this wind symbol."

"Me, too," I interrupted.

She cocked her head to the side. "Tell me."

"My dad arrived today. Unexpectedly."

Something sparked in Hulda's pale blue eyes. "An unforeseen visitor? Is an omen. Go on."

Maybe I was on to something? "He's an entrepreneur. And his latest business venture is wind energy."

"Wind energy?"

"Wind turbines, technically. He's been pulling together a deal to produce small wind turbines for residential application." I guess I'd heard my dad pitch the idea a time or two. I had the spiel down.

Hulda closed one eye and looked at me suspiciously. "What's it to do with our duties?"

"His company needs a factory. Their contract on a site in California fell through at the last minute. I never knew you owned the old paper factory in town until this weekend. I mean, it seems too much of a coincidence, doesn't it? It has to be a symbol."

Hulda was quiet for a long time. A very long time. I took it as a thumbs-down.

"Would you at least think about it?" Even I could hear the whiny ping in my voice.

"If it's important to you, I will," Hulda said. "But tell me, why such sadness about you today?"

Dang, her perceptiveness was eerie. "I now know what you meant when you called me 'the girl of the lake.'"

"This is not making you sad."

She had a future in interrogation if the whole first-chair-Stork-thing didn't work out. "It's Jack Snjosson. We've kind of gone back and forth on being friends."

"Ah." This she said as if it explained everything, which helped nothing, and may have only made me sadder. "Snjosson is an ancient family with roots that trace back many years, before the Icelandic sagas even."

Whose don't, around here?

"Their lands rose out of the farthest north," Hulda continued. "Legend has it they were a nomadic clan of Veturfolk, arriving every spring with white furs and eggs of the *geirfugl,* the great auk, to trade."

"Uh. That's interesting," I said.

"But do you understand, they're Veturfolk — Winter People?"

"No."

"Of arctic descent. Far above the timberline. A cold and unfriendly place."

So a lot like here.

"A warning," Hulda said in a grave tone. "Ice is at the core of their being."

Yowzer. Not exactly a stamp of approval. I guess grudges and legends chiseled in cold, hard stone stand the test of time.

"Is there possibly another who claims your affections?" she asked.

"Hardly one who claims my affections."

"A distraction, then," she said.

"Wade Ivarsson." I wanted to be careful. Wade was, after all, a relative of Fru Dorit. "I turned him down for the dance."

Hulda scrutinized me for a moment. "He was a mischievous child. Always clamoring for ways to be noticed. The Stork lineage can be difficult on boys. And a family with much sorrow." Hulda pressed her fingers to her temple. "But today we have other more pressing matters at hand," Hulda continued. "Have you had another dream?"

"Yes. One."

"Explain."

Nobody economized words like Hulda. Maybe I could learn something from her. I hoped to make quick work of this nightmare naming my own mother a potential vessel. "It's always the same. I struggle to get to the clearing, because there's something holding me back. This time it's the wind itself. It won't let me advance. In fact, it spins me around and steers me in the opposite direction."

"Once more the wind." This seemed to trouble Hulda. "What happens when you get to the clearing?"

"The baby is there. Happy as always. And then I watch as someone else appears. She sits in one of the chairs and pulls a cloak of grass and dirt over her shoulders." I paused, still unsure how to proceed.

"Go on."

"She is an older woman, late thirties. Recently returned to the area and newly divorced. She's in a new relationship, but who knows if it will last?" I sounded way too much like Fru Dorit at that first meeting. I momentarily considered foretelling that she'd soon dump him and his dishpan hands.

"Tell me something of her mind."

"Uh. She's a math teacher. Very analytical. Very exacting. In fact, she arrives with her hair tangled, presumably by the wind, which bothers her sense of order."

203

"Always this wind," Hulda said with a shake of her head.

"And then she, too, settles into some sort of dream-like state to watch the child," I continued. "So I guess that makes three. Three potential vessels now."

"But you say there are four chairs."

"Yes."

"Only the water element remains?"

"Yes."

"So many dreams." Hulda rocked back and forth, talking more to herself than to me. "Is unusual."

Naturally.

She pursed her lips. Deep vertical lines wrinkled the skin above her mouth. "This is important, Katla; think very hard. There must be someone else present."

I shook my head in bewilderment. "I don't think so."

"Time is such an important factor in our decisions. We must follow the laws of nature. The child must be placed very soon."

"I can't think of anyone else."

She continued to look at me coaxingly, as if leading me to some sort of revelation.

I started to get nervous. I was already on shaky ground, having suggested that my dad's business venture was fated for her old factory and concealing that my mom was the third vessel. I'd never been the halfway type.

"Hulda, I just thought of something." Acting had never been my thing. I just hoped spontaneity made up for lack of natural ability. "There *is* someone else present in my dream."

That got her attention. "Tell me," she said.

"You're going to think this is very strange. And it happened so fast I hardly thought it was worth mentioning."

She wanted a fourth, right?

"Go on." There was something eager and youthful in her voice.

I remembered the icy chute of the dream. My stomach relived it as I plunged onward with the fabrication. "At one point in my dream, I'm falling down a sort of frozen waterfall. I look to my side, and there, sitting on a rock, caught in a sort of wind tunnel, is . . ." I paused, desperately trying to think of something.

"Is?" I noticed Hulda's bony fingers gripping her chair.

"A mermaid." *Oh, God.* I'd panicked and the first crazy thing that had flashed through my mind had been my dad holding up his little can of coffee, but no way would Hulda fall for anything so absurd.

"A mermaid?" Hulda slowly bent her head from one side to the other, lost in thought. Finally she said, "A very powerful symbol. The mythological siren. Dating back as far as the goddess religions themselves. A creature of Vatnheim, the water kingdom. Describe her."

Oh, crap. "Uh. Long hair covering her breasts. Two tails."

Hulda gasped. "Split-tailed? Is certain?"

God help me. "Yes."

"What else?"

"She wears a crown." *Drinks a lot of coffee. Sometimes answers to the name of Ariel.*

"A crown?"

"Yes."

"You're sure of it?" she asked, trembling like a bobblehead.

"Yes."

Hulda sat back in her chair as if exhausted, as if exhilarated. She leaned over and patted my arm. "You go home. Get some sleep. Tomorrow is big day."

"How is it a big day?"

"Tomorrow, after school, you start scratching."

"Oh! Are you sure?"

"Yes. Though you may not realize it, Katla, your timing coincides with a day of great portent. Tomorrow is the autumnal equinox. Know that the changes of seasons are days of great significance and powerful magic. The signs are all there. Aslendigas Storkur Society meets tomorrow night."

Hulda rushed me up the stairs and gave me a big hug like something really special had just happened. I left her store feeling seriously guilty and hoped I hadn't done anything really stupid, especially considering that—*dear God*—there was a soul at stake.

CHAPTER TWENTY-FOUR

I let myself in through the garage door. The house sounded empty, though I knew my mom was home, since her umbrella was lying on the floor.

"We're in here," my mom called.

I followed her voice to the family room. She and Stanley were snuggling on the couch. She had her head dipped down in the crook of his shoulder, and it looked like it was a pretty good fit. I remembered the way my head had rested on Jack's arm during the car ride back from the hiking trip. It had been a nice feeling, both soft and solid.

"I talked to your dad," my mom said. "He said you two had a nice dinner."

I took a seat in the chair facing the couch. "It was great to see him. Thanks for calling him."

"Of course, honey. Your father and I are still friends. And when it comes to you . . ." She turned and faced Stanley. "We're still partners. And we both want to help you deal with any recovered memories you may have."

"How did you feel at school today?" Stanley asked.

"Good, I guess. Pretty normal." If getting a boyfriend by first period and then getting dumped after school was normal. And the whole mermaid thing—I wasn't about to go there.

"You've always been strong," my mom said. "When you're ready, there's a scrapbook that Amma kept with all the newspaper clippings. I put it on your desk."

"She made a scrapbook?"

"It was a really big story. Some believed it a sort of miracle. The scientific explanation has to do with the cold actually plunging the two of you into a sort of deep freeze, preventing your brain cells from dying. It's really a fascinating survival mechanism." No mistaking which version she believed.

"Still sounds impossible to me."

"Not impossible." My mom beamed at me like I'd just handed her a Valentine dripping glue and glitter all over the carpet. "Your dad and I have you to prove it."

Stanley squeezed my mom's knee after she said this. "I'm glad Greg's going to stick around for a few days," he said. "I'm looking forward to meeting him."

I felt kind of sorry for the guy. Their meeting would be rough on him. It would be hard to live up to my dad. I excused myself and headed up to my room.

It was not an easy night. I couldn't stop thinking about Jack. I wanted him to call. Even if it was to break our date, I'd know where we stood. And the idea of a photo was stressing me out. Did Wade really have one? Would he broadcast it? And on top of all this, I had my first Stork meeting the next day, a responsibility that triggered a nervous burn in my gut. Now that it was upon me, the decision seemed huge. I sat at my desk with my arms wrapped tightly around my shoulders, reading and rereading, unsuccessfully, an English assignment. The only thing that kept me from falling apart, literally ending up with body parts strewn about like dirty laundry, was puzzling through some of what Hulda had said. I focused on our discussion. And though I could feel myself almost choking with stress, and though I felt more alone than I ever had, I concentrated on Hulda's cryptic words.

For starters, the whole history of Jack's family. It was probably a sign of the level of my fixation that I could remember, verbatim, Hulda's comments about the Snjossons, and probably could have done a pretty good imitation of Hulda in the process. They were "Winter People . . . of arctic descent . . . from far above the timberline . . . a cold and unfriendly place . . . ice is at the core of their being." Did she know how charged our friendship had been? Was this her warning? Was Jack as cold and unfriendly as the arctic lands his family descended from? Was she telling me not to get involved with an iceman? Boy, I sure knew how to pick 'em.

I glanced over at the red scrapbook placed neatly on top of a pile of fashion magazines. I ran a hand over its linen cover. It was dusty and slightly frayed. I picked it up and walked over to the bed. I sat for many minutes against my headboard with the heft of the book in my lap. Finally, I found the courage to open it. I gasped. There, front and center on the first article, were large school pictures of me and Jack. They were the kind of smiling mugs so often used in news stories when the outcome wasn't good. Jack, this younger version, had a fuller face, too-large grin, and shooting cowlick. My own image, my fifth-grade school photo, had rod-straight hair parted down the middle and a shy smile. Another photo showed the scene of the accident: an ambulance pulled up close to the lake and surrounded by a crowd of people. I read the article entitled "Miracle at Elkhorn Lake: Two Children Fight for Life." Though the writer clung to the miracle theory throughout the story, citing both witnesses and medical experts, the incident had been barely twenty-four hours old. I noticed, with a shrug, the reporter had my name wrong. KATHERINE LEBLANC was printed under my photo. At the end of the article it was reported that "Katherine" had not yet gained consciousness, and Jack was listed in critical condition. Just yesterday, I'd have believed it the story of a stranger. I sat pondering how easily the outcome could have been different. "Tragedy at Elkhorn Lake: Two Children Drown." I shuddered and closed the book.

I barely slept, knowing the next day's events would be fateful. And though there was still some deep cavernous ache in my heart, I had, if nothing else, a small measure of self-respect. I was a fighter. If I'd survived a plunge into an icy lake — without breathing for twenty minutes, maybe more — I could survive tomorrow.

CHAPTER TWENTY-FIVE

My mom was cheerful at breakfast the next day. I supposed she had no inkling that she could, or could not, be pregnant. Nor, for that matter, did she know she was mother to a human Stork. She was, in general, a happy person — the kind who could always spot the sun behind the clouds. Her lightheartedness had eased the pain of so many of my childhood scrapes, cuts, and bruises, including those of an emotional nature. And her enthusiasm had always added worth to anything I brought home: a lopsided clay figure, a hairy caterpillar, or a good report card. I vowed, despite what the day brought, to channel this optimism. I realized then that, despite my parents' divorce, I had been lucky. She smiled at me over her bowl of yogurt topped with blueberries and something inevitably Kashi. She didn't even bother to comment on the Cap'n Crunch, whose contraband cargo I'd spilled into my own bowl.

She had a lunch date with my dad later today, but I knew, somehow, that the shade of her coloring had more to do with her date with Stanley last night than with the day at hand.

I pulled into the parking lot and instinctively took the first left, which circled me around the backside nearest the gym. My VW Bug seemed to have had a mind of its own. Daily, and without my input, it had chosen parking spots closer and closer to the second-row, third-from-the-left stall, which was habitually occupied by one beat-up old Ford truck with the faded SNJOSSON FARMS painted on its door. Today the truck wasn't there. I sank into the driver's seat of my little blue car, feeling a compression in my gut.

It was almost crazy to think that just twenty-four hours ago we'd walked hand-in-hand through the halls. There it was, only Tuesday, and so much had transpired. Not to mention my first Stork bestowal was later that day.

I trudged to first-period English. My blisters hurt. I was wearing my favorite pink Keen ballerinas, normally just as comfy as they were stylish. Even though I'd dressed carefully that morning, thinking I had achieved the new ruffian—punk goes princess—look, everything felt wrong. I forced myself to focus on the words as they exited Ms. Schaeffer's mouth. She had a very wide mouth, funny that I'd never noticed that before, nor the nasal quality to the sound it produced. I couldn't help it when, between periods, my neck craned of its own accord, always searching the halls. No sight of him, though. Not between first and second, nor second and third. Happily, I didn't cross paths with Wade, either. Pedro stopped me on my way to French.

"Have you heard from Jack?" he asked.

I shook my head, trying to hide my shame. "No."

"Do you have any idea where he went?"

"No."

"He didn't say anything?"

"No. Not really."

Pedro punched a fist into his open hand. "I phoned his house last night. His dad wouldn't tell me anything, except that he wasn't home. And didn't know when he'd get back. I really need to find him."

"Why?"

"He's in big trouble with Coach Carter. He skipped out on practice last night. That's an automatic benching for the next game."

"Oh. Homecoming."

"Yeah. Homecoming. And guess who's the backup quarterback?" Pedro said, pointing to his chest. "And trust me. This is not a good thing. Definitely not against Pinewood." Pedro crossed his arms. "It's probably none of my business, but did you guys have a fight or something?"

I hugged a book to my chest. "We did. About Wade."

"Wade?"

"I made a mistake the night before school started." I drummed my fingers across the surface of the book. "And when Jack asked me about him, I made it worse by lying."

"Oh." Pedro rolled his shoulders and looked at me thoughtfully. "Though I don't think you could shake him that easily."

"You didn't see his face."

"I can tell you this much — I've known him since we were kids, and it was huge that he put himself out there yesterday with you."

"Obviously not that huge. He hasn't called me."

"Trust me on this one — it was huge." His eyes darted to a wall-mounted clock. "Hey, I gotta run to class, but I'll see you at lunch."

I raised my eyebrows in response and then walked away. "Ice at his core?" was the new mantra I was chanting under my breath. Hulda's warning was something I could fixate on in an attempt to distract myself from the hole in my chest.

In Design, Penny told me that Wade and Monique had a big blowup in the hallway that morning. It'd been very loud, very ugly, and very public. Wade had said some really mean things, the kind of things one doesn't forgive. I kept waiting for Penny to mention photos of me circulating. She didn't, thankfully. Just the threat of them had done damage enough; I hardly wanted to deal with the cleanup their actual spill would entail. Ms. Bryant gave us free time to work with our partners. Penny must have pitched an idea or two at me—I could tell she was looking at me expectantly—but I just couldn't focus.

Jack didn't show up at lunch. I knew he wouldn't. Some internal sensor in me knew he wasn't in the building. Penny flashed concerned looks at me, but I just kept my head down and worked on my story—pretended to, anyway. On the way to our lockers, she suggested we hang out after school, maybe go to the bookstore or get some coffee at the Kountry Kettle. I invented an excuse, though I don't remember what. It couldn't have been very good. Worry creased her forehead.

Somehow I made it through the day. Just as I was about to leave, a group of girls caught my eye. They shifted, forming more of a horseshoe than a ring, and I got a good view of the person being consoled. It was Monique. I stopped, taking even my shadow by surprise. She looked haggard. Forget wind; the girl had had the sails themselves knocked from her mast. One of the girls placed a hand on Monique's arm, and I heard her say, "I was late last month and it turned out OK." I don't know how long I stood there thinking about that remark, but I must have made some sort of spectacle of myself. Next thing I knew, Monique was heading my way. My brain said go, but my legs, darn them, stayed put.

"Can I talk to you a moment?" Monique asked.

"I guess," I said, trying to prepare snappy comebacks in my head for what was sure to be an ugly confrontation.

"I owe you an apology."

To that I had no response, none — nothing in my upbringing, or formal education, or hours spent watching *The Hills* had prepared me for the haunted look in her eyes.

"I've been a bitch and I'm sorry." She fiddled with the buttons of her coat. "I heard you turned Wade down at the Asking Fire. Smart girl."

In my mind, I kept thinking that this was my chance to bring Miss Uppity down a rung. But I just couldn't do it; the nice bits of me won out. "I heard you did the same."

"Yeah, well, it took me a lot longer to figure him out."

"Come on, Monique," someone called.

"I guess I'll see you around." She hurried after her friends.

I walked to my car juggling so many thoughts and questions regarding the events of the past few days that I'm sure I dropped one. Seriously. I heard something splat. My first-ever Stork recommendation was only hours away; I was already nervous. As if the entire concept wasn't confusing enough, I now had one of the vessels changing her spots on me.

I'd had to pull together a really good excuse not to see my dad. He'd seemed pretty floored when I said I had an assignment due and had hours and hours of work ahead of me. It wasn't like me to be unprepared. Besides, I'd been begging him to visit for weeks. Even though he'd arrived unexpectedly, I could still hear the hurt in his voice when he responded to my library alibi. We made plans for the following day. I also asked him to the football game on Friday. My mom had been easier. She was, in general, a big fan of libraries. To me, it seemed as good a place as any to hide for a few hours—and start scratching.

CHAPTER TWENTY-SIX

I drove to Pinewood. I heard they had a nice library, and at least I didn't know anyone, so I couldn't make too big a fool of myself. The town was larger than Norse Falls, with newer buildings, but I couldn't help thinking that our downtown did a better job on the little things: hanging flowerpots, brick sidewalks, and bay-window storefronts. I settled into a dark corner on the second floor of the modern building with notebooks and papers spread around me, all of them completed assignments. I took a good bracing gulp of air and started scratching, as inconspicuously as possible. I felt like an idiot. Where to start? Under the bangs? Top of the crown? I seemed to remember the area above my ears being particularly bothersome, so I started there. Within moments, my head was crawling. It was awful, but once I'd begun, it had a mind—an evil one at that—of its own. Pain radiated from every follicle on my head. How did I not remember the extent of this misery? And how was I ever going to make it to nine p.m.?

I pulled Jack's mud-stained cap from my backpack and brought it to my cheek. It smelled musky and male. I enjoyed the diversion, no matter how brief. I pulled it over my head, liking its fit, though it did nothing to relieve the discomfort. It took me an hour to read a simple English assignment, the epidermis playing, apparently, an important role in the processing of language.

An older man settled at the table next to mine. He must have thought I had some sort of nervous disorder, or was in the process of an emotional breakdown. It took everything in me not to stop, drop, and roll across the wood floor.

I pulled a birthday card and envelope from my backpack and began a letter to my grams in Santa Monica. She didn't know e-mail from eBay, could handle a landline conversation, but considered the cell phone for 911 purposes only. She was definitely the snail-mail type and would be thrilled to get a note with her card. I don't remember what I wrote. All I could think about was the live wire of pain snaking across my head. In an effort to keep my mind off the slash-and-burn at work on my scalp, I tapped my toes. The old guy next to me shook his head like I was everything that was wrong with today's youth. I stuffed the card into the envelope, wrote out the address, and pushed away from the library table, quickly stuffing books and papers into my backpack.

Outside the library, a breezy evening offered a little relief. I remembered seeing a post office on the main highway only a short walk from the library, and hoped the exercise would be a small distraction. The building was dark, long past closed, but an old blue collection box sat at the corner. I saw a big logging truck coming down the road. It would be familiar to someone like Jaelle's husband, Russ, but to me it was new and wondrous. A pile of logs, at least twenty feet long, was stacked on the trailer of a big rig. They looked like fallen giants, those massive tree trunks, and it filled me with a sort of melancholy. I dropped my letter down the chute and stood, with my elbows propped on the blue box, thinking about Jaelle. She'd be a good mom. A baby was what she and Russ needed to get past this rough spot. It would force them both to grow up a little, settle down.

Then a series of events happened so quickly, I had a hard time processing it all. A very large and swiftly descending black bird smashed into the big rig's windshield — its wings crumpling like paper. There was a deafening screech of brakes, long and shrill and foreboding. Simultaneously, a breeze blew up from nowhere. In an instant, it lifted Jack's cap off my head. I watched as the hat skittered first at my feet and then with another gust was airborne, flying out of my sight, back toward the parking lot of the post office. As I turned to run after the cap, my attention was drawn across the highway, where I thought I saw — it couldn't be — Grim, flapping her arms like a madwoman.

In a few quick strides, I reached the cap. As I bent to retrieve it, nestled up against the brick building, I looked up in horror to see the truck skid sideways and jackknife, the cables holding the logs break, and the monstrous trunks scatter across the highway. At the corner, where I had just stood, the spill of logs buried the blue mailbox, as well as a parked car, and snapped a streetlight and street sign like toothpicks. I looked across to where Grim had been, but she was gone.

Horns blared and traffic stopped. Drivers got out of their cars. Shop owners and customers came out of the stores. The intersection was impassable. I walked shakily toward the confusion. Nothing that had been there a moment ago was left of the corner. I watched as the truck driver was pulled from his cab, apparently uninjured.

I pointed to the mound of fallen logs, addressing a woman holding a barking dog by its leash. "I was standing right there." My voice was hoarse.

"Me, too," she said. "We both would have been crushed!"

"Did you see that old lady across the road?" I asked, trying to control the trembling that rattled my molars.

The woman looked to where I pointed, but shook her head no. "I was watching the truck, and next thing

I knew it was skidding out of control. If it hadn't been for that young man . . ." She looked around in confusion. "Where did he go? I thought he was being rude, but he did push me out of the way."

"What young man?" I asked.

"He looked around your age. Big, with short brown hair. Or was he blond? It all happened so fast."

A police car, siren blaring and lights flashing, pulled up in front of the toppled truck, followed quickly by an ambulance. The lady and her dog moved back from the accident; I did, too, not wanting to get caught up in police reports or eyewitness accounts. Wringing Jack's hat like a sponge, I walked to my car.

I sat in the driver's seat for a long, long time, unable even to pull the keys from my pocket. I almost died five years ago in a frozen lake. By all accounts, I should have. This past weekend I blundered onto an unprotected bear cub, provoking its mother — charge-and-kill a common enough outcome of such a scenario. Now I had watched as the place where I'd stood, moments ago, was brutally swept away in a thunder of falling timber and twisting metal. I tugged Jack's cap over my aching head, thinking I really couldn't handle any more strange happenings — particularly those of a life-threatening nature.

CHAPTER TWENTY-SEVEN

I drove back to Norse Falls and parked in the alley behind Hulda's store. I don't know how I made it to nine. I felt like I was having an out-of-body experience, with just a shell of me rocking back and forth, while some spirit form of me watched from up above as that little blue mailbox was crushed, again and again. I thought about calling Penny—I sure needed a friend—but where would I even begin? *Hey, Penny. It's me. Had another near-death experience.* I toughed it out until, finally, my watch took a last begrudging lunge and I was out of my car seat with what felt like fireworks shooting out the top of my head. I used the back entrance. Not a soul was in sight, but as I opened the door, someone was at my elbow. Fru Birta. Where did she come from? And then immediately another entered behind her. And then another. Had my head not been about ready to launch, I would have gone back outside to have another look. I vaulted down the steps, probably too fast, and probably too furious, though that Pelican really should watch that cane of hers. I scrambled into the Robin's chair and immediately plunged my nose into the awaiting bowl of herbs, glorious nose-numbing, head-healing herbs. Relief.

I didn't lift my head for anything. A greeting's a greeting from any vantage point, right? The last to arrive was Hulda. I got the sense that this was customary. As she took her spot at the Owl's chair, the old women rose.

"In honor of the autumnal equinox," Hulda said, "it seems fitting to begin in praise of Sifa, Protector of the Harvest." She raised her hands in a gesture of offering.

"Sifa, balancer of dark and light,
We honor you this Harvest Tide.
In gratitude for Summer's bounty,
Under Winter's mantle we'll bide."

I couldn't help but cock my head from left to right. What the? Harvest Tide? Winter's mantle?

"My sister Storks," Hulda continued, "tonight we gather on a day of symmetry, moon and sun in harmony. And thanks be that another summer solstice is behind us."

Huh? Wasn't there a soul to be delivered? Having just escaped being pressed into paper, I wasn't in the mood to muse over the change of seasons. And was nobody else's head on fire?

"And more to celebrate this evening—is our newest Stork Katla's first bestowal." Hulda motioned for us to be seated. "Fru Birta, roll call if you will."

I lifted the bowl up and fanned its scent toward my nose as attendance was called. If I was to be a part of this hush-hush, ages-old tribe, I decided I should learn a few of their names. I scanned the group. Besides Hulda, there was suck-up Dorit. Birta, the horned-wimple-wearing Lark, was our bookkeeper. Marta, sporter of the Jackie Kennedy pillbox and brandisher of the cane, had the Pelican chair next to mine. And rounding things out was Svana, the Swan. Talk about typecasting: her hair and skin were parchment white, her neck was long and thin, and even her hand movements were fluid and graceful.

"Fru Grimilla," Birta called for a second time.

I looked across the table. Grim's seat was empty. Weird.

Hulda looked at her watch.

Fru Dorit said, "It's not like Fru Grimilla to be late. I wonder if she's sick."

I was torn. Everything had happened so fast. It had looked like her, but she was gone so quickly. "Uh. Fru Hulda," I said, "I think I saw Fru Grimilla in Pinewood a little while ago." I described the incident, the big black bird careening into the truck's windshield, and the old woman, who I thought was Grim, at the scene.

226

"What kind of bird?" Hulda asked ominously.

"Big and black," I said. "A crow, maybe, big enough to be a raven even."

A gasp worked its way around the room like a Dodger Stadium wave. I had to fight the urge to stand and lift my arms. It was definitely something I said.

"Are you sure?" Hulda asked.

"About the bird, yes."

"And about Fru Grimilla's presence at the scene?"

"It sure looked like her." Again, a ripple of surprise rolled over the women.

Hulda exhaled with a slump. "Katla, what you describe is a very serious accusation against Fru Grimilla. The carrion-eating Raven is the Messenger of Death, the chooser of the slain. It is the counterforce against which we operate to create balance. Our sworn enemy. Do you understand?"

Oh, no. "I'm not sure I do."

"Ravens are evil-born beings, masters of dark arts, snatchers of souls, an ancient cult rewarding immortality to those who execute three truly heinous covenants."

Ho, boy.

"Were this to be true," Hulda continued, "that Grimilla was indeed conspiring with a Raven, then she would be exiled, for all time, from the Storks."

God help me.

"Katla, your first bestowal of an essence is a moment of great mysticism. Many a Stork has had flights of fancy in the moments preceding her first meeting. I myself thought a Swan Maiden had granted three wishes." Hulda waved at the air. "And I'm still waiting for them." I briefly considered mentioning the black bird at the scene of our bear encounter, but what did it have to do with the issue at hand? Grim wasn't there that day.

"It all happened so fast," I said. "And another witness didn't see her. I think you're right. She couldn't possibly have been there and then disappeared in the blink of an eye. And I swear I never knew anything about Ravens. I honestly didn't mean to accuse."

"Is fine, child," Hulda said. "We do not doubt your integrity." She looked around the room, which had fallen eerily silent. "I suggest we proceed. Katla Gudrun Leblanc"—boy, Hulda could belt it out for such a small thing—"you have called us here today?"

And that was it. We were back on track. The first thing that went through my mind was how in the name of Elmer Fudd was I going to make it through any sort of talk or presentation? My wits left me. No joke. I heard the door shut behind them. Everyone was looking at me. I was expected to stand and deliver. Then I thought of how my mom taught me to tackle hard puzzles, or really anything daunting: start with a corner. I'd gone through a big jigsaw phase when I was young, doing puzzles way beyond my years, and often frustrating myself in the process. My mom had sat so patiently with me, always forcing me to come up with my own strategies, but still guiding gently. I just had to start small.

I stood, and though it felt like a thousand little drills were boring through my skull, I took a deep calming breath and started with a corner. "I have been contacted by an essence." I remembered that Fru Dorit had started with the essence. I could do that. "A girl. She will be shy and a lover of nature. She is destined to live in a cold climate." That wasn't so bad. Even my head felt a little better. "There are three possible vessels." My posture improved. "One is a sixteen-year-old girl who has been alarmingly deceived by her partner, an unfit parent." As I spoke, Hulda raised a single digit. "Another is a twenty-five-year-old newlywed." This time Hulda raised two fingers, a peace sign of sorts. "She wants a child," I continued, "though the relationship is temporarily strained, and the husband often away long stretches for work, and the mother is restless. This child could force them to settle."

"And the third?" Hulda asked, wagging three fingers, a flashing *scout's-honor*.

"A thirty-eight-year-old divorced mother of one. The relationship is new."

"And your recommendation?" Hulda looked at me kindly.

Weird how, in that briefest of moments, a million things flew through my head. I thought about how defeated Monique had been. I hoped Jaelle would know how to teach her daughter to puzzle through life with the skill and patience my mom had shown me. I thought about how content the baby had seemed in my dreams, and of my mom's own cheery disposition. And then it felt as if my thoughts were being guided by someone else. I resisted, formed thoughts, remembered intentions, strengthened resolve; yet my mind, and then my voice, continued of its own accord. "The divorced mother. She will love the child dearly."

The room got very quiet after that. I sat down and watched as, individually, the women held up one, two, or three fingers — a silent vote, predating the written word, possibly even language as we know it.

"Ah," Hulda said. "Katla's recommendation is approved."

I was too stunned to react. Though my scalp felt immediately better, I was confused by what had transpired. Then all of a sudden, as if a blanket had settled over my shoulders, I felt calm, and warm, and peaceful.

It didn't last long. Fru Grimilla came barging through the door, out of breath, and with a Barbie ski cap on her head. "I apologize for my tardiness," she said, fussing with the too-pink, too-small monstrosity that even Penny was too old to own. "There wasn't a hat of mine to be found in the house."

Uh-oh. I thought of our *Extreme Makeover: Minnesota Edition,* which concluded with Penny kicking a bag of hats under the bed. Could my life get any more complicated?

"What have I missed?" Fru Grimilla asked.

"Katla has recommended a thirty-eight-year-old divorced mother of one for her first vessel," Hulda said. "We have ratified this choice."

"Divorced," Grim said. "I do not approve."

Hulda opened her hands in a gesture of futility. "Is too late, Fru Grimilla; the decision has been recorded."

Old Grim's face went bug mad.

"Fru Hulda," said Fru Dorit, who had a very girlish quality to her voice for one so old and plump, "I, for one, would like to congratulate Katla on her first recommendation as a Stork. She showed great poise and maturity. I also wonder if we will be addressing the Raven charges against Fru Grimilla this evening?"

Just when I was beginning to really like suck-up Dorit, despite her relation to Wade, she had to go and add "pot-stirrer" to her résumé.

"Especially as this would be her second accusation." Dorit made a clicking sound with her tongue.

Make that pot-licker.

"What Raven charges?" Fru Grimilla shouted.

Crud.

Hulda clasped her hands together in what could only be described as prayer. "Thank you, Fru Dorit, for reminding us of our obligations." Though Hulda's tone didn't really sound all that thankful. "I remind everyone that past charges, once cleared, are null and void. New charges, should they be filed, would require a tribunal.

For now we seek only to discern if such action is necessary. Katla, again we ask you to describe the events of this evening."

Kill me now. Because the look of rage on Grim's face was certainly a promise to do it eventually, and the knit of her eyebrows hinted at a sooner-than-later resolve. I described the scene, truthfully, but with plenty of elbowroom for Fru Grimilla to add her own account.

When I had finished, Grim stood. "This is an outrage. I know not how to respond to such groundless accusations."

"Not accusations," Hulda cut in. "As you heard Katla say, she's not sure what she saw."

"It's true," I said. "It happened so fast. Even now, it's all such a blur."

"So, Katla," Dorit said, "do you charge Fru Grimilla with conspiring with the Raven?"

"No," I said quickly. "I don't."

"I should certainly hope not," Grim said. "For I promise to defend myself by whatever means necessary."

And we have a winner. "Like Fru Hulda said, I was probably just nervous and seeing all kinds of crazy things in anticipation of today's meeting." Sure wished I'd gotten the wish-granting Swan Maiden hallucination instead. Just my luck, I supposed, to conjure the Messenger of Death. The meeting adjourned with Fru Hulda tabling the Raven discussion for later. I remained in my seat for many moments recovering. Finally, I looked around. Only Hulda and I remained.

"I am proud of you." Hulda patted my hand.

"I made a mess of things."

"The first is always the hardest."

"Fru Grimilla hates me."

"No. She doesn't hate you. It's just that Fru Grimilla is very devoted, very passionate in her duties. To have her loyalty questioned is a great insult."

"I swear I didn't know anything about the significance of the Raven. But I have to say, it doesn't make me feel any better about my close call today. What if someone's out to get me? Because I'm a Stork." Contrary to popular belief, it did not help to talk about it. It only made it feel more real, as if the sound of screeching tires and the smell of burning rubber hadn't been sensory enough.

Hulda, lost in thought, twitched her forefinger back and forth in the air. "Ravens seek immortality. With dark magic, they coax both man and beast to do their evil bidding, to fulfill their devilish covenants. They risk everything in their quest. Do you understand the consequence of failure?"

"I'm not sure." But again, I wondered if I should mention the bear attack. How much more *beastly* could it get?

"Damnation," Hulda said in a low, rough voice.

That I understood.

"Storks, on the other hand, have a passion for both this life and the next. They are chosen to deliver souls. A great honor. A betrayal of this trust — it's just unthinkable."

"I guess that makes sense." And it did. Crotchety was one thing, but devilish was a whole 'nother country.

"Do not worry yourself. Only your sister Storks know your identity. You are safe within our ranks. Sometimes a big black bird is just that."

"Uh, Fru Hulda, what did Fru Dorit mean by a second accusation?"

"Did you not understand that she was cleared of this charge?"

"Yeah. I got that, but still, it struck me as important."

She tapped her chin. "Is old business, but it involves you."

"What? How?"

"The first accusation against Fru Grimilla came after your accident at the lake. There were reports of a coat of peacock blue at the scene."

"She was there?"

"This never was proven. In fact, she had a sewing circle with the Girl Scouts that day."

"But given these new charges . . ."

"Katla, listen closely to me. Fru Grimilla's name was cleared. This is old story with no relevance."

"But . . ."

"We speak no more of this," she said with a slash of her hand.

I had so many more questions: about the Ravens and their covenants, and about that day at the lake, but I knew better than to persist. She might need a leg up, but once in the saddle, Hulda was one big bad boss lady.

She then got a funny kind of proud look on her face. "Your recommendation for the vessel, I approve. You're a very strong girl. And you made a good decision. The earth element, a logical choice. A mother who is grounded. Of course, you knew this already of the vessel, and much more." Hulda squeezed my hand affectionately.

Somehow I suspected she, too, knew plenty about the vessel, including name, rank, and cereal of choice. Nonetheless, she seemed pleased with me. And while we were on the topic of family, I supposed then was the time to strike. "Uh, Hulda," I stammered, "do you think you'd be willing to meet my dad?"

"Of course, child. I should love to meet your father."

"Do you think you'd be willing to show him your factory?" My nose twitched. It always betrayed me in awkward situations. "Given the whole wind symbol from my dream."

Hulda took a long time to answer. It seemed like a bad sign. "An interesting interpretation, though I wonder its merit."

"My dad isn't exactly excited about it either."

Hulda perked up. "He resists?"

"Uh. Yeah."

"What are his reservations?"

CHAPTER TWENTY-EIGHT

"Did you sleep well?" my mom asked me the next morning. She looked just as sunny and calm this morning as she had yesterday, and the day before. I wasn't sure how long it took for our decision to kick in, but she clearly hadn't figured it out yet.

"Pretty good," I said, though I hadn't. As much as I trusted Hulda and wanted, badly, to believe that sometimes a big black bird is just that, the whole Raven thing — even just knowing they're out there — had me rattled. As did mailboxes. And logs, of any shape or variety.

"Did you get your project done?"

"Yep." I patted my book bag, which contained nothing more than a simple social studies assignment due that day.

"You sure looked beat when you got in last night." If only she knew. And then it struck me. She really did need to know. I looked down at the bowl of healthy kibble she was crunching. She definitely ate well, but I also noticed the big mug of coffee in her hand. She'd have to cut down on that, wouldn't she?

"I don't feel so great this morning." It was true. I woke with cramps. "By the way, I'm almost out of tampons. Can I take some from your bathroom?" That part was not true; besides, I wouldn't normally ask before raiding her supplies.

"Of course, honey. Get what you need." And then there it was. That flicker of realization. Calendar pages flipped across my mom's eyes. I saw them shuffle like cards.

"Oh." My mom tapped her bottom lip with her index finger. She lifted her chin. She was counting days; I knew it.

I cleared my breakfast dishes and made the phony trip to her bathroom. By the time I got back, my mom was a different person—or maybe, more precisely, an additional person. She was clearly flustered and distracted. I don't think she heard me say good-bye. If she did, she didn't respond before the door closed. I sat in my car and took a few cleansing yoga breaths. She'd be fine. It'd take a little while, but she'd be fine. She was the type who could roll with life's curves. That's why she was such an excellent mother. And Stanley, he was a good guy, even if a bit of a goof.

I drove through the parking lot twice. No beat-up truck. I felt as gray as the gathering clouds. I was beginning to sense a resiliency about myself, though. I lifted my chin as I walked, alone, to first period. Kids looked at me inquiringly and I flashed smiles at them, as if we were old pals. I heard about every other word out of my English teacher's mouth, and understood about half of those. I watched the halls carefully between classes. Nothing of interest. Though Monique did wave to me once. I supposed a pregnancy scare could knock the entitlement out of even the loftiest of stuck-ups. I also saw Wade. He gave me an odd look, though at least he didn't click an imaginary camera at me. Nor had I yet to hear of compromising photos circulating via cell phones or the Web. At lunchtime, when I arrived to Mr. Parks's journalism room, Pedro pulled me aside.

"Have you heard from Jack?"

"No," I replied.

"I called his house again. His dad just said he's unavailable. What kind of an answer is that?"

"I don't know." Pedro must have seen something in my eyes, though I tried very hard to look normal, knowing cheery would be a dead giveaway.

"Are you OK?"

"I'm good." I wasn't. I reached into my backpack. "Do me a favor." I held out Jack's cap. "Give this to Jack next time you see him."

"You give it to him," Pedro said.

"Nah," I said. "A good-luck charm, as it turns out, but I think I'm done with it."

Pedro took the hat from my outstretched hand.

Assistant editor Penny called the room to order and reminded everyone of the Monday deadline for stories. She seemed comfortable in front of the group. I thought that she was the kind of girl people underestimated. "Good work on your profile of Ms. Bryant, by the way, Jessica," she said. "Who would've known she could guess anyone's age to within twelve months? What a great anecdote. So unusual."

After everyone settled into their assignments, Penny took a seat beside me. She opened her notebook and flipped though a few pages. I grabbed her hand.

"What are these?"

"Some dress sketches." She seemed embarrassed. "You know, for the dance."

They were all shaded in seafoam green and floor-length.

"Are you making it?"

"My *amma* is helping me."

I grimaced. I couldn't help it.

"She's a good seamstress," Penny said. "And she's letting me make all the decisions. We're actually fashioning it out of one of her old dresses."

I didn't cringe this time, though it took everything in me not to. Poor Penny. I could just imagine what one of Old Grim's dresses looked like. "Which is the final version?"

She flipped the page, and I studied the drawing. Though it was traditional, I nodded my approval. "You will look stunning."

"I just hope I'm still going."

"Why wouldn't you be going?" I asked.

"My *amma* was so angry at me last night. She went out for like ten minutes and came back as mad as I've ever seen her. Apparently, she'd been looking for that bag of hats we joked around with on Saturday. You'd think I'd stolen a car or robbed a bank, the way she reacted. And she was only gone for a few minutes, so what was the big deal?"

I thought of the Stork time-bending phenomenon. The way an hour in the dungeon accounted for nothing on the clocks. A pretty clever device should you happen to belong to a clandestine organization. I also realized I'd achieved bronze, silver, and gold in the piss-Grim-off Olympics. My three-part performance included: bronze for conspiracy in the concealment of hats, thus rendering her late to council; silver for taking advantage of her tardiness and rushing through my first vessel recommendation in an effort to avoid her dissenting vote; and the coveted gold for a public accusation of being the Messenger of Death. Somehow I did not see the cover of the Wheaties box in my future.

Penny drummed her fingers across the notebook. "It's really weird, but for whatever reason, she doesn't seem to like you."

241

"Maybe she didn't like the makeover I gave you." Penny had been doing a much better job of styling herself, and I'd not seen a single sweater-vest since the night of the Asking Fire.

"It seems like it's more than that. She even wanted to know who you were going to the dance with, and when I said it was Jack, she had this weird reaction, like she didn't approve."

"Why would she care who I go to the dance with?" I asked. Was it me? Or was Grim worming her hooked nose into every corner of my life? And why?

"I don't know. I'm just going to make sure I don't set her off again this week." Penny traced the silhouette of her gown with a finger. "Did you get a new dress?"

"No." I probably answered too quickly.

"You're still going, right?"

I took a big breath. "We haven't really discussed it. And now he's had these two unexplained absences, so I doubt it."

"But has he taken back the invitation?"

"No. Not formally."

"What about your column?" she asked. "You need to be there for the article."

Just yesterday, I had pitched her a sort of red-carpet review of Homecoming's hottest and trendiest looks. "I've got a backup plan," I lied.

"You have to get a dress." There was an urgency to Penny's voice. Like dresses were a commodity more precious around here than balmy temperatures, or decent coffee.

"I've got an old one that will work," I lied again, but could tell by the way Penny scrutinized me that she wasn't convinced.

"Don't worry," she said. "He won't let you down."

I did worry. Jack was a no-show the entire day.

At the end of the day, just as I was closing my locker, Wade startled me with his sudden appearance.

"Boo," he said in a teasing tone.

"What do you want, Wade?"

"To apologize and promise to be nice."

"Just leave me alone."

"Hope to die," he said, crossing his fingers over his heart. "Monique said she'd take me back, but only if I change my ways. Make amends."

"You're getting back together?"

"Trying."

I shook my head. "You two have more ups and downs than an elevator."

"Do you accept my apology? There never were any pictures."

Bastard.

"Jack's on my sorry list, too. Haven't seen him around, though."

"Neither have I."

Wade looked at me with a funny expression, though I supposed atonement was a strange emotion to him. He took a step back. "Tell you what. I'll give you some time to think about it. In the meantime, you'll see I'm a new man."

As I walked to the parking lot, I thought about Wade's claims of being a "new man." And what had Jack once told me? That shiny and new isn't always better. Still, with Wade I figured it couldn't get any worse.

My dad was waiting for me. He honked and waved and pulled around to the curb. I could tell by the way some of the kids gawked that he was flashy for a dad, as was his car — for a rental.

"We're going to meet Hulda at the factory," I said.

He rolled his eyes, but asked for directions. It was just a little outside the downtown area. I drove past it often, but had never really taken a good look. Probably because there was a tall line of trees camouflaging the front of the square brick building. It had a decent-size parking lot, even if the pavement was cracked and sagging. Above the gated entrance, a large wrought-iron sign in an old-fashioned scroll said INGA PAPER MILL. We pulled in and parked in one of the spots closest to what looked like a formal entrance.

My dad took a long look around. He even sniffed with flared nostrils, never a good sign. I did my best to point out the positive. The building itself seemed solid and impos-ing, and brick was usually a sign of good construction, as it was an expensive building material. My dad had taught me that. He noticed that a few of the windows on the first floor were broken, but I reminded him that was an easy fix. I pointed out that the site was close to the river. A bonus, he countered, to manufacturing in the nineteenth century. I didn't dare mention the abandoned railroad tracks, though I saw him look at them with disdain. It was definitely going to be a tough sell.

We stepped into the office. It had a small front section with an old metal desk, presumably for a receptionist. A few chairs lined up along the window functioned as a small waiting area. Two glassed-in offices were positioned behind the reception desk. It was very cold inside. It obviously hadn't been heated in some time. And now was the time to sniff, as even I had to admit the air had a musty quality to it.

"Very small," my dad mumbled.

One of the office doors opened, and Hulda appeared, though I hadn't noticed her the first time I had looked through the glass. "Good afternoon," she said rather formally. She wore the same long gray woolen skirt as she had on every one of our encounters, but with a white blouse, which appeared clean and pressed, and a black tweed jacket, which almost seemed businesslike. She'd made an effort.

I introduced them, and then Hulda did that commanding thing at which she was so effective. "Follow me."

I almost wanted to chuckle when my dad scurried obediently behind her. How did she do that?

We walked through an unmarked door, down a

short hall, and ended up on the floor of a very large warehouse. It was an open space at least three stories high, with large equipment scattered about, and the remnants of a conveyor line. Enormous barn-size doors provided access to what looked like the back of the building, and light flooded the area from a large number of rectangular windows.

Hulda provided a quick history of the site. The factory was built by her father in 1940 and named after his wife and Hulda's mother, Inga. Hulda, a fifteen-year-old recent immigrant at the time, remembered the celebration of its opening day. The mill had been nonintegrated, meaning they purchased the wood pulp as dried bale, which was then converted to a slurry and passed through a series of presses, rollers, and driers. The end product, huge rolls of paper, had been newsprint quality. After her father's death, Hulda had closed the factory, as its old machines had become outdated and the factory too small to compete with the large integrated mills, which produced their own pulp. She seemed proud of her father's operation, which explained her refusal to sell the site.

She then took a deep breath and walked, with her hands on her hips, to the center of the space. "So you seek to harness the wind." She looked at my father gravely. "The wind is an ancient force whose powers are capricious. Think carefully of what we know as airborne — snow and rain, the obvious — but remember, too, plague, pest, and choking dust are carried on the back of an evil tempest."

Uh-oh. I was afraid of this. White Witch Hulda and her third eye. My dad gave me a what-have-you-gotten-me-into look.

"Yet," Hulda continued, "luck is ferried on the breath of the gods." Hulda pointed to my father. "So, Gregor, I understand your business partners are in Japan."

"My investors, yes." Funny how my dad's posture straightened as he spoke to Hulda.

"There are some important things you must share with your investors. First thing," Hulda said, stamping her foot on the concrete floor. "Solid bedrock underneath us here. Very stable foundation for a business. No?"

"Couldn't hurt." My dad opened his arms playfully.

"Also, the bamboo that bends in the wind is stronger than the oak that resists." Hulda looked at him expectantly. "I speak of change here."

"Change can be good, I suppose," my dad said, but I could tell he was just humoring her.

"One more thing. Listen carefully. Karma is the turning of the wheel and is very important to the ancient religions of the Orient. Is much like fate, but they believe karma is our will as we swim in the river of our past and present. We cannot change the course of the river, but the strokes of our swim influence our destination. This you must tell your investors."

"Uh. I'll tell them if it comes up," my dad said.

Hulda gave him a sharp eye and, again, his shoulders snapped back. I heard the ping. "You bring it up. You tell them at the Inga Paper Mill, and you must use the full name, an old woman told you that karma is the turning of the wheel." She pointed at him with a crooked finger. "You will see."

After that, Hulda cleared us out of the place like yesterday's newspaper. She walked us back through the reception area and to the front door. Her parting remark was, "I will think about this wind harnessing of yours. I will let you know my decision."

My dad and I walked back to the car with our hands dug deep in our pockets. Finally, he turned to me and said, "What was that?"

What was there to say? "That was Hulda."

"And you want me to enter into business with her? She'll let me know *her* decision?"

I got in the car. "I know. I know. She's a little odd." And wouldn't he be surprised to know the extent to which she was odd. Though it seemed to be a lost cause, I persisted. The thought of having my dad around on a regular basis was just too appealing. "Besides all the mumbo-jumbo, what did you think of the site?"

My dad started the engine. "Babe, there're abandoned factories all over the place. One's as good as another. I feel good about Palmdale, but if that falls through, we have a lead on something in the Phoenix area. Minnesota just isn't in our business plan." As we pulled out of the parking lot, my dad added, "Besides, I told you earlier. I refuse to set up shop anywhere I can't get a decent cup of coffee."

"Fine," I muttered.

He pulled onto Main Street. "Now how about some dinner? Is there anything besides the Kountry Kettle?"

"Not unless you're willing to drive," I said.

"Unlimited mileage, satellite radio, and GPS. We're heading south."

When I got home that night, my mom was watching the news. There had been an earthquake in the California desert that had been felt all the way to LA and Orange County. I sat down and watched with her for a bit. No fatalities had been reported, but a lot of damage had been done. The news reports showed everything from toppled store shelves to crumbled brick buildings to cracked road surfaces. My mom had always hated earthquakes. I was too young to remember the big Northridge shaker, but it was one of the things she often listed when asked why she left California. And even though she sat chewing her nails as she listened to CNN, I knew this wasn't the true source of her agitation.

"Where's Stanley tonight?"

"I canceled my date with him." Her voice faltered a little. "I was feeling kind of tired."

"Is everything all right?"

"I'll be fine," she said unconvincingly. "Maybe something I ate, or a touch of the flu."

I didn't press. I didn't even know if my mom had tested herself yet. "Dad asked me to see if you'd like to go to dinner tomorrow night, the three of us."

"I don't know if that's such a great idea."

My dad made me promise to ask, though even then I hadn't had high hopes. I looked at my sunken mom. Maybe I had been too hasty, too optimistic. This would change everything for her — her relationship with Stanley, her job, her energy level. I remembered then that she'd had a difficult pregnancy with me. Not that I remembered, of course, but there were stories about concerns for both of us. Remorse nagged at me. "It's OK. I understand."

She must have seen something register in my eyes. She hugged her arms to her sides, balling into something tight. "We'll see how I feel tomorrow."

I took one last look at the TV screen. More reports of earthquake damage were coming in. Fire engines were rushing to the scene of a blaze started by a severed gas line. I walked up the stairs to the sound of sirens.

CHAPTER TWENTY-NINE

On Thursday my mom called in sick, something she rarely ever did. I swallowed a good swig of guilt along with my chocolate milk and toasted bagel.

My morning didn't look much better. Jack's truck wasn't in the parking lot. I knew this for a fact because I circled it twice. With a sigh of resolve, I pulled into his vacant space. It felt wrong somehow, but also deliciously naughty.

I kept my head down through the parking lot; my backpack felt like an elephant catching a ride; even my hair hung in my face. I stepped out from between two cars when a truck pulled up alongside me.

"You parked in my spot." Jack had his window down and hung his left arm along the side of the door.

The first thing that went through my head was a little mental cartwheel. He didn't seem mad. "I didn't notice your name on it." I crossed my arms, hoping to still the jitters rocking me back to front.

"It's marked," he said, dipping his head a little farther out the window. "Not with my name so much, but it clearly states: for butt-ugly trucks only."

I smiled and pulled keys from my pocket. "You want me to move?" I said, jangling them.

"I want you to get in."

This caught me by surprise. "What for?"

"I want you to come for a ride."

"Skip?"

"I'm AWOL, so I may as well take a hostage."

I looked around guiltily. A couple of kids walked past. They looked at me and then Jack in the truck. If we were going to do this, we'd better do it before we had too many witnesses. I jogged around to the passenger side, opened the door, and jumped in. No sooner had the old door groaned shut than Jack was gunning it out of the parking lot.

I hadn't even had time to fasten my seat belt. I ended up sliding across the wide bench-style front seat, almost landing in his lap. He steadied me with his right arm protectively.

"Sorry," he said. He seemed to hold me like that for a moment or two longer than required, but then pulled his arm away with a kind of resignation. "Buckle up. It's a bit of a drive."

I scooted over to the far side near the window and fastened my belt. We drove in silence for a few minutes. I noticed we were headed north on the main highway out of town.

"Are you going to tell me where we're going? Or is this a real kidnapping?"

He looked over at me with a kind of half smile. "I'm not going to tell you where we're going, but I'll promise you this—you never have to worry about your safety with me."

Wow. As far as promises go, that was a whopper. The last thing I remembered promising was to get the clothes from the washer to the dryer. I hadn't. They were still there. Would probably need to be rewashed at this point. "Will you at least tell me where you've been?"

He drummed his thumb on the steering wheel. "I had to go north for a few days. Let's just get where we're going and I promise to explain it—all of it."

He turned on the radio. It was a country station. I groaned and turned the knob to an alternative rock station, *the* alternative rock station. A little grunt came from his side of the car, but he didn't comment, on that or anything else. It reminded me of being with my *afi*. The way the two of them settled into silence like an old couch, with room for me.

The scenery changed from shops to homes to fields

to woods on both sides of the highway. We pulled onto a gravel road marked with a faded sign that read ELKHORN LAKE PUBLIC PARKING.

I swiveled in my seat. "Is this . . . ?"

"Yes. Are you OK with that?"

I looked around. Nothing seemed familiar. "Yes. I suppose." The narrow access road was still wooded, though now the drive was winding and pot-holed. Finally, we pulled into a paved lot with a view over a calm lake. "So this is the place," I said once we'd parked.

"This is it."

"What are we doing here?"

He scratched at his head. He was capless today. I liked it when he was capless. He wore an old blue T-shirt so faded whatever team or business it had supported was no longer legible. It clung to his ropy shoulders, which were taut, seemingly with purpose. "It seemed like the right place for part of what I want to tell you."

"For part of?"

"Let's walk." He opened his car door, and I did the same.

We came to the edge of the parking lot and crossed a small grassy area. Several benches lined the edge of the small clearing with a view out to the lake. He sat, as did I.

"I had to go away for a few days," he said finally. "To sort a few things out."

"Oh."

"It's just . . . after the whole thing with Wade, I didn't trust myself."

"Or me?"

He turned to me quickly. "Is that what you think?"

"You made it pretty clear."

He lowered his head into his hands. "No. I didn't. I screwed it all up. Would still be screwing it up, if it wasn't for Pedro."

"Pedro?"

He lifted his head and dropped his hands to his lap. "Stubborn bastard. Wouldn't stop calling my house. Finally showed up last night, uninvited. Wouldn't leave until I saw him. Wouldn't leave until he put my cap in my hands."

"Your cap?"

"You called it lucky."

A light flutter began in my chest. "I did. I know it sounds crazy, but I think it was."

"You don't know how much that meant to me. I'd been convinced of the opposite."

"The opposite?"

"Yes. Of being some sort of curse."

"How could you think that?"

"Because ever since you've come back, I've been half-crazy: confused, distracted, and a mess of emotions. And you have to admit, when we're together, wild things happen. So when the whole thing with Wade came up, the fact that his hatred of me was all the more reason to hurt you, it was some sort of last straw. And I just couldn't stand the thought of him touching you, hurting you. I lost it. I'm sorry, but I did. I snapped."

"I thought you were mad at me. For lying."

He spun wildly to face me. "Mad at you? No. I was mad at him, and myself, but not you."

"But you just took off. You could have called or something."

He placed a hand over mine and traced light circles with his thumb. "I was in a bad place. I needed to sort some things out. Besides, I'm not really a phone guy."

"I'll say." I felt suddenly dizzy, and a small spasm racked my shoulders.

"I made things worse. I know that now. And I'm sorry."

"Me, too. For lying. I was ashamed of my behavior. I made a big mistake and I just wanted to bury it."

"Not such a big mistake," he said, dropping his other hand over mine. "Wade has a way of manipulating people. You figured him out a lot quicker than most. I'm just sorry he hurt you."

"For the record, Wade didn't hurt me; I hurt him. Got him good. It stopped there."

"That's my girl." He pulled me into a hug. "I knew it. Anyone who could survive what we did could take a punk like Wade."

"He apologized, you know. He now says there never were any pictures."

Jack ground something at the base of his throat.

"He says you're on his sorry list, too."

"I'll believe that when I see it," Jack said.

I didn't want to talk about Wade, or think about Wade. I settled into Jack's embrace. He held me like that for a little while, and then pulled me to my feet.

"Come on, let's go down by the lake. I'm not done yet."

There were a dozen or so wooden steps leading down to the water's edge. He held my hand as we crossed a muddy flat area adjacent to the beach. It was mostly a pebbly shore with several large rock formations to our left. A wooden pier, now vacant for the season, led out to the tinny gray waters. Jack led me to one of the larger rocks, which provided a flat surface and view. We both sat for a few moments taking in the scenery. I closed my eyes and could picture it cloaked in snow, the lapping waves frozen in time, and the chill air ringing with the voices of skaters and the slap of hockey sticks.

"You wore a red coat," Jack said, pulling me from my reverie.

"You remember?"

"I remember everything. All of it. I want to tell you, if you think you could stand to hear it."

"Yeah. Sure."

He looked at me with an odd expression, tentative and probing. "You might think I'm crazy."

"Trust me," I said. "I'm not one to throw stones."

He hunched his shoulders and looked out to the

water. "I'd never seen you before, but the moment you stepped onto the ice, I couldn't take my eyes off you. I'd never seen hair so blond, or skin so white, or any girl so pretty, ever."

I gulped. It was wake-the-baby loud, but Jack just continued.

"I was twelve and had never really taken an interest in girls before, but this hit me like a bolt of lightning. I followed you around the ice for a good half hour, but you were completely oblivious. When you skated off to be on your own, it felt like you'd taken the sun from the sky."

Oh, my. His voice was intense and he was still looking out over the water and away from me, as if he couldn't bear to look me in the eye. "I didn't notice you," I said honestly.

"I know. It didn't matter. I was smitten." He rolled his eyes and looked at me sheepishly, obviously embarrassed by his word choice. Then he just kind of shook it off and continued, "I stayed on the side of the lake closest to where you had gone off to twirl and jump. My friends were angry that I'd left our hockey game. I didn't care. I heard the ice crack and knew immediately what it was. You were gone in an instant. Nothing but a vertical slab of ice bobbing in your place."

I scooted closer to him and put my hand in his. It was warm. He wore no jacket, as usual, and I felt the heat of his body as I drew myself next to him.

"I was to the spot where you'd last been in a dozen strides. I could see your red coat deep under the surface.

258

You were thrashing underwater. I dove headfirst without thinking of anything but staying close to the girl in the red coat. I got to you in just a few kicks. I was upside down, just as I'd dived, and I'll never forget the look of panic on your face as I drew near. I righted myself next to you, which was right when it started to feel like my chest was going to explode. I took your hand. You'd lost your gloves, and your skin was so cold I almost thought it was too late. We kicked to the surface. I held your hand as tight as I could, pulling you up with me. When we got to the top, we hit solid ice. We'd drifted from the hole. I had no idea which way to go. I felt along the ice for what seemed an eternity, but it was frozen solid. There was no sign of movement above. I didn't even know if anyone had seen either of us fall in. And then we started to sink. You were so still and resigned, but your eyes held on to mine with such intensity. I thought my lungs were going to explode. I thought we were going to die. I thought we were going to go to heaven together. I remember thinking that you looked like an angel with your hair fanned out around your face." Jack turned to me and stroked upward from my chin, tracing the line of my jaw.

I couldn't help myself. "I'm nobody's definition of an angel."

"You may be mine," he said. His fingers trailed over my earlobe and then down the tendrils of my hair. "How're you doing?" he asked. "Am I freaking you out?"

"Fine. And yes."

He laughed and then leaned in and kissed my neck. It was our second kiss. Yes, I was counting. And no, I didn't want it on the neck. "Do you want to hear more?"

"We live, right? Because it's not looking very good."

He laughed again, and I knew in that instant it was a sound I wouldn't want to live without. "We continued to sink. It was almost like floating. We held hands and gazed at each other intensely. You were so peaceful, so accepting, until I felt a calm come over me. My chest stopped hurting and we both stopped kicking and we were just kind of suspended there looking at each other."

"And then what happened? Are you sure we live?"

"You closed your eyes and I thought you died. It was like dying myself. I felt hopeless and angry. And then you reached out your other hand, the one that wasn't holding mine, and closed my lids. I reopened them, but you shook your head at me, all the while not opening your own eyes. Within a moment or two, I could hear something around us. Murmurs, or whispers. And then I didn't need to close my eyes anymore, because something wrapped around them from behind: a leaf or cloth. I couldn't tell what it was. I felt no pain and no fear, but I was aware of the passage of time. I knew we'd been under for a long time, too long. And then something encircled me, from under my arms, and we were gliding effortlessly and upward. We still held hands, and it was all that kept me from kicking to be free of whatever had taken hold. We came up in an entirely different section of the lake from where we'd gone down. That's one of the mysteries of the event. No one knew where or how we'd surfaced. The rescuers were looking for us clear across the ice. You were frozen, wracked with chills. I managed to call and wave to someone. And then we were descended upon by a mob of people. They pulled you away from me. All I could think was that they had no right. And then you were gone. I was told I couldn't see you in the hospital; you were too sick, in a coma. And then they took you back to LA, and all we ever heard was that you had some sort of trauma-induced amnesia."

Jack stood and pulled me to a stand. "You think I'm crazy, don't you? I just told you I heard whispers under the water, and that something pulled us up. You're probably thinking I suffered some sort of brain damage that day."

"No. I'm not."

"Do you remember anything about our time under the water?"

"No. I remember skating, and falling through the ice, and the cold, but nothing more."

"The lake is glacier-fed, but that only explains the depth and cold. The rest . . ." He looked at me for a long time. "Have I scared you? I pretty much bared my soul just now."

I took a deep breath. Funny how just a week ago I'd never really given the concept of soul much thought. "I'm not scared."

"What are you?" he asked tentatively.

I moved closer to him, burying my head under his chin. "Humbled. Incredibly grateful. Flattered. And what was that word you used?" I turned my face to his. "Oh yeah, I remember. Smitten."

He kissed me then. And on the right place this time. And his touch was anything but cold. My lips were on fire. A surge of white-hot heat coursed through me. It seemed even the weather felt the charge of our emotions. Winds whipped around us. I could feel my hair lift and fall across my face and his. It didn't matter. I could have stayed like that forever. I wanted to stay like that forever. He was the first to let go.

"Do you believe in fate?" he asked.

How many days ago had Hulda asked me that same question? How much had happened since then? "Yes."

"It's hard to explain," he said, "but from the moment I laid eyes on you skating, I felt this unshakable sense of fate, or destiny, or whatever you want to call it."

"I know someone who calls it karma."

"Karma it is, then." He rested his chin on my head.

"Wow," I said. "My head is spinning." It was true. I could feel the gray matter orbiting behind my eye sockets, which explained my blurred vision and lightheadedness.

"There's one more thing you should know about me." He pulled me away and looked into my eyes. I flinched. It was pure reflex. I seriously didn't know if I could handle anything else. Something shifted in his look; he hesitated, cleared his throat, and then said, "I'm partial to red. You don't happen to have a red dress for the dance, do you?"

I wondered if it was really what he wanted to tell me. It didn't seem to need that kind of build-up. Part of me was relieved, though. This I could handle. "Red?"

"Yes. And simple. Clothes don't have to be all that complicated."

"Red I can do. As for simple, I make no promises."

He replied with a kind of half laugh, half groan and pushed me a few inches away from him. We stood face-to-face, with just a light wind rushing through the space between us.

"So we're still going then? To the dance?" I asked.

"Of course we're going. You want to, don't you?"

"So much has happened since you asked me, and you never mentioned it again, and then you were gone. I honestly didn't know."

"Now you know. And you, of all people, can depend on me." He looked at his watch. "Almost lunchtime. We'd better head back. I've got to plead my case with Principal Henrich, and then with Coach Carter."

I looked wistfully out to the lake. I knew that something momentous had happened here. Both five years ago

CHAPTER THIRTY

It was so hard to go back to school and attempt anything that remotely resembled attendance. Jack's words looped through my mind over and over. This guy, for whom my feelings had been increasing exponentially, had confessed an attraction to me, a commitment to me, which was nothing short of epic. I buzzed through what remained of the day like a drunken fool. Even a visit to the guidance counselor to discuss my unexcused absences for first through fourth period did nothing to dampen my mood.

Jack found me in the hallways between classes. I honestly don't know if we elicited the same kind of stares and reactions. I saw nothing but him, heard nothing but him. After school he met me at my locker.

"I'm off to beg Coach Carter for forgiveness," he said.

"What do you think he'll do to you?"

"I definitely see a few penalty laps in my future, and I'll probably be benched for tomorrow's game."

Pedro, accompanied by Penny, appeared at Jack's side. "Dude, don't even say it."

Jack balled his shoulders forward. "Rules are rules. I'm prepared for the worst."

"No way." Pedro tugged on Jack's arm. "Come on. You'd better be early today. And I'll talk to Coach Carter myself if I have to."

As Pedro pulled him away, Jack looked back at me pleadingly. I must have responded with a toothy grin.

"You're all smiles," Penny said.

"I can't help it," I said. "I'd sing if I could carry a tune."

She giggled. "Told you he'd be back." She tugged at my sleeve. "I like your outfit today. It suits you."

"Thanks." I looked down. The boots Jack had vandalized, Levi's, one of my mom's Nordic sweaters, and a Gap down vest. I remembered being on some sort of autopilot that morning. Fumbling around the laundry room for clean jeans and then fingering my mom's pale yellow sweater and thinking it fit my mood.

"So, I guess you're going to the dance. Good thing you had a backup plan for a dress."

Yikes. A dress. I wondered how on earth I'd have time between now and Saturday to drive to a decent store. "Good thing," I mumbled in return.

266

I pulled a notebook from the top shelf of the locker and stuffed it into my satchel. "My dad's going to the game with me. You want to come with us?"

Penny scrunched her mouth to the side. "I should probably meet you there. My *amma* is still angry about those hats. You'd think they were the Crown Jewels the way she's acting. And it's weird, but she's got it into her head that it was your idea to hide them. Why would she think that?"

I'd been thinking a lot about Grim. About how mad she'd been at my first Stork meeting when I'd been ushered into the second chair. Had I not arrived, would it have been hers? Had I spoiled her chances forever? Would she prefer me out of the way — for good? And what if she really had been at the scene of the truck accident? The only things that kept the bogey in my head at bay were Hulda's faith in her and a constant memo-to-self that Grim was Penny's grandmother and guardian, and a Stork, neither of which she'd jeopardize for anything. I hoped. Though it was not entirely lost on me that, besides *Raven,* the agent of death went by the nickname *Grim* Reaper. "Beats me," I said. "Parents usually like me."

"I guess I have been a little different since I met you," Penny said. "A little more rebellious."

Perfect. Because the motive Grim had against me felt incomplete. Corrupter of her sole surviving progeny rounded things out nicely. "I never meant to get you in trouble."

Penny waved her hand in a dismissive gesture. "Are you kidding? I wouldn't trade this last week for anything."

Had it only been a week? Of course it had, but how was that possible? It felt as if the whole time-bending Stork phenomenon was compressing the days of the week and hours of the day even outside of council.

I closed my locker just as Wade and Monique passed by arm in arm. "Hi, Penny. Hi, Kat," Monique said with a smile.

"So, I guess they're back together," I said.

Penny shook her head. "Can you believe it?"

"Somehow I can."

"They're like new people. Monique even spoke to me before PE today, asking me if I was going to the dance, what color my dress was, and, of course, if I'd remembered to vote for queen. Still, that wouldn't have happened a week ago."

"I guess a lot can happen in a week." I thought just how crazy and true that was.

After school, I walked over to Afi's. He went to take one of his power naps, so I tucked in behind the cash register. He left the book he was reading, *Moby-Dick,* on the counter. As a bookmark he had travel brochures to the Bahamas. One was for a deep-sea-fishing charter service out of Nassau. Lately, Afi had been talking a lot about missing the water. A lot for him, anyway. He'd spent the first nineteen years of his life in a small coastal village in Iceland and claimed it was seawater, not blood, that tinted his veins blue. Within a few minutes—and to my surprise—my dad came walking through the door. His collar was up, like he'd been pulling on it, and his hair was tousled, like he'd been tugging at it.

"I've been looking for you. You're not going to believe what an extraordinary day I've had." He paced in front of me distractedly.

"Why? What happened?"

"It's crazy."

"What?"

He threw his hands up. "I had a conference call with the investors today. They were very agitated. They'd heard about the earthquake out in Palmdale and wanted to pull the plug on the deal, then and there. They kept talking about omens and bad luck. And how the Japanese believe in signs and need a solid foundation. The whole thing was going to fall through because of a little tremor. I had to think quick. Two years of work and a lot of money was about to go south."

"What did you do?"

"I told them about that crazy Hulda and her factory. It was the first thing that popped into my head. And you're not going to believe it."

At this point I figured even Ripley himself had nothing on me, but I tried my best to look curious. "Believe what?"

"They bought all that crazy stuff she said about karma

turning the wheel, which they immediately interpreted as a wind turbine. And I knew the factory was on a bedrock foundation. How in the world had that even come up?"

"Hulda's kind of funny like that."

"There's more," he said. "When I told them the name of the factory was the Inga Paper Mill, they just about flipped. *Inga* is the Japanese word for fate or karma."

Now that, I wasn't expecting. "Wow!"

"I'll say." My dad ran his fingers through his hair, leaving it in spiky tufts. I didn't know if I'd ever seen him this keyed up. "And now I've got to get hold of Hulda. I don't even have a verbal agreement with her, never mind contract."

"Hulda can be hard to pin down. She shows up in her store across the street from time to time, but besides that . . ." As I was saying this, I looked across Main to see none other than Hulda in the front window of her store. I sat there, mouth open, as I watched her place a square red-and-white For Sale sign in a front and center position. "You won't believe this," I said. "Even I don't believe it. She's there right now."

My dad turned to follow my gaze. "Excellent. Let's go talk to her."

Afi must have heard the excitement in my dad's voice. He came shuffling out, rubbing his back. He shook Dad's hand affably. I could tell he wasn't the type to get involved in whatever had transpired between my parents. "What's all the clamor out here?"

270

"Look, Afi." I pointed to Hulda's. "It's for sale."

Afi scratched his head. "Well, I'll be."

"Dad and I are going to talk to Hulda about her factory. I'll get the scoop while I'm there."

My dad and I hustled out of the store. I heard Afi ask, "What about the factory?" on my way out, but figured we'd catch him up with the whole story later.

The chimes tinkled above Hulda's door as we let ourselves in. She was sweeping a century's worth of dust and dirt, and it swirled about her in a thick, smoky haze.

"Ah. I've been waiting for you." Hulda propped the broom against a wall. "Follow me." She waddled down an aisle of ginghams. It was alarming how small and frail and stooped she appeared from behind. I instinctively squared my shoulders, remembering my mother's they'll-stay-that-way warnings. She headed toward the back. Panic burned in my tummy. Was she really going to take my dad to the dungeon? He was already spooked by her; no need to set the stage. She stopped at the door and passed her hand over the crackled painted letters of the word OFFICE. Pushing the door open slowly with an eerie creak, she motioned my father forward. "After you."

I took a deep bracing breath and followed my father into the office. *Huh?* I spun around twice. No winding stairs, no basement room, just a battered wooden desk and chair, two folding metal chairs in front of them, and an old bookshelf stacked with pattern books. I touched one of the walls, the one where I thought the stairs should logically be, and tapped.

"Kat, what is wrong with you?" my dad asked.

I looked at Hulda, who had a wry smile on her face. "You like my office? I don't think I've taken you back here before."

"I was expecting something different," I said lamely. My dad looked at me like I'd sprouted alfalfa from my nose. "I thought there was access to the basement from here."

"No basement in this building," Hulda said. "Nor in any of the shops on Main Street. Too close to the river. Flooding can be a problem." She smiled at my dad. "Factory up high, you noticed. Never flooded, ever."

Now that I thought about it, Afi didn't have a basement. Only the storeroom in the back and the attic rooms up above. I wanted to laugh and smack myself, hard. How could anything about Hulda still surprise me?

Hulda took a seat behind the desk; my dad and I sat in the wobbly chairs.

"So," Hulda said, folding her hands, "you still want to harness the wind." It wasn't a question.

"I had a very interesting conversation with my investors in Japan. I shared with them what we discussed at our last meeting." My dad crossed and then uncrossed his legs. "You didn't happen to know that *inga* means *karma* in Japanese?"

"Of course," Hulda said matter-of-factly.

My dad opened his eyes wide, but then continued. "Then maybe I don't need to tell you they were impressed. They thought it was a good omen."

"And you told them about the bedrock?" Hulda asked.

"Yes," my dad replied.

"Interesting events in California lately," Hulda said ominously. "Native American legend believes that the world sits on the back of Big Turtle. Mostly we don't feel him move, but when he is bothered or frightened, we have earthquakes."

"Big Turtle reached the news in Japan," my dad said. I was amused that he was starting to play along with Hulda.

"Fascinating, this tale of Big Turtle." Hulda looked at me pointedly. "The legend holds that a young girl from Sky World sat down under the branches of an apple tree. There was a rumbling, and the ground opened, and she would have fallen to her death, except two swans carried her on their backs to Water World, where Big Turtle made a new home for her on his back. This girl, Sky Girl, took on many qualities of the birds who saved her, and totem poles and carvings depict a powerful half-bird, half-woman creature in her honor."

"Sky Girl should pay more attention to where she plops down," my dad said, clearly having surrendered all attempt at logic or formality.

"This is the thing." Hulda shook her finger at him. "Sky Girl was drawn to the apple tree."

"Her destiny," my dad said.

"Precisely," Hulda replied.

My dad did manage to talk business with Hulda. She was surprisingly knowledgeable about contractual leases, land sales, business permits, and all the various boring details my dad seemed keen to finalize. In the end, he negotiated a verbal agreement on a five-year lease, details to be hammered out lawyer-to-lawyer. It surprised me a little that Hulda had a lawyer. I half expected her to refer him to her shaman or numerologist.

"Hulda," I said, "I noticed you put a For Sale sign in your window."

"Ah," she said. "Winds of change have come to Norse Falls. Remember the bamboo that bends is stronger than the oak that resists."

"Who are you going to sell it to?"

"Whoever makes the best offer," Hulda said, as if it were perfectly clear and as if she were always so plainspoken.

We walked out of the office, and as I walked down one of the cramped aisles, my finger trailed slowly across the bolts of beautiful fabric.

"You see something you like, you take it," Hulda said. "I'm donating the rest."

I inhaled sharply. "I do need something for the dance on Saturday."

"Any particular color?" Hulda said with a sparkle in her eye.

"Red."

"I have just the thing." Hulda directed me to a different aisle, one with velvets and satins. She pulled out a bolt of nubby raw silk. It was a beautiful Chinese red. She walked to another aisle not far away and returned with a sheer tulle overlay in the same color. "What do you think?"

"It's perfect."

"You know your *amma* — she had many red dresses. Red was her favorite color. And she and your *afi*, they liked to go dancing."

That I did not know.

"You have a peek in her old steamer trunk," Hulda said.

My dad had wandered to the front part of the store. "Kat, I'm taking off. Gonna make a few calls," he called back to me. "We'll talk later."

"I understand the school is putting on a performance of *The Snow Queen* this spring," Hulda said. "I'm going to donate materials to the costume department."

"That's a great idea. I'm in Ms. Bryant's design class. We're already working on a semester project of costume and set designs."

"Do you know this story of *The Snow Queen*?"

"A little, I guess."

"Did you know that Hans Christian Andersen based this on many of the sagas that came from the Nordic peoples?"

"No."

"Oh, yes. Story is of the evil sorceress who rules the Winter People. Her snow palace is a mysterious castle of ice. Legend has it that she seeks to recover her errant peoples."

"Uh, that's interesting."

"It's very curious," Hulda said, "the way so much that is held as myth or children's stories are common themes found throughout cultures of the world."

All of a sudden I felt as if I should have a pen, notebook, and possibly class syllabus.

"I just spoke of the Native Americans' tales."

"Right. About Sky Girl."

"Good. You are paying attention." Hulda walked along the back aisles of the store, as if looking for something. I followed. "This is very important, Katla. It is no coincidence that, throughout the world, ancient cultures share similar beliefs in realms separate to our earth. There is, of course, a common faith in a creator and a heaven to which the worthy will ascend. We know also of a netherworld to which doomed souls will be condemned."

Again with the damnation? As if recent events hadn't sufficiently rattled me.

"So much of this I learned at the knee of my own *amma*," Hulda said. "I know your grandmother was sad not to have the chance to entertain you with the stories passed from Stork to Stork."

"Stork to Stork?" I asked.

There was a funny glint in Hulda's eye. Did she just tell me my *amma* had been a Stork?

276

"Good," Hulda said. "You're listening again."

Busted. I felt like I'd been caught passing notes or sleeping in class.

"Our Stork legends tell of Niflheim, a land of ice—Vatnheim, a watery kingdom—and Asgard, a world of sky. And of course, Midgard, our earth, the one which man, in bodily form, inhabits. Once upon a time, a bridge between these worlds was accessible—on significant days and in special locations—to the extraordinary among us."

Even though Hulda was using words like *legends* and *tales,* her tone was pulpit-pounding.

"The passage was closed," Hulda continued, "when Ravens were found gaining entrance to Asgard, the airy home of Odin and Valhalla, his majestic hall of warriors, where empyreal powers are granted."

Did she just describe a world-of-sky, power-disbursing hall of warriors?

"Katla, these stories were not shared with you in your youth, but is not too late for you to learn the old legends. If you are interested, I will tell them to you."

"Uh. Sure. That'd be nice." Because it sounded more like required reading than elective.

"Good. The tales of Niflheim, the ice realm will be good for you to know. Especially if you're going to make good design for school project, you have to understand the nature of this coldhearted Snow Queen." Hulda ran her hand along a rack of satins, stopping at a blue so pale and crystalline it appeared to be made of glass. "This is good color for Snow Queen." She held it out to me.

"Thanks. I guess." Hulda seemed to be in a good mood. And I didn't get many opportunities to talk to her alone. "What else can you tell me about my *amma*?"

"Such a good person. Such a good friend. She suspected you were special, a herald of change, and foresaw great things for you. She entertained her sister Storks with tales of your childhood interest in birds. She even boasted of your claims to communicate with winged friends." Hulda winked. "We all had a good laugh over these stories."

It didn't sound so innocent to me anymore. It meant that my *amma* had unwittingly disclosed my Stork destiny and made some sort of prediction. And if there was already tension between my *amma* and Grim, then her resentment of me must have been cooking for years. Hulda was still smiling, so I figured I'd press for more info while I was at it. "Uh, Hulda, do you mind if I ask you something else?"

"Ask."

"What did my *amma* and Fru Grimilla fight about?"

"Ah. This again. They fought about the accusation that Fru Grimilla had been present at your accident."

"So my *amma* thought she could be a Raven?"

"Originally, yes. But I promise you this was resolved and your *amma* was eventually satisfied with Fru Grimilla's whereabouts that evening."

"How?"

"It's not for me to reveal."

"OK. One more question, Fru Hulda, if you don't mind? Who would have been named second chair if I hadn't shown up that night?"

Hulda exhaled. "I had not decided. I was waiting for a sign."

"Was Fru Grimilla being considered?"

"Yes. Why do you ask?"

"It's just . . . she always seems so mad at me, and if there had been bad blood between her and my *amma* . . . Plus, there have been some fairly strange things going on. Close calls. What if I upset the chain of command?"

"Do you trust me?" Hulda asked.

"Of course."

"Then I tell you I would place my own life in Grimilla's hands. I know her to be loyal and devoted to the Storks. As I know all of my sister Storks to be."

I felt only slightly better, but was glad I'd asked. *Sometimes a big black bird is just a big black bird* was the chorus to my new theme song. I filled my arms with the three bolts of fabric, some trim, and a pocketful of glittery buttons.

I waved good-bye to Hulda and was backing out her door, when a well-dressed, middle-aged man with a map approached me on the street.

"You wouldn't happen to know the best way to the Lodge at Cedar Pole, would you? Or at least get me to Highway 116?" he asked.

"Sorry," I said, juggling the slippery materials. "I'm the wrong person to ask." I motioned with my head back toward Hulda's door. "You should ask Hulda, the woman who owns this shop. She'd know."

The man thanked me, and I heard Hulda's door chimes jingle as he stepped into her store.

Afi was scratching his head in confusion when I got back.

"Holdout Hulda's really going to sell?"

"Looks that way," I said.

"Well, I'll be." His milky blue eyes were glazed. I could see that this had really startled him. "A day to go down in the record books." He looked at the stack of fabrics in my arms. "What's all that?"

"I'm going to the Homecoming dance Saturday night. With Jack Snjosson. I need a dress."

"Snjosson?"

"Yeah. We're kind of friends. Maybe even a little more than friends."

"Like I said. A day for the record books."

"I was wondering if there might be any old dresses of Amma's I could look at. Hulda said you guys used to go dancing."

"There's an old wardrobe full of her things up in my attic. You're welcome to whatever you find."

"Thanks." I kissed him on the cheek. "You're the best."

He blushed and rubbed his face.

* * *

of Grim's old dresses. Shame on me for pitying her this necessity. Once again, I'd underestimated my new friend's ingenuity. I held the dress against my front, looking in a full-length mirror propped up against the wall. With a fitted silk underlayer and full tulle skirt, it would be quite elegant, and simple. Simple for me, anyway. And the red was perfect. I remembered my *amma* wearing a lot of red. I wondered what bird she had represented at council. A red bird? A red finch? A scarlet macaw? A cardinal? Something about the last one felt right to me. There had always been an unusual number of cardinals at her bird feeder.

I checked my watch. Five o'clock. I had a lot of sewing ahead of me. I scooped the dress up and headed toward the steps when an old trunk caught my eye. Hadn't Hulda told me to look in Amma's old steamer trunk? I knelt down over the large flat-top case, running my hand along its faded dark leather. The brass latches and dime-size tacks were tarnished, but I could tell that this was once a beautiful piece of luggage. It looked exactly like the type of chest people used to take on long voyages. I fiddled with the catch and opened its creaky hinged lid. The first few layers I sorted through were linens, gloves, velvet jewelry boxes and pouches, a medium-size hat box: all the sorts of things I'd expected. Then, at the bottom of the trunk, I found a cloth-covered book tied with gros-grain ribbon. At first I thought it was a calendar or almanac, as it was divided into the twelve months of the year. The more I looked at it, though, the more I came to see it as a keeper of important dates—dates that repeated year after year. Each month began with an old-fashioned illustration of a girl in clothing suitable to that time of year and surrounded by the flora and fauna of the season. The pages following each month were numbered at the top and then lined below. Thirty-one pages for January, twenty-nine for February, thirty-one for March, and so on. On each page, and in varying colors of ink, notations had been made. People's birthdays, anniversaries, and holidays—including many I'd never heard of—were all recorded on their respective dates. My sister Storks were all there. And as much as I intended to surprise Hulda on February twentieth with some small token, and giggled to read that glum old Grim was a summer girl, their birthdays were only a small part of what was making me cluck with happiness. The fact that my *amma* used their bird names—the Owl in February and the Peacock in July—filled me with smug satisfaction.

I continued to thumb through the pages, a little creeped out to find that the dates of deaths were marked as well. Other notations were in such a cramped hand and so lengthy that I hardly knew what to make of them. Paging through the book, I thought I recognized a few mentions of signs of the zodiac, and planet names. Another thing stood out: the calendar dates corresponding with the solstices and equinoxes had far more entries than any other. I remembered the fuss Hulda had made over the autumnal equinox—just two days ago—and her small chant to Sifa, Protector of the Harvest. March twentieth and twenty-first, the two possible dates for the spring, or vernal, equinox, had references to Ostara's Dawning and what looked like a poem or song. June twentieth and twenty-first, the summer solstices, were also crammed with long passages, something about the Tropic of Cancer, and first covenants, and deaths — an unusual number of deaths. As I read through the list of names for that day, one jumped out at me: Hanna Ivarsson, Wade's little sister. The inclusion of her name in Amma's private book punched the wind from my lungs. I recalled the conversation with Jaelle about Dorit acting so odd on the first day of summer.

I descended the creaky attic stairs with Amma's book hidden in the folds of the red dress. I was a ball of nerves — curious and confused by the book and its mysterious entries — but also so thrilled by the revelation that my *amma* was a Stork that I chirped. I did. It felt surprisingly familiar.

CHAPTER THIRTY-ONE

The atmosphere at school on Friday was electric. Nobody could talk about anything but the big game that night and the dance the next. Even the teachers were wearing school colors: green and gold. Everyone was certain that this was our year to beat Pinewood. After a long meeting with Coach Carter, Principal Henrich, and Mr. and Mrs. Snjosson, Jack was allowed back into the lineup for Saturday's game, though, as a compromise, he was benched for the first half.

Jack and I were on our way to the cafeteria when we ran into Wade.

"Jack," Wade said, blocking our path, "we didn't get a chance to talk yesterday. Coach Carter had you tied up for most of practice."

"What do you want, Wade?" Jack asked.

"To make nice." Wade flashed us a smile. I really hated his smile. He showed teeth, but somehow the other components—twinkling eyes, soft facial lines, relaxed posture—were missing. "First, I'd like to apologize for my recent behavior. I've been a class-A jerk and almost lost Monique in the process. I don't deserve it, but she's forgiven me. Can you?" Wade held out his hand. "Will you shake and accept my apology?"

I could see the muscles in Jack's jaw and neck tighten, and for many moments he left Wade's outstretched arm just hanging there.

"I'm really trying here," Wade said, turning up his palm.

Finally, Jack exhaled and shook Wade's hand in one brief pump, though I noticed he didn't say *Apology accepted*.

"Good man," Wade said. "I also wanted to personally invite you both to an after-dance party at my family's barn. My parents are going all out, chicken and ribs."

We didn't even have a chance to respond before Wade jogged off, calling over his shoulder, "It's all settled then. See you guys later."

Jack and I exchanged looks. I interpreted his as a lingering mistrust of Wade. Mine was that, with an extra roll of the eyes conveying that "all out" was not chicken and ribs.

It was positively raucous in Mr. Parks's room during lunch. Happiest of all was Pedro. The pressure of an entire game as quarterback now lifted, he was a new man.

"Have you guys heard about Wade's party?" Pedro asked.

"We've heard. Is that where you guys are going?" I asked.

"It does sound like fun," Penny replied.

"Everyone's talking about it," Tina said.

"The whole night's gonna be a blast," Pedro said.

"Matthew's dad's lending him his car," Tina said. "We'll be traveling in style."

"I'll be looking sweet in my new threads," Pedro cut in.

Jack pulled me away from the group. "I won't be showing up in anything fancy. That truck is as good as it gets."

"It's fine. I don't care."

"I have a suit, but it's an old one of my dad's."

"They're just clothes." This out of the mouth of a girl whose tenth-grade yearbook quote was, "I accessorize, therefore I am."

"What would your friends in LA think?"

"What does it matter?" It didn't matter. Not one bit. I couldn't believe how distant malls and beaches seemed.

"You won't be embarrassed?"

"I won't if you won't." I motioned with my arms to an imaginary skirt. "Did you know vampire drool is an actual shade of red? And Fredrick's of Hollywood has a whole line of *Pretty Woman* formal wear?"

His eyes grew to the size of Frisbees. "Uh. I think my parents will want to see a picture of us."

"You are so gullible." I elbowed him in the ribs, hard. "Just don't wear flannel, and I'll do my best to keep it simple."

I thought about Wade's party as I walked to my next class. If money was an issue for Jack, this, in place of dinner at a restaurant, was at least free. And in a crowd of a couple hundred kids, Wade would be easy to avoid.

Fifth period was canceled for an outdoor pep rally. Jack and I walked toward the stadium together. He gave me a quick kiss on the cheek before veering toward the field to stand with the football team while I herded up the bleachers with the rest of the student body. The cheerleaders kicked things off with a pom-pom routine, then they held up a huge paper banner for the team to crash through. The principal spoke, as did Coach Carter. Pinewood was maligned in word and thought, and I wondered if they, too, were riling up an angry mob. Thank goodness the announcement of Homecoming King and Queen came next. I'd never been a big supporter of such popularity contests. They seemed to reward the most vapid of individuals. Five girls, Monique among them, were called forth as this year's court, as were five guys. I couldn't help feeling thrilled as Jack took his place as one of them. Maybe things were different here. Though barrel-chested Wade, grinning like a hyena, was a thorn. The king was announced first. Jack was clearly surprised and embarrassed. He looked up to me in the crowd as he received his scepter, raising it in something like a salute. I smiled and blushed and was flattered, mostly by the knowledge that his eyes had followed me to my seat. Wade, to my surprise, smiled, clapped Jack on the back, and was the first to shake his hand. Next the queen was announced. Monique cried like she'd just been crowned Miss America. A week ago I might have audibly scoffed. The new me, the forgiving me, applauded politely. I reminded myself that I wasn't the only one who had had a tough week — a pregnancy scare and a roller-coaster relationship would be tough on anyone.

After the assembly, Jack found me at my locker.

"Your Highness." I bowed.

"Don't." He rolled his eyes. "It's weird enough."

I flicked the brim of his cap. "Guess you'll be trading this in for a crown now."

"No, but I will be exercising my authority."

"How so?"

He pulled me into him. "I want you to stay close to me." It was an order, something I would normally defy on principle, though I somehow liked this one's nose-to-nose delivery. Had me at attention, anyway.

"Is that a command?"

"Yes."

"Impressive," I said. "On the job for less than an hour and already taking charge."

"My duty to serve and protect." His voice was a low growl in my ear.

"I'm kind of impressed with your subjects," I said,

pulling away and closing my locker with a loud bang. "I figured new-and-improved Wade or at least one of his henchmen would have been elected. It shows a certain amount of independent thinking on the part of Norse Falls."

He pulled my hand playfully. "What are you trying to say? That you're surprised a guy like me can win?"

"No." I laughed. "It's just that you don't necessarily align yourself with the in crowd."

He pulled me alongside his body, his hand sliding around my waist. "I align myself with you."

Which really only proved my point, but I decided not to argue. Instead I simply enjoyed the weight of his arm on my hip bone.

CHAPTER THIRTY-TWO

It was fun taking my dad to the football game. He refused to dress in school colors, but it didn't matter. I wore enough green and gold for the two of us. We sat with Penny and Tina. I could tell by the way they kept sneaking glances that they were a little in awe of him. He did that to people. Soon enough, though, he had them giggling and blushing. He did *that* to people, too—females, anyway.

Jack did his penance and sat out the first half. I could hear the tightness in the crowd's cheering and their collective gasps every time Pedro put up a pass. The first quarter was weak; even I let the occasional sigh of disappointment escape.

Early in the second quarter, Pedro handed off for a series of successful running plays that got us close enough for a field goal. The kick was good, and we were up three–zero. Our fans went crazy. I had to hand it to the Norse Falls Falcons. They had spirit to spare.

With a minute to go until half time, Pedro threw a pass to a receiver downfield. The throw seemed short and about to be intercepted. Just as the ball had wrung what it could out of its draft of air, a wind sworled down the field. The ball tipped off the fingers of the Pinewood player and into the hands of our receiver, who ran it in for a touchdown. The crowd went nuts.

Sitting on the bleachers, I discovered that I had a new skill. When Jack was present, I had the uncanny split-screen ability to watch both him and whatever it was I was supposed to be focusing on. Jack paced the sidelines the entire time Pedro was at the helm. When Pedro threw, Jack's arms went up. When Pedro got crunched, Jack's entire body balled into something small and hard. And on that last play, the one where the wind marched down the field, I noticed something odd. Whereas the entire stands seemed to hold their breath as it seemed a turnover was inevitable, Jack appeared to bellow something, though I couldn't hear what, given the distance separating us.

Special teams took the field, and I watched Jack chest-bump Pedro when he jogged to the bench. Our kick for the extra point was good, which put us up ten to nothing and sent the crowd into a frenzy. The team ran off the field for half time to a roar of approval from the entire home side of the bleachers.

My dad high-fived Penny, telling her, "That boy's got game." Penny puffed up with happiness.

The half-time show began. Matthew played trumpet for the marching band, and Tina told us how hard they'd worked on a new routine. I saw my dad snicker a little bit when one of the twirlers smacked a member of the horn section with her baton. Thank goodness for the rubber tips. She got some serious air speed on that projectile. My dad did manage to keep his amusement mostly to himself. I could tell, though, that it took some restraint. I liked the show. I liked how they kept it simple. Our marching band in California had gone to state finals three years in a row and was known for their theatrical productions complete with moving sets, costumed characters, and complicated themes. Maybe CliffsNotes or a doctorate on Wagner would have helped, but, personally, I never got it.

The Homecoming court was introduced, followed by the king and queen. Monique traversed the field on Jack's arm. I didn't like it. Nor did I like it when my dad said, "Now, there's a pretty girl." Though even I had to admit she looked very attractive with her curls bouncing under her crown as she glided over the grass, and her belted jacket accentuated her curves. I took comfort in the fact that Jack looked straight ahead and escorted her some-what robotlike to their spot in the semicircle. Though his stiffness could have been from the pads — he, as well as two of the four king's men, Wade the biggest hulk of them all, wore their football uniforms.

"So that's him?" My dad craned his neck for a view down to the field.

"Yep."

"I never did get to meet him, you know, five years ago. Not formally, anyway. Saw him in the hospital, but he was just a skinny kid, and looked half-dead at that."

I was surprised how much my dad's remark cut. To hear Jack described as "half-dead" sent a blast of cold mist down my spine. It did. Fog crept out from under my pant legs.

"You cold, hon?" my dad asked.

"A little."

He shook his head. "How're you ever going to make it through a winter here?"

I looked out to the field, where Jack was jogging off to rejoin his team. That's how.

The second half was scoreless. Jack did manage to pass for some decent yardage, but the team was stopped twice just shy of the five-yard line. I was a little let down. Maybe because I'd heard about Jack's golden arm. Maybe because I had some silly girlish notion of showing my dad my shiny new toy. Maybe because it just seemed like there had been a couple of missed opportunities. Twice it seemed Jack had his sights on an open wide receiver and had even stepped back for the pass, but then had changed his mind and ran it himself or passed to someone in the thick of things. He constantly had his eye on the scoreboard and seemed to be checking on our ten-point lead and the time left on the clock. And the defense, led by Wade, was on fire. Pinewood couldn't find a hole. We beat them ten to nothing. The moment that final second ticked down, Jack hoisted Pedro onto the team's shoulders.

After the game, Jack met up with my dad and me at the Kountry Kettle. The place was packed with people celebrating the big win. Jack slid into the booth next to me, his jeans sidling up along mine.

"Great game," my dad said.

"Thank you."

My dad held out his hand. "Greg Leblanc."

They shook. "Jack Snjosson."

I could tell my dad was impressed by Jack's handshake. My dad put a lot of stock in handshakes, as well as shoes. It was a good thing Jack's beat-up sneakers weren't visible under the tabletop.

"You boys sure can play both sides of that ball."

"My friend Pedro had a great first half. I knew he could do it."

I glanced over to where Pedro, Penny, Matthew, and Tina had a table at the back of the restaurant. Kids, and even adults, were stopping by to high-five or shake Pedro's hand.

Jaelle bustled over with two mugs in one hand and a coffee pot in the other. "Coffee, Ice?" she asked.

"Ice?" my dad asked.

"Her nickname," Jaelle said. "That hair is ice-white."

Jack lifted a strand of my hair that curled just under my chin. He rubbed it between his thumb and forefinger. "Ice. I like that."

A look of surprise batted my dad's lashes. He wasn't used to seeing me in this way.

"Yes. Coffee. Please. It was freezing in those bleachers," I said. Jack, with what seemed like pure instinct, dropped his arm over my shoulder and rubbed. Again, my dad looked uncomfortable. I didn't move away or shake Jack off. He was a part of my life in Norse Falls. My dad needed to know that.

"How about you, Greg? Coffee? It's a fresh pot." Thank God for Jaelle and her diverting could-sell-toothpaste smile.

A frown weighted the sides of his mouth. He was not a big fan of the Kountry Kettle's coffee. But then he returned Jaelle's winning grin. "Why not?"

Jaelle turned to Jack. "The usual?"

He looked a little flustered, but then he lifted his shoulders and said, "Sure."

"Crazy night," I said to Jaelle. "How're you doing?"

"Nothing I can't handle," she said with a swipe of her free hand.

My dad watched as she walked away. "There's something about that girl I like," he said.

My eyes widened. "Dad, she's married."

He shook his head at me. "Not like that. I saw the ring. Not to mention the age difference. But there's something very efficient yet personable about her."

Jaelle returned and set a very large glass of milk in front of Jack.

"That's your usual?" I asked.

He smiled sheepishly. "I don't do caffeine."

"Never?" My dad's tone was incredulous.

"Never," Jack replied.

"Not even Coke or Pepsi?"

"Nope." Jack drank half his milk in a single gulp.

My dad had an amused look on his face. I just hoped he continued to be kind. "So what's good here?" he asked. I recommended the potpie, Jack the meatloaf. We talked about the game again. Jack couldn't say enough about Pedro's contribution and how he finally conquered his nerves as backup quarterback.

"So if he's the backup, why didn't you start?" my dad asked.

"I was benched for missed practices."

I wanted to pipe in and elaborate, but how would that sound? Well, Dad, there's a little more to it than that. I was careless, put myself in a compromising position—and then lied about it, riling Jack up in the process. To complicate things further, Jack and I have been on some sort of destiny-ordained collision course. Things, bizarre things, happen when we're together. We're either each other's curse or lucky charm. He thought the former, so left to protect me. But don't worry, Dad; I'm pretty sure it's the latter. Though I'm still not too crazy about big black birds.

My dad let it drop, but I could tell he was disappointed. "And your family has a local farm?"

"Yes."

"That must be a lot of work."

"Harvest is always rough. Coordinating the extra hands and delivery schedules, but we're lucky to have a successful orchard. Some of the smaller farms in the state haven't made it."

My dad launched into a Darwinian theory of economic policy, an evolve-or-get-out-of-the-way view of things. I could hear myself—the way I'd probably sounded that night in Afi's store.

When Jaelle returned, my dad ordered a chef's salad, no ham, no egg, dressing on the side. He took a quick sip of his coffee and grimaced. "So, Jack, has Kat told you about my business plans?"

"A little. That's great news about the factory being leased." I had told Jack about the wind turbines earlier that day. He had been genuinely excited about the prospect of new families coming to town.

"Should liven things up a little around here," my dad said.

"The school district sure could use a boost in enrollment," Jack replied.

"I imagine some good-paying jobs wouldn't hurt, either," my dad said.

"Did somebody mention jobs?" Jaelle topped off my dad's cup.

"I haven't had a chance to tell you yet, Jaelle," I said. "My dad's going to refit Hulda's old factory to produce wind turbines."

"Are you hiring?" Jaelle asked.

"I will be in a few months." My dad looked appraisingly at Jaelle. "What kind of experience do you have?"

It took Jaelle about two minutes to get herself an interview as my dad's office manager. And another one minute to get Russ and a few of his crew interviews for the turbine assembly floor. Jaelle walked away with a very pronounced sashay.

"I knew there was something I liked about her," my dad said. I honestly didn't know if he was talking about her negotiation skills or the swing in her hips. Nor did I want to know.

"Here's a good-looking group." I looked up to find Wade standing over our table. "Great game, Jack." Wade held out his hand.

"Thanks. You, too." Jack shook, but his posture was rigid.

"Looking forward to seeing you two at my party tomorrow."

Jack and I exchanged looks. We had talked about it earlier. How would it look if we were the only ones not to go? Was this new-and-improved Wade to be trusted? After much debate—nothing had been settled.

"We'll be there," Jack said, his voice low and deep.

Matter settled.

I introduced Wade to my dad, who complimented the defense. Wade swelled like a balloon animal. "The only thing we let through was their white flag."

I watched Wade saunter off and join a large group of football players, cheerleaders, and other various members of the school royalty—Queen Monique included.

Jaelle delivered our meals, and Jack tucked into a big scoop of mashed potatoes.

My dad ladled dressing onto his salad. "So, Jack, you're a senior, right?"

Jack swallowed and wiped his mouth with his napkin. "Yes."

"Any plans after graduation?"

Even I hadn't asked Jack this. I knew my dad was curious about the guy and had my best interests in mind, but it felt like a challenge.

"College."

Gotta love a guy who boiled things down to a single word.

"Anywhere in particular?"

"University of Minnesota, possibly. Walden, probably."

"Walden," my dad said. "That's where Kat's mom teaches."

"I know," Jack said. "It's close enough that I could

commute. Save money. Maybe transfer to a bigger school junior year."

I felt funny finding this out via my dad. I wished he hadn't asked. I wished it had come up in a personal conversation between me and Jack. One where we shared our goals and dreams. And I also wished Jack hadn't mentioned money constraints, not because I judged. More because I saw my dad's eyebrows lift ever so slightly, because he judged. I was thankful that my dad hadn't pressed, wanting to know a prospective major, a five-year plan.

"Did Kat tell you about the Sorbonne?"

"The Sorbonne?" Jack asked.

"The famous university in Paris," my dad said. "It's where she wants to do college. Perfect her French, so she can get a top job in fashion."

Jack didn't know this. Not even my mom knew this. It was a little secret between me, my dad, and my grams, who was more than happy to bankroll my college experience if it took me to Paris, her hometown. It seemed like a don't-get-too-attached warning from my dad.

"Nothing's settled yet," I said quickly.

"Still. Sounds exciting," Jack said, but there was a dullness to his words that betrayed him.

My dad paid the bill. Jack offered to pay his share, but my dad waved him away dismissively. He would have done this anyway, but I could tell Jack didn't like being taken care of. Jack and I said good night in the presence of my dad. It was a little awkward. I wanted more than just a hand squeeze and a wave. So did he. I could tell.

It was a quiet car ride home. My dad was humming along to the oldies station. I was thinking about Jack. I both hated and loved the way he now preoccupied my every thought.

We pulled up in front of the house.

"Is that Stanley's car?" my dad asked.

"Yes."

"I won't come in, then."

My dad and Stanley had yet to meet. My mom didn't want it. Not yet, anyway. And seeing as my dad had a flight out tomorrow, it wasn't imminent. My mom did know about the lease on Hulda's factory. She'd been pretty surprised and not necessarily in a good way. I hadn't factored in her wish for a fresh start, away from my dad. She recovered quickly, though, for my sake. She'd seen how excited I was about having him around.

I gave my dad a big hug good-night. It was such a relief that he'd be back soon. A part of my day-to-day. I promised to call him on Sunday and let him know how the dance went. I wished he'd offered some small compliment of Jack. How he seemed like a hardworking kid, helping out his family. Someone who gave credit to others, like Pedro, and didn't crave the limelight. Someone who would get his degree, one way or another. Someone who drank milk, because he always drank milk, and didn't try to affect airs. I also wished he'd had more good things to say about Norse Falls in general. How he liked my new girlfriends, Penny and Tina. That it was nice of me to help Afi out. That it was a nice place, with nice people. I knew all this would come later, but still, I wished my dad had seen these things.

CHAPTER THIRTY-THREE

I had already waved my dad away from the curb and was just holding my key to the lock when Stanley came bustling out. He murmured a very terse greeting and made an all-business beeline to his car. I knew something was wrong. I walked through to the family room. My mom was on the couch with her head in her hands. I could tell she was crying.

"Is everything all right? What's up with Stanley? Did you guys fight or something?"

She looked at me quickly, wiping away tears. I thought for a moment I'd get the type of denial all parents give their kids in tough moments, the kind of denial I got when the marriage first started to crumble, but then something in my mom's eyes changed. "He's disappointed."

I dropped my things on the floor and sat down next to her. "Do you want to tell me?"

She took a big breath. "I suppose you'll find out soon enough." She looked away, obviously embarrassed. "I'm pregnant. Thirty-eight, divorced, and pregnant."

"Oh." I tried to act surprised. "How do you know?"

"I took one of those tests," she said. "Technically, three of them." She shook her head from side to side. "What you must think of me."

"It's OK, Mom. Why would I judge?"

Tears welled at the outside corners of her eyes. She let them roll down her cheek. "Because I made a big mistake. A very big mistake."

I scooted a little closer to her. "You and Stanley will work it out. He's probably a bit surprised. He just needs some time."

Big glugs of tears streamed down my mom's face. "Except I'm not completely sure it's Stanley's."

No need to feign surprise now. "What?"

"It's just your father and I . . . when I went to San Francisco to sign the papers . . ." She waved away some imaginary foe. "It's his fault. I should have just signed them and left. But he had champagne, and a really nice suite with a view, and one thing led to another."

"You and Dad?"

She dropped her head back into her hands. "It was so stupid. And I was already seeing Stanley, so really terrible of me."

"You and Dad?" I couldn't help myself. I was stuck on this point.

She straightened. Big black drips of mascara now stained her cheeks. "Please don't read too much into this. There is no 'me and Dad.'"

"But you just said . . ."

"That it was a big mistake."

"So is it Dad's?"

She bit her lip. "I don't know."

"It could be Stanley's?"

"Yes."

"Mom!" How many teenagers got to have this moment? A reverse *Juno*.

Her head sank farther. "It's terrible, I know."

"Did you tell Stanley?"

"Yes." The reply was muffled by her palms.

"All of it?"

"Yes."

"What did he say?"

"He was very quiet. And then he left."

I put my arm around my pregnant mother. "It's all right, Mom. I know it probably doesn't feel like it, but it will be OK. You'll make it OK. Because you're a great mother. And you always wanted another baby, right?"

"Not like this," she sobbed.

"Stanley will be back. He's that kind of guy. He'll be back. And then he'll be excited about the baby."

"What if it's not his?" She looked at me with fear in her eyes.

"It's his," I said.

"How could you possibly know that?"

There had been the briefest of moments when I'd been filled with the hope it was my dad's. My full sister. It had passed quickly. I knew too much about this baby: a nature lover, like Stanley, and destined to live in a cold climate. And that floral wreath of bright orange marigolds — Stanley was a redhead.

"Because you and Dad tried forever. It just wasn't in the cards for you two."

"I hope you're right. Your dad never wanted more kids. We tried, but he'd gone along unwillingly." She obviously saw the alarm in my face. "Not that he doesn't love you, doesn't love being your dad, but that's enough for him."

"Are you going to tell Dad?"

"I suppose I'll have to."

"Did Stanley say anything at all before he left?"

"That he needed to be alone."

"Do you love him?"

She picked at a bit of fluff on the arm of the couch. "I think so. We were getting there, anyway."

"You need to tell him that."

My mom squeezed my knee. "Look at you. When did you get so wise?"

"I guess a lot has happened to me lately."

"What have I done?" She shook her head. "First the divorce, then the move, plus the skating ordeal."

Heaping onto that Stork duties, the stupid night with Wade, my developing feelings for Jack, and my newest affliction — blackbirdophobia — I supposed it was the kind of load that'd either break you or make you. I looked down. I appeared to be in one piece. "I'm OK, Mom. Keeping busy. Adjusting to the new place, new kids." It was true. I was finally adjusting.

CHAPTER THIRTY-FOUR

Saturday morning, I tugged the last few stitches into the hem of my dress, tied it off, and trimmed the thread. After sailing it over the dress form next to my sewing machine, I stood back and watched the gathered tulle skirt float back into place. It was a great dress for dancing. It was a great dress *period.* I sat on the edge of my bed contemplating the way it differed from its backdrop: a huge bulletin board of elaborate sketches, magazine-clipped couture photos, and fabric swatches. Glancing up, I saw my mom leaning against the doorjamb.

"It's beautiful, honey," she said.

"Thanks."

"You know, I think I remember that dress of Amma's." She stepped into the room.

"You do?"

"She wore it to a New Year's party," she said, fingering its beaded bodice.

"She wore a lot of red, didn't she?"

"Sure," my mom said. "It was her favorite color."

"I think it's mine, too, now."

"You two always were a lot alike."

Birds of a feather, I said to myself.

"You did a great job on the dress," my mom said. "Amma would be very proud." She dropped her hand to her tummy. It seemed unintentional, but still, a kind of head count of everyone there — my mom, me, my sister, and even my *amma.*

It had been my idea to work at the store that day. I was too nervous and excited to sit around the house. Driving down Main, I noticed that downtown was hopping. I saw a couple of girls with updos coming out of the Mousse Head Salon, and Paulina, the owner of the used bookstore, waved to me as she rolled a cart of half-price books out to the sidewalk. Just as I was pulling into a parking spot in front of Afi's, some movement across the street caught my eye. Hulda was replacing the For Sale sign with a Sold sign. Huh? I bolted across the two lanes, not even looking for cars, and bustled into her store. She stood near the entry with her arms crossed and a sly look on her face.

"You sold the store?"

"Yes."

"To the developers? Afi didn't say anything."

"Not to the developers."

"What?"

"I got a very interesting offer. Something different. I think you'll be pleased."

"What? Why me?"

"Is sign of the mermaid. Just as you saw it."

"What mermaid?"

"Split tail. Bearing crown. Just as you saw her."

"Fru Hulda. You've lost me."

"The coffee place. The Starbucks."

"Starbucks bought your store?"

"Yes."

"How?"

"A man came in here lost. Was Thursday after meeting with you and your father."

"Oh, yeah. I saw him. He asked me for directions."

"He was needing to find some fancy lodge up north. His GPS not working. Anyway, he took a good look around this little town. It reminded him of northern Michigan, where he used to pass his summers as a boy."

"So who is he?"

"He's some big-shot with the coffee. Big enough to place a store."

"Just like that?"

"Oh, no. Took a few calls. Lawyers talking to lawyers. Another team coming next week. Hulda knows, though.

I make them very good offer. Tell them of new important business coming to Norse Falls, new jobs." She winked at me. "Hulda can be very persuasive."

"I can't believe it."

"Katla, you're the one who had the vision."

"Uh, right, but I didn't think it meant Starbucks." Technically I didn't think it meant anything, because I made it up. And then I wondered what Hulda meant by persuasive. Was the guy back home somewhere wondering what hit him? Having to explain his spontaneous and illogical decision to a boardroom full of angry executives? At this point, I put nothing past Hulda.

"Is good news, yes?"

And it was. Not only was my dad coming to town; so were nonfat caramel macchiatos. "Yeah. Great for me, but what about the rest of the stores?"

"This is good for everyone. New jobs. New prosperity. Some old stores stay. Some new come in. Is mixing of past and present. Compromise. Winds of change."

"Wait till I tell my dad." And Afi. And my mom. And Jack. Holy cow. What would he think?

Hulda continued to look at me with an odd expression. "So. Tonight is big dance."

"Yep."

"Red is a good color for you. Red is a warm color. Red is color of the heart. Red is the breast of the robin."

"The robin?" This sparked my interest.

"The harbinger of spring."

312

So I was the sign of change. How appropriate. And red was my *amma*'s color, and now my color, too. "The dress came out great. I love the color."

"Not just for special occasions. Red is color of the heart all the time."

Yeah. Sure. I filed that one away. Knowing Hulda, it'd come up somewhere, sometime.

CHAPTER THIRTY-FIVE

The last half hour before Jack arrived was straight-up torture. I was so nervous. And I felt I was forgetting something—like half my outfit. Dress, shawl, shoes, that was it. I hadn't realized how hard it would be for me to keep it simple. I looked in the mirror, turning one way and then another. What was missing? What could I add? A few bangles on my bare arms? A big cross or a couple strands of beads at my white throat? A silky tank under the sleeveless bodice? Ankle bracelet? Hair jewelry? Body glitter? I realized, with a start, that I normally presented quite the façade.

I heard the doorbell ring, and my confidence spilled to my toes with a splash. After a big calming gulp of air, I padded cautiously down the stairs. My mom and Jack were sitting in the living room, chatting calmly. It probably wasn't easy for her. She'd had a rough day. She'd phoned Stanley, but he hadn't called her back. Plus she wasn't feeling well. She was nauseous and tired. Still, she was the one who'd remembered to run out and get Jack a boutonniere. It was sitting on the kitchen table in a little plastic sleeve. And she was the one maintaining the conversation with Jack, who I could see, on closer inspection, was as keyed up as I was. His knee was jostling up and down in the leather club chair by the fireplace. He stood as soon as I came into view, and instantly all my nerves melted away. He looked so happy to see me.

"This is for you." He held out a red-rose wrist corsage.

"Thank you." My mom ran to get his boutonniere, giving us a moment to just kind of stand there and stare at each other with dopey looks on our faces.

"You look beautiful," he said.

"You look pretty fly yourself." The suit was old, and a little large for him in the waist and through the shoulders, but clearly of good quality and classic design. The starched white shirt and red tie were a nice contrast against the charcoal of the pants and jacket.

"Here it is." My mom handed me the lapel corsage, expecting me, I supposed, to pin him. His eyes grew wide as I approached with the spinal-tap-worthy needle. He dodged one way and then the other to ward off my advance, and deserved — if you asked me — the poke he ducked right into.

My mom snapped a few photos. She scribbled down his parents' e-mail address, promising to send them copies. She looked wistful as she watched us walk down the front steps and out to his truck. I knew it would be a hard night for her, one growing up, another growing in her tummy, and home alone.

"Have you heard about Hulda's store?" I asked after we'd been driving for a short time. He hadn't. And wasn't entirely thrilled with the prospect of Starbucks coming in. He reiterated all his old arguments: the loss of their small-town individuality, non-local products, and another piece of history lost forever. I didn't want to argue. Not that night, anyway. We pulled into the lot. He parked in his usual spot, cut the ignition, and then just sat there.

"Is something wrong?" I asked.

"Just the opposite."

"Shouldn't we go in? I mean, you are the king. I wouldn't want to keep your queen waiting."

He pulled me across the front seat, alongside him. "There's no queen on earth who could tempt me over you." His kiss had me numb and dizzy and seeing things — like the benefit to spending the evening in his truck. He stopped and held me at arm's length. "There's something I'm going to tell you tonight."

"What?" Though I had a suspicion it would be the I-love-you declaration. It seemed a little soon, but maybe not after everything we'd already been through. Besides, what else could there be?

"Later. I need to get my nerve up."

"Just tell me."

He shook his head. "No, because now I've got the added advantage of keeping you waiting." He opened his door. "Shall we?" He then helped me out his side, taking a good, long look at my outfit. "Simple and elegant," he said. "I knew it would suit you. And red. You look great in red."

Amazingly, we entered the gym through a giant whale's mouth. Once through, I stopped to take in the transformation of the space. The decorations committee had really ramped up the whole Enchantment Under the Sea theme. There were nets and seashells dangling above us. Huge hanging cutouts of fish swam along a track in the ceiling. Murals of sandcastles, and coral reefs, and spiny sea creatures covered the walls. It was impressive. There were obviously some talented artists around here.

Penny and Tina came running toward me, with Pedro and Matthew following behind. There were compliments offered all around. Penny looked stunning in Grim's vintage dress, and I wondered how on earth there could have ever been an occasion where Tall-and-Dour had worn seafoam-green chiffon. Tina confessed that her dusty-rose organza number had been the bridesmaid's dress at her cousin's wedding. It suited her. A muted pink was a good color against her auburn hair.

"So are we still on for Wade's party after the dance?" Penny asked.

"That's the plan," I replied.

"My *amma* asked me about a thousand times if you and Jack were coming with us out to the barn."

"Why? Because she didn't want us hanging out?"

"I don't know," Penny said. "It's like she needs me to map out every little detail of the evening. Especially if it involves you. It's like she's going crazy. It's a wonder she didn't want me to pre-schedule our trips to the bathroom."

I made a decision then and there not to drink too much punch that night. And not just because the long gown would be an awkward bundle to hike up and over a toilet bowl.

A lot of kids were already on the dance floor. It was a song by the Black Eyed Peas that rocked.

"So are we going to dance?" I asked the group.

Matthew took Tina by the hand and headed toward the throng. Penny and Pedro followed.

I looked at Jack. He just stood there.

"I don't fast dance," he said.

I put my hands on my hips. "You asked me to a dance and you don't dance?"

"I don't *fast* dance," he repeated as if it were clarification.

"Unbelievable." I may have tapped my toe impatiently. "No exceptions?"

He shook his head.

"What am I supposed to do?"

He gestured toward the floor. "You can still dance."

"Seriously?"

He shrugged.

I shook my head and turned to watch the dance floor. It was just too tempting. "I'll be back in a few," I called over my shoulder, dropping my shawl and clutch on a chair, and leaving Jack standing off to the side. The DJ played a series of fast songs. Pedro and Matthew hung with us for the first one, and then tagged off to join Jack. I kept an eye on him. It amused me. He stood with his hands in his pockets, watching me.

The next song was a rap number. Penny had some serious booty action, and I folded over with laughter. When I stood back up, Wade had joined our group. It made me uncomfortable, and I looked around for Monique, who I expected to be at his side any moment. At first he sort of danced with all three of us, but then made it pretty clear that I was the object of his attentions. I felt awkward, particularly with Jack watching, but I figured it was just a fast dance. At one point in the song he put his arms on my waist and kind of shimmied behind me. It didn't seem like a big deal. Everyone was whoopin' it up. I know I'd danced with guy friends like that back in LA. Next thing I knew, Jack took me by the hand and was leading me off the dance floor at a very, very brisk pace. We walked straight out one of the gym doors and into the evening air. Unbelievable. A cold front had picked up in the short time we'd been indoors. How could it change so suddenly? Winds swirled around us, lifting my hair and the gauzy overlay of my skirt. I shivered without my shawl.

"What's wrong?" I asked.

"Wade," Jack said. "That's what's wrong. I didn't like the way he was looking at you. And then when he grabbed you from behind . . ." Jack stood with his arms crossed, obviously trying to keep a lid on something. "I couldn't take it."

"Jack."

He shook me off. "I know. I overreacted. I'm sorry."

"You know I don't like Wade."

"I know that." He seemed to be calming down.

I snuggled into him. "Let's get something straight. I'm with you. Period. Everyone else is just wallpaper."

He relaxed and put his arms around me. "You still don't know."

"Know what?"

"How vulnerable you make me."

"Vulnerable?"

He took a deep breath, lowered his head, and spoke softly into my ear. "It killed me; your first day at Norse Falls almost killed me. I thought for sure you'd take one look at me and know me."

"But you know why now. I didn't remember anything."

320

He pulled me into the contours of his body. "I begged my dad to let me deliver the apples that night. He didn't want me to. Said it'd be best to let sleeping dogs lie." Jack shuddered. "But I couldn't do it. I couldn't stay away."

"I'm glad you didn't."

"I couldn't believe my bad luck when that piece-of-junk truck broke down. I just kept thinking: What if I missed you? What if you'd closed up?"

"I hadn't. Plus, we'd have come together somehow, right?"

"I don't have to tell you how shattered I was when you still didn't know me."

I groaned. "I can't believe I picked a fight with you that night."

"It didn't matter. It was contact. Better than nothing."

"Are you calming down now?" I asked.

"Yes. But now you know."

"Know what?"

"How defenseless I am."

"I bet Wade doesn't think you're defenseless."

"Good."

"So is this what you wanted to tell me?"

"Not even."

"So?"

"Soon. I think I've got some kingly duties to attend to first."

When we got back into the gym, Penny came running toward us. "Where have you guys been? They've been paging Jack on the microphone for like five minutes."

Once Jack was accounted for, the entire Homecoming court was assembled onstage. All ten of the senior royalty were introduced, but only Jack and Monique were seated on thrones. The DJ went into a slow dance and it was announced that the Homecoming court would have the first dance. I had to stand there and watch Jack dance with Monique, a slow dance, their crowns tilted together, his right hand at her waist, his left encircling her hand. I was beginning to understand just what had bothered him about Wade singling me out. He looked up at me a few times, feigning a pained expression. On his third glance my way, I tapped an imaginary watch. I could see his body shake with laughter. It helped to ease the tension, but still I was impatient. Finally, the song came to an end. Jack pulled away from Monique and walked over to the DJ, engaging him in a brief conversation. Then the DJ announced that the next song, another slow one, was "king's request." Jack walked over to me and pulled me onto the dance floor without a word. "Helpless" by Neil Young wailed from the speakers. I imagined there were kids who had never heard the song before. I only had because my mom was a big fan.

"This was your request?" I asked.

"Yes." He pulled me into him, already closer than he'd held Monique.

"It's old," I said. "Old-Testament old."

"I like it." He pulled me closer still. "Plus, it's fitting."

"Helpless?"

"It's what I am with you." His breath tickled my ear.

"You are not helpless."

"Yes. I am. And it's not just a feeling. It's a state of being."

"Jack, you're anything but helpless."

He pulled me away a little, holding me by the shoulders. "I'm not lying to you. I'm incapable of lying to you. If I lost you again, it would . . ." He looked away. "I couldn't . . ." He pulled me back into him and sang along with Neil. "Helpless." He wasn't much of a singer, but the whole baring-of-his-soul thing he had down to a science.

"You could have at least gone for the k.d. lang version," I said. "A little hipper. A little more orchestra, less harmonica."

"I'm impressed. You know the song." He looked me in the eye. "But by now you should also know I'm loyal. A traditionalist."

"I wouldn't want it any other way."

The next song was another slow one. I was on to him the moment he twirled me, quite effortlessly. Doesn't fast dance, yeah, right. "If you can dance like this, you can dance to anything."

"I said I *don't* fast dance, not that I couldn't."

"I should have guessed. I should have known by what Penny said."

"What did she say?"

"She said you were good at everything."

He laughed, a big throaty *haw-haw*. "Did she?"

"Did you know she had a crush on you?"

"Yes."

"And did you know that a lot of girls had crushes on you?"

He exhaled impatiently. "Yes."

"And Monique last year?"

"Hard not to notice that one."

"Penny thought you were oblivious, or above it all."

He pulled me closer. "I am definitely not oblivious. Nor above anything or anyone."

"What then?"

"Nobody got hurt," he said. "While I was waiting for you."

"How could you know I'd come back? I didn't know I'd come back."

"I just believed. And held on to that for as long as I could." The way he was holding me, both his arms now low and around my waist, I knew he was the kind of guy who could, and would, hold on for a long time, a very long time.

We danced one more slow number. With every step, the room spun off and the world fell away until we were entirely alone. The spell was broken when Wade and Monique danced into our view. I might not have noticed had Jack's grip not suddenly become viselike. I tugged his ear with my left hand and nestled into the cleft under his chin in response. He relaxed, but still kept me close. It was a night I didn't want to end. *Magic* was a term I had never used lightly. To say an evening was magic sounded corny, but it was. Anyway, I figured by now I, human Stork, had a little authority in that department.

When the entire dance floor broke into the "Cha-Cha Slide" and then a couple of ditties circa *Hee Haw,* Jack and I watched. I can dance to rap, rock, disco, and even show tunes, but I draw the line at country. The rest of the evening flew by quickly. Everyone was getting ready to take off for the party. We told the gang we'd see them there and headed to the parking lot. Just as Jack was backing up, Wade appeared at his window.

"Good thing I caught you," Wade said. "Not sure if you got the directions around the detour." He handed Jack a flyer. "There's some construction out on the county road, so it will be faster to come in the west side of the property." He leaned casually against the driver's side of the truck. "You know how these large properties are. Access trails from every point of the compass."

I didn't know anything about the properties around here. My family's lot in LA had been forty by one hundred — feet, not acres.

Jack took the paper, looked it over, and said, "See you out there."

CHAPTER THIRTY-SIX

Jack pulled his truck onto the main highway north. After about a half hour, he pulled onto a smaller two-lane county road, which quickly became a gravel road, off of which we turned onto a private drive, and then were essentially four-wheeling down a one-lane trail with dense firs and pines slapping the truck from both sides. I hadn't expected such a remote location for the party, and although I understood we were coming in on an alternate route, something didn't feel right.

Soon, however, there were lanterns lighting the path, and then we saw Wade's car and Wade himself off to the side of the lane. I still couldn't shake the foreboding feeling. Had I been asked to describe it, I'd have said we were being watched or followed, but that was unlikely at this point. NORAD probably couldn't have tracked us up here.

Jack pulled to a stop, cut the engine, and we got out of the car.

Wade walked over to us with a big smile on his face. "You guys are the first to arrive."

That seemed unlikely. We weren't the first out of the parking lot.

"Not everybody got the news about the detour," Wade said. "It'll take those cars a little longer."

"Where's Monique?" I asked.

Wade pointed to a spot in the distance lined with glowing lanterns. "She's helping set up. We had to go to a plan B on location. My parents were worried the old barn couldn't handle the crowd. We've relocated the party to a nearby field."

Something about an evening of detours and plan Bs didn't settle well with my tummy, but as I hadn't eaten since lunch, I attributed it to nutrient deficiency. And chicken and ribs sounded pretty good right about then.

We followed Wade along the lighted path. The night air crackled with life: rustling trees, the hum of insects, the smell of moss and wet leaves, and shadows of trees pressing in around us. The city girl in me was way out of her element, not to mention that I was wearing a floor-length dress and strappy high-heeled sandals and had nothing more than a shimmery shawl for warmth. I sorely missed my Nike sweatpants, Columbia fleece, and redesigned-by-Jack Timberlands.

The remote location and absence of others started to worry me, but the music I heard carried over the night air was reassurance of a gathering ahead. We finally came to a stand of tall spruce trees. Most grew tightly together, but there was an opening between two central trees over which grew an arch of twisted vines.

"Follow me." Wade beckoned with a wave of his hand.

Though I took no more than three steps, my heel negotiating nothing more than a two-inch differential, my stomach plunged as if I'd been dropped from the top of the Empire State Building. Cold air rushed past my ears, my eyes watered, and I felt dizzy and nauseous. I tumbled to the hard-packed ground, my hands splayed in front of me. The next thing I knew, Wade was standing over me, tying thick ropes around my legs to match the ones already pinning my arms to my sides. Even though I kicked with every sinew of muscle in my calves and thighs, it took him but a few moments to hobble me.

"Stop it!" I screamed.

Wade laughed, an evil and menacing sound, but he didn't speak as he cinched a final knot around my legs, bunching my ridiculous tulle skirt and ensnaring me like a fish in a net.

I looked around frantically. We were in a clearing where a ring of four trees had been cut down to form a small, intimate circle of chairs. I gasped. It was so eerily like the scene from my dreams that I could feel my heart rattling within my rib cage. Huge lanterns lit the perimeter and country music filled the air, but this was no party, nothing public, anyway.

I heard a groan from the center of the grassy area. I turned my head to see Jack, also tied with thick ropes, struggling to stand. Wade picked a rock up off the ground and strode over to him. I watched, in horror, as Wade slammed it over Jack's head. He crumpled to the ground. It took me several seconds to realize that the anguished sound buckling the air around me was my own scream.

In another moment, Wade was standing over me again. He grabbed my legs and dragged me farther into the clearing.

"What are you doing?" I yelled. "Are you crazy? Let go of me!"

Wade dropped my legs roughly to the ground. "I suppose a few explanations are in order." He stopped, looked to where Jack lay unconscious, and slapped his palms together in a gesture of satisfaction. "You two were such easy marks, but I suppose that's the nice thing about the truly good; they're so trusting. No need, even, to use my persuasive powers."

A part of me knew I needed to calm down, take a moment to figure things out, buy myself—and Jack—some time. Another part, the majority share, was in a full-throttle frenzy and wanted to exercise one of the few things I still had use of—my voice. "What the hell do you want?" I yelled, trying to push to a sitting position, not an easy task without the use of my arms.

Wade strode over to me and kicked me back down to the ground. "Be good," he said, "and I'll explain. Be bad, and you'll both pay." He took a seat on one of the stumps, as if he had all the time in the world. "Where to even begin?" he said casually. "I suppose the basics—who, what, when, where, and why—are in order. Let's start with *where*. Do you like the location? We're not technically on my family's property anymore, but you two didn't know any better. It was once a place sacred to the Chippewa. It's in private hands now, a hunting property; the owners have no idea what they've got."

He leaned back and crossed his legs. "And how was your trip through? I only ask because the first time I stumbled onto this place I ended up flat on my face. You should have seen the two of you." He tried to keep his tone light, but I could see the tension twisting through his neck and throat. "You're at a portal. Not accessible to just anyone. Had I tried to take any other two lumps from the dance, they'd have found nothing but more trail and trees on the other side."

A panic began at the base of my skull, soaking steadily down through my shoulders and along my spine. I stretched to look at Jack. He still wasn't moving.

"How about *who* next? You know I've heard about you Storks for years."

Oh, my God. How much did he know?

"My bird-brained grandmother thought she was preparing my sister for her destiny, so she told us all about the legends, the realms — all of it. And about the good forces as well as the evil."

With the mention of evil, a shiver racked me.

"And lately," Wade went on, "it's just gotten worse. She's obsessed with the Storks, you in particular. Stupid woman led me straight to one whose death would complete the third and final covenant — the only one Hanna's death didn't fulfill."

I fought for breath. I couldn't help it. Did Wade just say he killed his sister? And that he sought to fulfill initiation covenants? Where had I heard that before? From Hulda. Realization dawned on me. "You're a Raven?" I gasped.

"How easily shocked you are. As startled as those old birds were. They questioned me about Hanna's death, under the guise of pity or concern — for me, of all things. To have witnessed such a horrible thing at such a tender age. In the end they were convinced I knew nothing more of the significance of the summer solstice than I knew of the geological classification of the rock face I pushed Hanna over. Little did they suspect I'd attempted all three covenants at once: starting with first kill on the solstice; next, murder of one related by blood; and third the removal of one born to greatness. My delusional grandmother had been convinced her Hanna was exceptional. She wasn't — but you are. Aren't you?"

I was paralyzed with fear.

Wade wagged his finger at me. "Killing you has

proved difficult. Why did that bear charge in the wrong direction? Beasts are normally simple to manipulate. And how did you escape that truck when I had the driver so completely under my control? Maybe I've become somewhat lazy, wasting my skills to keep Monique under my thumb. Or is it that I've encountered an able opponent in you?"

So, Wade had some kind of power. An ability to persuade would explain how he'd managed to kill his sister and get off scot-free. And me, too, nearly. He was likely to finish the job here, especially as he saw me as an "opponent." It wasn't easy, but I remained still and let him do the talking. All the while, I kept looking over to where Jack lay unconscious. I was choking with fear for his life as much as my own. How hard had Wade hit him? With the distance separating us, I couldn't even tell if he was breathing.

Wade then stood and walked to the perimeter of the clearing where hay bales were stacked neatly. He picked one up and carried it back to the center, talking as he went: "My grandmother, the family tyrant, was so eager to prepare Hanna for her destiny, she both neglected and underestimated me. From her, I learned of the Ravens and their gift of immortality."

My peripheral vision became a kaleidoscope of raging fears. A minute ago I thought I'd been dealing with the school jerk and bully. I now realized I was up against something bigger.

"What do you want?" I asked, my voice hoarse with terror.

"At first, I was thrilled to think the elusive third covenant was within my reach. To my absolute delight, however, I realized you two offer even more."

"What are you talking about?" The rope was too tight. My fingers were going numb. I squirmed to readjust by even the smallest of margins.

"Which brings us, quite nicely, to the *why* — you two offer passage to the other realms. Legend has it that in Asgard, at Valhalla — home of the great Odin — warriors are rewarded with great powers."

"Wade, seriously, untie me so we can talk." I wrestled again with the ropes. They didn't budge. "You're not making any sense. I can't offer you passage to anywhere."

"You can't alone, but the two of you together, now that's a different story." Wade continued to gather bales and bring them to the clearing. It seemed he was shaping some sort of ring out of them, with Jack at its center.

I looked again at Jack; he still wasn't moving. "Why do you need us?"

He stopped, balancing an armful of hay. "The mysterious Vernal Incantation. My silly grandmother telling me how, for hundreds — if not thousands — of years, magical creatures gathered at portals throughout the world on the day of the spring equinox. The only day each year when the bridge can be lowered."

"Today's not the spring equinox. It's not even the fall equinox."

Wade dragged another bale into the clearing. He had completed a tight circle around Jack. He then pulled a metal canister of something from his pocket. It was lighter fluid. My hopes plunged.

"No, it's not, which is why we can skip the *when*. All those idiots, for all that time, were looking for a convergence of time—not of people." Wade walked in a loop, dousing the hay. "And you are more than a Stork, aren't you? You are the Robin, the sign of spring."

I inhaled quickly, audibly. Could Dorit really be so careless with her tongue?

"And Jack, rumor has it, is one of the Winter People." Wade set the canister on the ground, walked to the edge of the clearing, and returned with a flaming torch. "It's really quite simple once you contemplate the Vernal Incantation as referring to beings, not dates. I had to congratulate myself on that one: pegging you two as the personifications of spring and winter. So instead of a calendar date, you two conveniently made a Homecoming date. And it's all foretold in a funny little poem." Wade held the torch to the side of his face, creating an eerie hollow of incandescence. He spoke in a rhythmic chant:

"Heimdall, keeper of the Bifrost Bridge,
We call you lo this keening.

Sound Gjallar, your trusted horn,
While Spring from Winter is weaning.

A key we offer you, Brave Heimdall,
Ostara's Dawning, it's ken by.
To Water, to Ice, or to Asgard's Sky,
Open passage 'fore the Frost doth die."

I knew where Wade had perfected the poet's cadence he'd skillfully affected at the Asking Fire: at Dorit's knee, learning the Vernal Incantation.

Wade then touched the torch to one of the hay bales. It caught instantly with a whoosh and crackle, and quickly ignited the entire wheel of straw. "If the *what* isn't clear to you yet," he said, his eyes sparking like the flames below him, "your presence at Jack's death will open the legendary portal—the Bifrost Bridge."

The fire encircling Jack was growing. Flames, ferried by the night winds, licked high into the air. The heat had to be tangible.

The smoke burned my throat and stung my eyes. The smell made me sick to my stomach. I watched, in both relief and dismay, as Jack stirred, moaning and pulling at his constraints. "Stop it!" I yelled to Wade. "He'll burn."

Wade's nasty laugh again permeated the clearing. "What better way to kill winter than with fire and heat?"

Once more, Jack moved and groaned.

"Jack!" I yelled, though my voice was now choked with tears. "Wake up! Can you hear me?"

Wade approached the growing fire, now dangerously closing in on Jack. With a flick of his wrist, he sprayed more lighter fluid over the blaze. The flames kicked high into the air.

"Getting closer," Wade said. "As one of the Winter clan, his tolerance of heat is much lower than yours or mine. A degree or two increase in body temperature, while an annoyance to most, is fatal to poor Jack here. The heat from this fire is cooking him alive. Another wonderful tidbit my grandmother shared with me." Wade paced, watching and rubbing his palms together. "Roasting nicely."

As if he heard, Jack howled in response.

I momentarily rejoiced that he was coming to, though everything seemed to be building much too quickly to some sort of finale. I had to think fast. What good was soul delivery in a situation like this? *Not much,* I thought with a spill of panic. And birds? Where was my guardian eagle now? I closed my eyes to the immediacy of the situation, not easy with Jack moaning in pain. I suddenly found myself in the clearing of my dreams, the place where my newly discovered gift had felt its most powerful, its most magical. A light breeze lifted tendrils of my hair; sunlight warmed my cheeks. As I gazed in wonder at my mystical woodland clearing, I sensed that I was at the origin of my magic. Two steps took me to one of the stump-carved chairs; I ran my hand over its nubby bark. I approached the earthen bed where the baby had lain. Kneeling to gather a fistful of leaves and soft petals, I was overcome with an extraordinary sense of determination and resolve. I felt my instincts rising and with them the memory of an ancient voice. I opened my mouth, and I cawed. I called to the eagle, the owl, the gull, and even the arrogant peacock. I had no idea what emanated from me, whether the cries, screeches, and squawks were audible in the real world or just my dream one. I feared I was wasting precious time, but I couldn't stop. What I experienced was visceral and primitive, a distress call predating language itself.

When I opened my eyes, I could barely see Jack for shooting flames, but I could still hear him. He was in agony, but at least alive.

And then Wade loomed over me. He sneered and heaved me over his shoulder like a duffel bag. I continued to fight, squirming and twisting, but it was useless with the thick ropes binding me. From this elevated position, I got a look at Jack, whose entire body was convulsing in pain. I noticed blisters on his face and arms.

"You'll need to come with me," Wade said. "You are, after all, Ostara's Dawning—the key. All we need now is for his last few gasps of life. He really can't take the heat."

I screamed. It was loud and shrill. I felt my throat strip with ribbons of pain, but I continued screaming. I heard a thunderous sound—and then birds rushed in from every direction. They dove at the fire, hundreds of them, the weight of their bodies suffocating the flames, extinguishing the light. Their wings flapped in angry snaps and they gouged at Wade with diving beaks and sharp talons. Wade continued to carry me like a sack, using my body as a shield against the attacking birds. They buffeted and bumped me, but spared me their beaks and claws.

A river of air, loud and angry, roared down on us, and I watched in wonder as a milky substance materialized in the sky, lowering and descending in a cloudlike swell. A bridge appeared through the mist. Wade tightened his hold on me with one arm, while pawing at the air with his other, as if he could quicken the descent of the billowy span. It soon lowered to the ground, and although birds dove at us from every angle, Wade stepped onto the bridge. There was a flash of light, then a cracking sound boomed from above, and I felt a jolt that knocked me out of Wade's arms and onto the cold, hard ground. I looked up to see Wade crumble to the ground, clutching his chest in shock and agony.

Confusion gripped me as the birds descended, pecking and nibbling at me. It took several moments before I realized I was unharmed and free of the ropes. I looked around. Feathers and birds choked the air and blanketed Jack's body. Hundreds more lay dead in the smoldering ashes. I stumbled to him, stepping over carcasses large and small, and through burning embers. Though the birds had picked him free of his bindings, Jack wasn't moving, wasn't breathing, and the skin on his face and arms was bright red and shiny. I fell to my knees, choking with emotion and afraid to touch him. I assumed the worst. Tears ran down my face.

"A catastrophe! I tell you, Fru Hulda, a catastrophe!" The harsh voice of Grim filled the air. "How long was the portal open? What has been wrought this horrible night?" That acidic tone was pure joy to me. I lifted my head and saw her and Hulda step into the clearing.

Hulda rushed over to Jack. "Quick," she commanded. "The white clay, the *aurr,* from the base of the ash. And the herbs. Did you bring them?"

Hulda sifted through a leather bag stuffed with leaves, berries, barks, and small medicine bottles. She extracted a mortar and began adding ingredients, crushing some with a pestle, and crumbling others with her fingers. Grim rushed to a nearby tree and began pawing at the ground, filling her apron with clumps of mud. She firmly pushed me aside and began pressing the white paste onto Jack's burns, with long, quick strokes covering his arms and face. Hulda continued with her potions, adding a single drop from a bottle of inky black liquid, and a healthy glug from another containing something yellow and foamy. A sharp scent filled my nostrils. Hulda held the concoction under Jack's nose. I sat back on my heels, watching and feeling useless as the two women tended to Jack, who didn't seem to have the slightest flutter of life in him.

"I fear we're too late," Grim said in a sad voice.

"He used his last spit of life saving our Katla," Hulda said. She caressed the white mud over his face in tender strokes.

"No!" I yelled, throwing myself on Jack's chest. "He's not dead. Jack, you're not dead. We survive. Remember? We find a way to survive."

My grief-stricken body was so racked with emotion that I didn't notice the rise and fall of his chest. But then Jack coughed and moaned in pure anguish. Never had the sound of misery and suffering been so welcome.

"Praise be," Hulda said.

I was crying too hard to form coherent thoughts, never mind words or sentences.

"Let us do our work now, Katla," Hulda said.

I scooted back again.

Hulda continued to hold the mysterious rub under his nose, while Grim pressed the salve into his burns. Jack was soon covered in a ghastly white plaster; his breath was ragged, and he rocked in spasms of pain. The two of them muttered softly to each other. Grim moved back and forth collecting armfuls of leaves. Soon, over the layer of white clay, there was a blanket of foliage covering him. And then they chanted something in Icelandic over and over, their voices plaintive and solemn. For a long, long time I didn't dare interrupt them, or ask questions, or get in the way. I was vaguely aware of other movement in the strange clearing. I thought I recognized Fru

Birta—in a long, white hooded coat, and others similarly clad—dragging and lifting and clearing things from the scene, one of which I realized was Wade's heavy body.

Finally Grim began to brush the leaves from Jack. Hulda, using the tails of her apron, wiped the thick clay from his arms.

He stirred and slowly opened his eyes. "What happened?" he asked, his voice parched.

"A terrible thing," Hulda said. "A breach of many years' peace." Hulda waved at the air in front of her. "We don't talk of such things now. Now we focus on healing." Hulda continued to wipe the clay from him.

I gasped as I realized he was unscathed: no char, no blisters, no twisted skin.

Jack struggled to a sitting position. Color returned to the bits of him visible through the splotchy dried mud. "What about Wade?"

"Dead," Hulda said.

Jack clutched his knees to his chest. "That was intense," he said, looking up to where I stood.

I hurried over, crouched next to him on the ground, and threw my arms around him. I started to cry again. He rubbed my arm up and down in response.

"Fru Hulda, Fru Grimilla," I said, wiping my eyes and struggling to control the shake in my voice. "I can't thank you enough. How did you do it? How did you heal him so fast?"

"Ah," Hulda said. "We are in a place of great power

here. Magical forces swirling over special beings have strong healing powers."

"And how did you know to come?" I asked.

"Your call of distress, of course," Hulda said.

Jack reached out and pulled my hand into his. It was warm and strong.

Hulda straightened her skirt. "Come, Fru Grimilla. Our work is finished."

They walked to the edge of the clearing, Grim's hawkish voice drifting back. "I wait all night at my post in the cold barn, and then this sudden change in plans. I'm telling you, Katla is not an easy charge to protect. No patience. No protocol."

It was kind of nice to know that despite everything I'd just put her through—acts of heroism and magical healing—old Grim wouldn't let it change our relationship.

CHAPTER THIRTY-SEVEN

Jack pushed himself up. I rose to my feet. We collapsed into a bone-melting embrace.

"I've never been so frightened," I said.

"He almost took you with him."

"I thought you were dead."

"Wade had to be stopped," Jack said.

"He was evil. Something called a Raven."

"You're a Stork."

I gasped. I didn't know how much he'd overheard or been conscious of. Enough, obviously.

"I knew before tonight," he said.

"How?"

He took a big breath of air and held me at arm's length. "Maybe we should start with that thing I wanted to tell you."

"It's about time."

"Sit down," he said, gesturing to one of the stumps.

I sat, which was just as well. I really felt quite weak.

"Have you heard of the Veturfolk, the Winter People?"

"Hulda mentioned them to me."

"Do you know I'm one of them?"

"Yes."

"Technically, I'm more than just one of the Veturfolk."

"What does that mean?"

He stood in front of me and gestured to himself with a small pull of his arms. "Make me mad."

"What?"

"Make me mad."

"What? That's silly. After all we've been through."

"Just play along. Tell me something that will make me angry," he said. "Better still, tell me something that will make me jealous."

"You're talking crazy."

"Just do it. Tell me about some guy in California."

"OK. There was a guy named Ethan. We went out for six months."

Winds began to rustle through the trees. A blast of arctic air lifted the tails of my shawl.

"Wow," I said. "That came out of nowhere."

"Finish your story."

He was starting to scare me a little. Why would he want to hear about another guy? Nonetheless, it seemed important to him. "He had long hair. I like long hair on guys."

The air temperature dropped precipitously. The wind continued in intensity, but was much colder. Something fluffy and white danced at the corners of my eyes.

"Is it snowing?" I hugged my arms in tight.

"Kat, I'm trying to tell you something."

I was entranced by the flakes falling around me. "It's snowing in September!"

He took me by the shoulders. "Focus, bird girl."

That snapped me out of my winter wonderland.

"Now tell me something you like about me," he said.

"What?"

"Just do it." He touched my mouth lightly.

"I like everything about you."

He smiled and slowly traced my lips. "Go on."

"You're in my head. Every minute of every day ever since you walked into Afi's store. But almost unbearably since the Asking Fire. And what I know now about the lake. And knowing the way you protect everything that's dear to you—your town, your school, and me—I can't imagine my life without you."

Suddenly, it was warmer. A light breeze tickled my cheeks. And it hit me like a Louisville Slugger.

"Are you doing this?" I held my arms up.

"Yes."

"You're changing the weather?"

"Yes."

"How?"

"Well, it's not something I have much control over, but it's what I've been trying to tell you. I'm more than just one of the Veturfolk. When we didn't die in the lake, my grandmother was the first to suspect. Even as one of the Winter People, the cold should have killed me—us."

"What saved us?"

"My special immunity to the cold was part of it. But as my grandmother explained it to me, there was a combining of forces. Yours and mine."

"Oh."

"Kat, I felt wings under the water that day of the skating accident. I know it sounds crazy, but I did. Besides you, my grandmother is the only one I've ever told."

"What did she tell you?"

"She told me all about the Storks. She thought there could be no other explanation to what I described. That you had to be one of them."

"You knew?"

"I knew. And this is how I've known that our destinies are entwined. We both have abilities, special abilities. And I'm convinced now when combined, some sort of immunity. Do you get it, Kat? We're stronger together."

Got it. Loud and clear. As if tonight hadn't been

evidence enough, I thought about the incident at the lake, the bear encounter, and the way Jack's cap pulled me from harm's way. As I momentarily basked in that knowledge, questions pecked at me.

"But if an ordinary ancestor of the Winter People would have died in the lake, what are you? *Who* are you?"

"I'll give you a hint. My last name, Snjosson, means *Son of Snow*. That makes me *Jack Snow*."

"I don't get it."

"Sometimes known as Jack Frost."

"Jack Frost?"

"Yes."

"For real?"

"Well, not *the* Jack Frost. A gifted descendant is probably a more accurate description, though I'm sure — besides my grandmother — there isn't a living soul who believes the old tales are true."

My hand covered my open mouth. It started to snow again. Thick flakes fell like confetti. He pulled me to my feet. How had I been so oblivious? Had I been so consumed with my own abilities that I hadn't noticed the personification of winter breathing down my neck?

"I believe."

"Thank you." He squeezed my hand.

"What about Wade?"

His shoulders dropped. "That was lightning. I didn't mean to kill him, but I had to do something."

"You saved me. You saved yourself. Wade would only have hurt more people. What else could you have done?"

"Still. I didn't know I could. Up till now, it had only been small things. But lately, under stress, my powers have been growing."

I remembered Jack's reaction to the threat of a compromising photo. "Monday's electrical storm?"

"That was me."

"And the blast of air that hit the bear cub?"

"Guilty. Fear is a powerful emotion."

I started to laugh. I knew it was inappropriate. But as I stood there looking at the two of us, our clothes singed and in tatters, our faces smeared with dirt and mud, and having survived our second, my third, brush with death that week — it all hit me as funny. It was a crazy reaction, but I was OK with that. We were alive, together, and still had our feet firmly planted on the realm known as earth, or Midgard. I guess I had been paying a little attention to Hulda after all.

CHAPTER THIRTY-EIGHT

Jack and I rehearsed plausible stories to explain our appearance. And as punch-drunk as I was, I made up some doozies, but still none of them came even close to the truth.

Never the halfway type, I thought we should go with an alien encounter, burned clothing from an otherworldly fuel source. Jack, Mr. Practical, thought we should go with an engine fire, of the earth-based combustible fossil fuel variety. Though how we'd explain rolling up in his truck — old and ugly sure, but the same old and ugly we'd departed in — he was still working out.

We had just pulled to the front curb, when my mother came running out of the house.

"Oh, my God," she said. "We heard about the barn fire. The police phoned. They've been trying to account for all the kids. Thank God you're OK. You weren't answering your cell phone."

Barn fire?

"I lost my purse," I said. I had. But at the portal to another dimension, not at a barn fire.

My mom cupped her hand to her mouth. "Look at you two!" she said.

We did, indeed, look like we'd just stepped off the set of *Back Draft II: Barn Burner*.

"It was chaos," I improvised.

"Penny called twice," my mom said. "She was worried about you. Said she couldn't find you."

"We were looking for her, too. It just got too crazy. Sirens going, girls screaming and crying, people running around, and fire everywhere."

One of Jack's eyebrows raised in a don't-overdo-the-drama arch.

Somebody, clearly, never had a Broadway Barbie.

"The police cleared the scene," Jack said. "So we never heard. Was anyone hurt?"

"You didn't hear about the Ivarsson boy?" my mom asked. "Someone saw him running back into the barn. Maybe trying to help the rescuers. He hasn't been seen since."

So that'd be the story. Odd that he'd be made out as

some sort of hero. I supposed Hulda, who was certainly behind the cover-up, had her reasons.

"Have you talked to your parents yet?" my mom asked Jack.

"No."

"Why don't you come in? You can phone them from inside," my mom said. "Stanley just made a pot of coffee. I know it's late, but why don't you ask if you can stay awhile. I know I, for one, couldn't sleep."

"Stanley's here?" I asked.

We started walking up the front steps. My mom slipped her arm through mine. "He came over as soon as he heard about the fire."

I squeezed my mom's hand. "That's great."

While Jack called his parents, my mom opened first the kitchen window and then the sliding glass door. It took me a few minutes to realize she was airing out the space. From me and Jack. We smelled like a couple of chimney sweeps.

Jack hung up the phone, reporting he could stay.

Be-prepared Stanley, who, I had to admit, was probably once a top-notch scout, offered Jack the loan of some workout clothes from his car. The two of them went outside in pursuit of the gym bag.

I walked to where my mom stood pulling coffee mugs from the kitchen cabinet.

"So what did Stanley say?" I asked.

"That he doesn't care whose baby it is. He just wants

to be a part of my life." She rubbed her flat tummy. "Of our life."

I noticed her sweater. "Is that new?" I fingered its ribbed sleeve.

"I saw it yesterday in Walden," she said. "Somehow it spoke to me."

"What color would you say that was?"

She tugged it over her hips. "Yellowish green. I guess chartreuse is what it's called."

"It's a good color for you," I said. "And I'm happy for you and Stanley. I really am." I gave my mom a big hug. "He's a good guy. He'll be a good dad."

"He thinks he is the dad." My mom grinned and shrugged. "He says he had a dream about us."

He had no idea who he was dealing with in that department; my little sis and I were a few steps ahead of him there.

"What about Dad?" I asked.

"He'll be told I'm pregnant. And he'll be told I'm with Stanley. And he'll be told he's forgiven, finally forgiven. I've been very angry, but I know now we're all capable of mistakes. Some worse than others, but I'll admit now I made mine. Even with your dad."

"I think he'll be happy for you, Mom." And I did. My dad had his faults, but he wasn't spiteful. "Have you told Afi yet?"

"Ugh. That was not an easy conversation. He was still shocked by the news that Hulda had sold to Starbucks.

He'd been so sure the big development deal would go through. He had his mind set on retiring and moving to Florida. And then I sprung the news about the baby on him."

"Florida?"

"I know." My mom shook her head in bewilderment. "What the heck would he do in Florida?"

"He'd be a fish out of water," my mom said. "But he claims he aches for the sea."

"He'd die of heatstroke."

"He wouldn't have lasted," my mom said. "He'd have come back here to his friends, his town."

"So do you think he'll stay now? With the baby coming?"

"I think he will," my mom said. "I think he'll keep the store for a while longer. He may not know it, or admit it, but he likes to keep busy."

I went upstairs to clean up. I washed my face, hands, and arms, ripped a brush through my tangled hair, and changed into my favorite PJs, despite Jack's presence.

By the time I got back, Jack was sitting at the kitchen table in a too-large Walden University T-shirt and too-short sweatpants with a half-full glass of milk in front of him.

I sat down.

My mom handed me a mug of coffee. "Decaf," she said.

Jack rubbed my collar between his thumb and forefinger. "What would you call this fabric?" he asked.

"Flannel," I said reluctantly.

"Hmmm. That's what I thought." He pointed to the design on my pajamas. "And what would you call these things?"

My breath caught. "Snowflakes."

"With all the excitement," my mom said, "I forgot to even ask about the dance. How was it?"

"Great," I said, though it felt like an eternity ago.

A waft of cool air came in through the still-open patio door.

"They're calling for another storm," Stanley said.

"I heard it was going to miss us," Jack said. "That we'd have a nice day tomorrow."

"About time," I said.

"Just look at that sky," my mom said. "You don't see stars like that in LA."

Jack made a small motion with his head toward the backyard.

"You want to go check out the stars?" I asked him.

"It's cold out there," my mom said. "Put on jackets. Or bring a blanket."

I put on a down vest. Jack, I knew, required nothing.

We cuddled together in a chaise longue on the back patio.

"Better," he said. "It was getting warm in there. I think I'm still recovering from the . . . incident."

"You really can't take the heat, can you?"

He shook his head.

"What do you do in the summer?"

"I have to be careful."

"So I guess you and me on a steamy beach somewhere . . ."

"Out of the question."

I pouted. "I guess there's always a cozy ski chalet. The two of us on a bearskin rug in front of a roaring . . ."

He shuddered.

"Sorry," I said. "My bad."

"To be honest, I'm just looking forward to settling into a nice normal routine. With you, first and foremost." He kissed my neck. "And football, and the paper."

"Are you going to hold me to Monday's deadline?" I asked.

"Absolutely."

I groaned. "At least I've decided on an angle. I'm going to write about how old dresses can be given a face-lift, a new purpose. I noticed a lot of the girls wore vintage dresses that had been updated. I'll use this as a kind of metaphor for change."

"Change?"

"Yes. And compromise. A blending of old and new."

"I think I know where you're going with this." There was both skepticism and resignation in his voice. I hoped more of the latter.

"Change is inevitable, you know. The downtown couldn't have stayed that way forever."

"I know."

"And you have to be willing to bend."

"I know. I'm getting there, anyway."

"It doesn't mean you have to wipe away what was there. Like I said, compromise."

"It can be a good thing," he said.

"New isn't always bad." I smiled at him, winningly, I hoped. "I was new once. Remember?"

"Yes."

"And you got used to me."

"I got more than used to you," he said. We kissed. It was long and hot. I pulled away, with a start, remembering his weakened condition.

"You OK?" I asked.

"More than OK."

I settled back into the crook of his arm. "About that nice normal routine you're looking forward to."

"Yeah."

"Do you think it's really possible?"

He sighed. "I kind of see your point."

"It's OK, though," I said. "Because we're stronger together."

"We are."

"And we belong together?"

"We do," he said.

"So bring it on, right?"

"Bring it on." His voice was gravelly.

"Because we'll be the likes of something even Hollywood hasn't seen."

"What's that?" he asked.

"A power couple. The real thing."

Jack traced his forefinger across my jaw, behind my ear, cupping the back of my neck in his hand and pulling my face to his. "You said 'we'll be'—future tense."

"Did I?"

"So you think we'll have to put it to use again?"

I thought about Wade opening a portal to which Jack and I were the key. I thought about Hulda, mysterious Hulda, and the stories she still wanted to share with me.

"I do."

"I like the *we* part, anyway," Jack said, kissing my neck.

I did, too. The *we* part I could definitely get used to. I felt warm and flushed and snug. There I sat with a modern-day Jack Frost, and all I could think was I'd never be cold again.

ACKNOWLEDGMENTS

My IOU forever list includes:

Jamie Brenner of Artists and Artisans, my agent extraordinaire, who received a one-page query on Tuesday and signed me on Friday. I am proud to call Jamie a partner and friend. And *the call* is a wondrous life-changing thing.

Jennifer Yoon, my keen-eyed editor. I am grateful to Jen for embracing *Stork* and wrapping it in the prestigious Candlewick Press jacket. Her savvy edits made the story stronger.

Chantal Corcoran, Dawn Mooradian, Kali VanBaale, Kimberly Stuart, and Murl Pace, the red-penned members of my critique group. These women are wickedly talented writers, tireless supporters, and ever-after friends.

Elaine Peck — my vivacious, can-do mother — who gave her girls the sky. Jennifer Peck and Valerie Devine, my bookend sisters, best friends, and early readers. I am in your debt for a rich history of Barbie world-building and beach-towel fashion shows.

And finally, hugs, kisses, and love always to the three Delsol men in my life: my husband, Bob, and sons, Ross and Mac. Thank you, thank you, thank you.

A MYSTERIOUS STRANGER WILL TEST KATLA AND JACK'S LOVE.

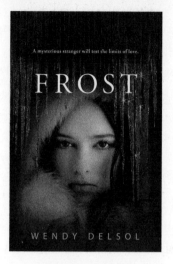

FROST

by **WENDY DELSOL**

There was one thing, and one thing only, that could coax me into striped red tights, a fur vest, and an elf cap: Jack Snjosson. Make that Jack Snjosson in a Santa suit. Our high-school paper's for-charity lunchtime food drive offered an up-close-and-personal with the old fellow in exchange for a nonperishable. Jack, as the paper's editor in chief, was the unanimous choice for the red suit. Never the look-at-me type, he resisted, digging in deep the heels of his old work boots until he devised a scheme requiring company in his misery. My current ensemble was the result. As the paper's fashion editor, I found playing elf more than a little embarrassing, but at least I got first crack at Kris Kringle.

An excerpt from Frost

"Uh, Santa," I said, "aren't you going to ask me what I want for Christmas?" I scooched my striped limbs into the velvety folds of his lap.

"Tell me, what is it you want from old Saint Nick?"

"Santa"—I buried my face into his beard and whispered into his ear—"all I want for Christmas is . . ."

I couldn't help drawing out the moment. It was just too much fun and too surreal, even if my definition of *surreal* had all-new meaning since September. It was still hard to believe everything that had happened in just three short months. I really thought I was losing it when, shortly after the move from LA to Minnesota, I discovered that I was a Stork: a member of an ancient flock of soul deliverers. Things only got more complicated when I met Jack. Turned out he had a pretty nifty talent of his own. As a modern-day descendant of Jack Frost—uh-huh, *that* Jack Frost—he had the ability to control the weather. All the same, had you told me three months ago that I would ask Santa—and not even the real thing, instead my seventeen-year-old, bony-kneed, mahogany-haired, gem-eyed boyfriend—for what was possibly the only thing you couldn't get at the Beverly Hills Nieman Marcus, I'd have said you were cracked.

"A white Christmas," I said.

"And have you been good?" fake-Santa asked.

"Mostly."

He groaned. Because of his special ancestry, heat was

An excerpt from *Frost*

Jack's kryptonite. The heavy costume was uncomfortable to him; my proximity made it worse. Not to mention he wasn't really the PDA type and there was a line of at least twenty can-donating do-gooders—all girls—waiting their turn.

"Thanks, Santa," I said, kissing him briefly on the cheek and springing from his lap.

His face went candy-apple red. It was, as always, our combustible combination that tested his abilities. He made it through the rest of the lunch hour without incident, while I, his elfin helper, handed candy canes to both the naughty and the nice. When his lap was finally girl-free, he stretched, peeled off the press-on whiskers, and headed in my direction.

"Were you trying to kill me?" A much younger Jack seized me by the shoulders.

"What?" I asked, all innocence. "I was your helper." I shook my satchel of goodies as proof.

"You were no help at all."

"Ungrateful," I said.

"Unthinking."

"Unworthy," I countered.

"Unbelievable," he said, though his tone had softened considerably.

"Ah-em." I looked up to see Penny standing behind us. "I just wanted to thank you guys for all your help. We collected ten boxes of food."

"That's great," I said.

An excerpt from *Frost*

"Are you two still gonna help us load the van after school?" Penny asked.

"We'll be there," I answered for both of us. In the three months since our fateful Homecoming adventures, Jack and I had become a unit. Nothing like almost getting sucked through a portal to another dimension by an evil soul-snatching Raven to fast-track a relationship.

I watched Penny walk away with a Prancer-like lope. She deserved the bounce in her step. She'd worked hard to promote and organize the food drive. I was glad it had been successful and was happy to have assisted by printing up flyers and plastering signs throughout the school.

Jack took advantage of my diverted attention and coiled a thick swath of my hair around his fist. "And what's this about wanting a white Christmas?"

"I do. Now that I've embraced living a stone's throw from the North Pole, I actually do."

"You? The California Girl? Not liking this mild winter?"

"It's wimpy," I said, laughing. It was true. Now that I lived in Minnesota, the recent start-of-winter warm temps and lack of snow seemed pathetic.

He arched his eyebrows. I loved the way it flared the blue of his eyes. "Wimpy, huh?"

An excerpt from *Frost*